Louisa's mouth captured Rayann's, and Rayann melted, twisted. Louisa was over her, her deliberate mouth moving from lips to forehead to chin and returning to Rayann's mouth, tasting deeply, then brushing with the softest press of lips. One hand unbuttoned Rayann's shirt, then the strong fingers slid inside. Rayann shuddered and reached for Louisa, wanting to feel her skin gliding under her fingertips.

Louisa caught Rayann's hand in her own, and held it down with gentle pressure. "Let me do this," Louisa said in her low voice. Her fingers claimed the tender flesh of Rayann's stomach, then slid upward, around to her back, dexterously unhooking Rayann's bra. Her lips came to Rayann's again as her hand moved under the bra, around Rayann's ribs and cupped the softness she had freed.

About the Author

Karin Kallmaker was born and raised in California's Central Valley, and came of age during what she terms the cultural toxic waste zone of the 70s. When she's not working, she's tormenting her loved one, writing, reading or watching very bad science fiction movies. Her second favorite way to pass a rainy afternoon is with good chocolate, good books and good music. Her popular lesbian romances, *In Every Port, Touchwood,* and *Paperback Romance* will increase in number to four in September, 1993 with the publication of *Car Pool.*

Touchwood

BY KARIN KALLMAKER

The Naiad Press, Inc.
1993

Printed in the United States of America on acid-free paper
First Edition
Second Printing August, 1993

Edited by Christine Cassidy
Cover design by Pat Tong and Bonnie Liss
   (Phoenix Graphics)
Typeset by Sandi Stancil

Library of Congress Cataloging-in-Publication Data

Kallmaker, Karin, 1960—
   Touchwood / by Karin Kallmaker.
      p.   cm.
   ISBN 0-9541483-76-2
   I. Title.
PS3561.A41665T68   1990
813'.54—dc20   90-6238
                                                          CIP

For November Maria
[It was a chartreuse Volkswagen.]
The Second Is Spilling Over

Acknowledgments

My thanks to my parents who taught me to love books
and to the bookstores who proudly keep us all supplied
with books by and for lesbians. This book was made
possible in part by the insight and diligence of Christi
Cassidy and Katherine Forrest, a.k.a. "the editing
process."

Touching

The trees have kept the sun in their branches.
Veiled like a woman, evoking the past,
Dusk goes by weeping . . . And my fingers
Follow, quivering, the line of your thighs.

My clever fingers linger with the shudders
Of your flesh under your soft petaled gown . . .
The art of touching, complex and curious, equal
To the dream of perfumes, the miracle of sound.

I follow slowly the contour of your thighs,
Your shoulders, your neck, your unappeased
   breasts.
My delicate desire holds back from kisses:
It grazes and swoons in the white voluptuousness.

from *Muse of the Violets* (Evocations)
by Renée Vivien [1877–1909]
Translated from the French by Catharine Kroger

Reprinted with permission

1

Wormwood

Numb with shock, Rayann backed out of the bedroom.

Look again. Maybe this is just a hallucination.

No. The soft noises, the moaning — too real to be anything but here and now.

She shut the front door with a faint click, then walked quickly down the stairs to the street. She didn't look back, didn't know if Michelle had seen her or heard her strangled gasp. She didn't want to know if Michelle had stopped, if Michelle would follow her, if Michelle would try to explain. Explain? No explanation, there could be no explanation.

She heard Michelle call her name, then scream at her to come back. *So she heard me . . . I'm surprised, since she was so intent . . .* Rayann began to run.

How long has this been going on? How many have there been? How many times has Michelle poised in just that way, with just that look, but not over me? She said I was the only one. Said she loved me —

Market Street, finally. Sides aching from the uphill run, Rayann stumbled out of the late-afternoon chill into the Muni station, fumbling in her backpack for three quarters and a dime. *Damn, not enough change.* In a panic, she fed a dollar bill into the change machine but the machine rejected it. With shaking hands she smoothed the edges and unbent the corners. *Why didn't I buy a Fast Pass?* Because she didn't have enough cash and Michelle hadn't been to the ATM recently. Finally, a bill went in and she scrabbled her change out of the dish, then ran to the turnstiles. She didn't stop to wonder where instinct was taking her. She pushed the button for a transfer and kept running.

Blame? She blamed the penny pinchers at the old college. They declared it wasn't sufficiently cold to waste energy on heating yet. The chill of the classroom had been too cold for extension students with only a marginal interest in wood sculpting. Too cold for the housewives who'd figured out they wouldn't have enough time to make all the Christmas presents with which they'd intended to amaze and astonish their friends. She'd hurried home through the cold, damp afternoon, reveling in the richness of the fall air, knowing Michelle was off-duty. She had wanted to sit for a while in front of a cozy fire. Wanted to surprise Michelle with extra hours together — lately there had been so few.

The bar looked the same. The women looked the same. Her reflection in the mirror behind Jilly looked the same — wide hazel eyes, indifferent brown hair curling and brushing at her shoulders, shoulders too wide for her size-twelve frame. Maybe she was paler than usual. Her nose was red but it was probably just the cold. She ordered a Tanqueray and tonic. Jilly brought it.

"Y'look tired," Jilly said.

Rayann shrugged. She couldn't talk. She carried her glass over to the jukebox. Leaning on it, she thought of Bette Davis leaning on the piano in *All About Eve*. *Fasten your seat belt, Rayann, it's going to be a bumpy night.* She took a healthy swallow of her drink and promptly choked on it. *Some Bette Davis you are — do you think if she'd caught her lover like that she would have run?* Coughing, she managed another swallow, then drained the glass in three more. Gin wasn't going to solve anything, but it might ease the pressure before she exploded.

So what are you going to do about it? Fight for her? Rayann pictured herself as a female Gary Cooper, facing some nameless blonde interloper who stood framing her womanhood at the end of a long, dusty street. Rayann started to giggle, realized she wouldn't stop once she started and went to the bar for another drink. She ignored the puzzled look Jilly gave her as she went back to lean on the jukebox again.

A young couple came in, a blonde and a redhead, hugging each other, holding hands, making lovesick eyes — so young and in love it hurt Rayann to watch them. She doubted either of them had said goodbye to their teens, and noticed Jilly doubted it too, though she didn't kick them out. Jilly gave them a stern look as she brought them club sodas, her eyes daring them to try to order anything else. Rayann remembered that look when it had been directed at her a long, long time ago.

The baby blonde danced by herself over to the jukebox. The redhead's eyes never left her — the gaze was proud and indulgent and proprietary. The blonde looked Rayann over and Rayann wondered if she were assessing Rayann's hands or her mouth, thinking maybe she wasn't too bad for Pushing Thirty.

The blonde scanned the record list. "Wow, it's got Melissa," she said. Her fashionably tousled curls looked as if she had just come from bed. The half-dozen earrings piercing her delicate lobe winked at Rayann. "Half these people I never heard of. Like what are Vandellas, anyway? But I love Melissa. She's *been* there, you know."

Been where? What do you know about anything but here and now? Just wait until three years of your life melt away in less than a heartbeat. Rayann was at most only twelve years older, but she felt as if she had as much in common with this woman as she did with an infant.

The child-woman dropped in a quarter, pushed some buttons and danced back across the floor to her waiting partner. The redhead glanced briefly at Rayann, then away with a shrug of her leather-clad shoulder. She knew Rayann was no threat.

Three years with Michelle and Rayann had forgotten all about the games. For three years she had spent most of her time at a table-for-two in the tea room, not in the bar. For three years there had been only one woman.

The interminable, endlessly-only-you love song on the jukebox finally faded to a close. The records whirred, clicked, and the low beat of Melissa Etheridge pulsed against Rayann as she leaned on the jukebox and wondered how long it would be before Michelle looked for her here. She couldn't let Michelle find her. *That's assuming that she cares enough to come looking. No sign of her yet, and she has a car.*

Her hands flat on the top of the jukebox, Rayann kept time with the bass, lightly slapping the beat. Melissa's whisper surged into throaty, burning agony, and the jukebox throbbed the anguish of an unfaithful lover. *She has been there, or she's a real good faker.* Rayann swallowed the last half of her drink as Melissa cried "Bring Me Some Water" — Rayann screamed with her in silence, beating the bass line on the jukebox with her palms, then with her fists.

Firm hands pulled her away from the jukebox. "Stop it, stop it! What's wrong? Ray? Look at me!" Jilly's fingers dug into Rayann's shoulders.

Over Jilly's shoulder she saw the baby blonde and the redhead on the dance floor, hip-to-hip, crotch-to-crotch, frozen with hands in each other's back pockets as they stared at Rayann. Everyone was staring at Rayann.

4

"Rayann, what's wrong?" Jilly persisted.

"A lie." She pointed at the young couple and their happy-ever-after eyes. "A goddamned lie." Jilly looked at them, and Rayann slid away from her, around the jukebox, out the door. She ran.

Her mind and body still remembered the combination journey from the bar to the house where she'd grown up. Muni, transfer to the Noe Valley bus, then to the one that took her up to Diamond Heights. She walked slowly through the neighborhood — wide streets, stately, columned houses set back with impressive spreads of lawn between them and the world. The streets were silent and empty of cars despite the rush hour gridlocking the rest of the city. Rayann could almost feel the burglar alarms monitoring each door and window.

She stood in the driveway of her mother's house for a moment, mentally sketching a memory of her mother standing next to the car, hollering at her to shake a leg — they were going to be late for dancing lessons. One of the last things she and her mother had done in a mother-daughter-it'll-be-fun manner was to take the dancing lessons. How ironic that Rayann had been more comfortable leading. How ironic that the boys at the country club had found it impossible to dance with her. Instead of making her more socially adept, dance lessons had underlined how out of step Rayann had been with her mother's world.

Not long after that had been the day she had learned why the other girls' bodies intrigued and embarrassed her. The day she had seen two women holding hands as they walked and not told herself they were probably just good friends. The day she had realized why her gym teacher, a client of her mother's, an older cousin, a waitress, a Naval officer in dress blues, her mother's secretary — women in all their differing guises — attracted her with their common strength, power and grace. The day she had felt no need to look further outside herself, only within.

5

Shaking herself out of pointless reverie, she walked briskly up the drive as if she belonged there. There had been several times when Rayann had wanted to throw the key to her mother's house away, or, when severely tried, actually at her mother. Now she was glad it was on her key ring where it had been since she was ten. It still fit the lock and the sound of the empty house was soothingly familiar. A warning alarm shrilled and she quickly punched in the code.

Rayann put her backpack and keys on the entry table, then hung her coat on one of the teak pegs protruding from the wall-mounted coatrack. Smiling fondly, she traced the delicate maple leaf border on the mounting board, remembering the hours spent working out the pattern with her mother, then the time spent actually carving the teak. The task had been fun and she knew her mother loved the finished product. But the fun had been before Michelle — before the memorable evening she had brought Michelle home and said, "Mom, there's something I've been meaning to tell you."

Turning away, Rayann sighed. The gin had succeeded in making her woozy, but at least Melissa Etheridge was no longer moaning over and over in her head.

On the refrigerator was the usual note from the housekeeper explaining what was prepared for dinner and heating instructions. Her stomach growled, and Rayann wondered if salad, curried turkey slices and fruit compote would stretch to two. She looked at the neatly wrapped containers. It might. She also looked, to no avail, for the pie or cake that had always been left in the refrigerator by all the previous housekeepers ever since Rayann was a little girl. *Mom must be getting diet-conscious.*

She found some cardboard-flavored crackers and carried them with her from room to room, then up the curved staircase, munching loudly to fill the empty spaces, but making sure she left no trail of crumbs. It had been almost a year since she had been home. Excuses not to come to dinner and not to make the holidays had been easy when Michelle's schedule was so erratic to suit classes and residency.

6

The thought of Michelle sent angry, despairing shivers through Rayann. *What am I going to do?* She sat down on her old bed, looking around the room that was unchanged from when she had lived at home. She had moved out midway through college, just after changing her major from business administration to art. Her mother had been disappointed, but after years as a marketing executive Ann Germaine was too appreciative of the powers of creative design not to encourage Rayann in her chosen field. She had only cooled her encouragement — and financial support — when Rayann had expressed a desire to make a living as a wood sculptor. Rayann had been infuriated by her mother's suggestion that she was being impractical. *Damn it, another thing she was right about.*

In their last real fight, when Rayann had still cared enough about what her mother thought to argue with her, her mother had said that Rayann was too dependent on Michelle for love, support and money. She'd said something about eggs and baskets, and Rayann had been livid, retorting that if Michelle were a man, her mother would think it only *too* appropriate for Rayann to be completely dependent on her husband.

It only occurred to her now, as she finished the last cracker, that she had agreed with her mother about being dependent. Gender aside, she was too dependent on Michelle. That was abundantly clear.

What am I going to do? Michelle — who paid the rent, owned the car, bought the food, paid for the vacations — was in love with someone else, or at the very least, in lust with another woman. *I've been trusting the happy-ever-after feeling and since it was expedient, I let her own everything.* Rayann's own balance sheet was as devoid of value as Michelle's commitment. What kind of options did she have? Rayann rolled over on her back and decided to be rational, at least for the moment.

Option One. Forgive and forget. Impossible. She would never forget the sight of Michelle's arms around another woman's body, her mouth wet with another woman's passion. The artist in her had caught that image

7

permanently. Someday, as therapy, her artist self might sketch it. Then the non-artist self would burn it or throw darts at it or stick pins in it. No, forgetting was out.

Option Two. Just forgive. Rayann studied the muted geometric pattern of the wallpaper as she considered this option. She might be able to forgive, if Michelle promised to be true. Rayann laughed harshly, startling herself as her voice broke the stillness of the room. *Get real. She was doing it with another woman in YOUR bed, on YOUR favorite sheets. Don't get angry, not yet. Think!* She rolled over onto her stomach with a groan. Thinking was so hard. *So, can I forgive Michelle?* Forgiving would be hard, if not impossible.

Option Three. Leave her. Even as Rayann considered the idea, she was amazed at how her mind had divided into pieces, all objectively examining different options. One part wanted to run back to the apartment and throw a couple of dishes around, while her logic said violence would help nothing. Another part wanted to plead for understanding and forgiveness, though her anger reminded her that Michelle was the one who ought to beg. Yet another part of her wanted to step back and make a concrete plan, think things through, concluding with a sound decision based on all the facts available. *She was going down on another woman in your bed on your favorite sheets. That's a little beyond heavy petting. What more do you need to know?*

Another part of her brain told her to aspire to something better while the small part that kept track of mundane details remembered her empty savings account. She needed a place to live (not to mention a reason), which would require a job. She was not destitute, or homeless — for which she was thankful — but at the age of twenty-nine it was not pleasant to discover that she had no foundation to build on. *Most of the people I went to college with are probably vested in pension plans by now.*

Knowing that Michelle was more than able to meet the rent, Rayann had given up her budding career in commercial art and graphic design to be a full-time artist, with Michelle's encouragement and approval. It would give them more time together, they had agreed. It would strengthen their relationship, they had said.

Deep inside, where her mind would not go, a raw hurt pulsed. She wanted to give in to it and cry. She wanted to feel the pain and have a grand catharsis of weeping and wailing, tear her hair and beat her breast.

She heard the whir of the garage door opening, then her mother's key in the lock. Instantly the house seemed filled with sound and energy. The quick click of heels tapped through the kitchen, then stopped in the foyer.

"Rayann? Where are you?" Her mother's modulated voice did not sound surprised. But then again it rarely did.

"In my room." *It is my room, isn't it? I wonder why she didn't turn it into a sewing room or a guest room?* Though they were muffled by the thick carpeting, Rayann could make out the rapid footsteps as her mother ran up the stairs. Her mother always ran up stairs. Rayann sat up and smoothed her hair, aware that she would be unkempt and far too casual by her mother's standards. As she had expected, her mother was wearing a designer suit, tailored perfectly for her petite frame.

"Hi," Ann Germaine said. She studied Rayann for a moment, then said, "Want to have some dinner? Feel like going out?"

"What about the dinner in the 'fridge?" Rayann surprised herself by laughing as they agreed on pizza.

Her mother slid off her jacket. Even after a day at the office her jacquard silk blouse was crisp and fresh — a look Rayann couldn't achieve at any time of the day. "Pepperoni and mushroom?"

Rayann nodded, then followed her mother to her bedroom and stretched out on the bed while her mother called the pizza parlor — the number was programmed to speed-dial, Rayann noted — and then changed into designer sweats that nevertheless appeared comfortable and practical. Rayann felt as if she were in high school again while her mother chatted about clients and potential accounts.

9

After three pieces of pizza her mother finally relaxed in her chair at the dining room table and studied Rayann without speaking. Rayann slipped forward in time again. She was not in high school anymore and she couldn't go on pretending everything was normal.

"I caught her with someone else, Mom."

"Oh, honey," her mother said. She leaned forward to pat Rayann's hand. "Are you sure? Are you sure it was her?"

"Oh yes. I got home early. *In flagrante delecto* I believe is the phrase."

"Was it a . . . woman?"

Rayann resented the tiny hesitation and snapped, "She's still a lesbian. So am I."

Her mother took a deep breath, let it out, then said, "You know your room is always there for you."

It was what Rayann had been hoping her mother would say. She wasn't going home tonight. She didn't have enough courage, and curiously, not enough anger. "I don't know what I'm going to do, Mom. But knowing I can come home if I have to helps."

Rayann woke early, startled, but then oddly comforted by the clunk-thunk the plumbing made when the hot water was turned off upstairs. A few minutes later she heard her mother's blow dryer. She could almost pretend she was seventeen again, but not for all the money on earth would she be seventeen again. She'd have to come out again, for one thing, and she'd probably still end up right where she was.

She searched the dresser and found some of her old clothing. Her panty size hadn't changed since she'd lived at home and when she found a pair it didn't matter that they said "Sunday" and were covered with little hearts. *Images from a previous life.* She showered quickly, then dressed in the sweater and jeans she'd worn the day before, and hurried downstairs to share a cup of coffee and some breakfast with her mother.

"Mmm." Rayann hung her nose over the steaming cup of French roast she'd poured. "This smells wonderful. What else is in it?"

"A little vanilla bean," her mother croaked, glancing up from the *Wall Street Journal*.

Rayann smiled as she sat down with her English muffin, hot from the toaster. She'd forgotten her mother's voice took two cups of coffee to warm up.

"Made any plans?" Her mother folded the paper away.

"No." Despite lying awake for the better portion of the night, Rayann had come to absolutely no conclusions. But staying away for the night should show Michelle that Rayann wasn't totally dependent on her. "I'm going to go home and talk to Michelle. I don't know if we can save anything."

"Do you want to save something?"

"We've had three years. I'd say it was worth a try."

"If things don't work out," her mother said slowly, "and you have time, well, I know three groups who are hoping to find a graphic artist who'll help design some publicity pieces. There's the Center for Chronic Fatigue Syndrome, and —"

"I don't do graphic design anymore." Rayann's tone was flat. A practical voice inside said they might be good opportunities, while a creative voice said they sounded like fun — but it meant the life with Michelle as it had been was over. The dream of being an *artiste* was over. She wasn't ready to admit that yet.

"I know you haven't done it for a while, but this would give you a chance to get your hand back in, get your name circulated — *if you have the time for it now.*"

"I don't know that I do."

"Dear, I only meant if you don't work things out with Michelle then you would have something to look forward to —"

"Jobs you arrange for me?" Rayann couldn't keep the bitterness out of her voice. This was an old argument. Her mother hadn't changed.

"Jobs I'm only letting you know exist. And these aren't even jobs — just high-visibility *pro bono*

11

opportunities. You don't have to take them." Her mother quietly pushed back her chair and carried her plate to the sink.

"Good. Don't plan my life for me yet, Mom. It's too soon for you to start dancing in the streets because I left Michelle."

"I'm not dancing —"

"You never liked her."

"No, I didn't, but I still l—"

"So don't try to lure me away. It won't work." Rayann stood up and marched to the sink with her coffee cup. She rinsed it, then smacked it down on the counter.

"You're being very unfair to me," her mother said quietly. "I'm not trying to lure you away. I'm just trying to let you see your options."

Options. Rayann wailed inside. She was tired of considering her options. She wouldn't be doing it at all if Michelle hadn't — "The primary of which is giving up this lesbian silliness and finding a man, right?"

"I said nothing of the kind." Her mother's voice was clipped as she picked up her briefcase and suit jacket.

"But you were thinking it." In her anger, Rayann could see her mother was upset at having been found out. "You sent me all those books, remember, about how I could be cured, remember?"

"I'm not going to argue about what I've already apologized once for. You do what you have to do," her mother said. She walked quickly to the door that led to the garage, then turned. "Your room is there if you need it."

Rayann was so angry at her mother and — and everything that she practically snarled her response. "As long as I behave the way you want me to, right?"

"I made no conditions," Ann Germaine said. "But if this is how you're going to behave, then maybe I should." She shut the door quietly behind her.

* * * * *

Anger quickened Rayann's stride. Her mother had been doing the same old thing, trying to break her and Michelle up. She didn't need her mother's help. Michelle and she would work this thing out. Michelle's 300Z was in its parking space as it had been the afternoon before, covered with early morning mist. As she approached the building a car U-turned and came toward Rayann. She glanced disinterestedly at the driver and then froze. The driver was the woman Michelle had been in bed with.

That bitch spent the night! Rayann felt speared by the truth — Michelle had not cared enough to come looking for her. Michelle had gone back to that woman, had gone on making love to her. *She couldn't care less about me. Three years —*

The pain slowed her steps and she leaned on the Z while she gasped for breath. Her vision cleared after a few minutes and her body went blissfully numb. *What am I going to do?* Bette Davis would have known. Straightening her shoulders, Rayann walked resolutely up the apartment steps. *What a dump*, she thought contemptuously. *I'm going to get the hell out of here and good riddance.*

Even before Rayann's steady hand turned the key all the way, Michelle was pulling open the door.

"What did you for—" She broke off with a noiseless gasp. Rayann looked at the shining blonde hair with the red glints, attractive long, dark lashes fringing pale blue eyes. Her courage began to fail her. She had forgotten Michelle was beautiful.

"Where the hell have you been? I've been worried sick!" Even in anger, Michelle's voice was beautifully pitched. So often Rayann had imagined how comforted Michelle's patients must be by that lovely voice.

"That's rich. I saw her driving away. Did she adequately fill the void my absence created?" Rayann headed for the bathroom. She'd just pack some clothes.

"You could have at least called. I don't care how angry you were."

13

"'Angry' isn't quite the right word," Rayann said, her tone as aloof as she could manage. "And why would I call? To say I was fine and tell you to enjoy yourself?" She stopped in the doorway of the bedroom. Her favorite sheets. Lilacs and roses intertwined like legs and arms. Rayann realized she would never have known about the other woman if she hadn't seen her with Michelle. She realized then that yesterday probably hadn't been the first . . . indiscretion.

"Are we going to be rational about this? Aren't you even going to look at me?"

Rayann kept her back turned. Then the love she had felt for Michelle began to throb. *Is this what love feels like when it's dying — or is it coming back to life?* "Was she the only one?"

"It was a mistake."

Rayann turned to study Michelle's expression. "What was a mistake? What I know I saw? Just an optical illusion maybe? Or going to bed with her? Was that a mistake? A mistake that lasted all night and well past breakfast?"

"It was the first time."

Rayann saw the corners of Michelle's eyes crinkle slightly, then relax again. "The first time with her or just the first time in our bed?"

"You're not going to listen to me, are you?" Again the slight crinkle.

Rayann suddenly knew that the little facial change she'd never noticed before meant Michelle was hiding something. She frantically searched her memory. *How many times when she didn't come home after her shift and said she'd filled in for someone else — how many of those times did her eyes do that? How many lies have there been? Just how stupid am I?* "You're answering questions with questions. But the answers don't matter because I'm leaving."

"Look, Lori was a mistake. I invited her home for a

drink because our shift was absolutely shitty and one thing led to another."

"I really didn't want to know her name." Rayann went to the closet and rummaged in the back for one of her suitcases. She'd fill the medium-sized one. When she set it on the bed, Michelle leaned across and held it closed.

"What do I have to say to make you believe me?"

Rayann looked down at Michelle's hands. She wanted to snatch the suitcase away and heave it against the wall. And then break everything until there was nothing left worth having. In a whisper, she managed, "I believe you've slept with every woman from here to Denver. I think every time I look at my friends I'll wonder which of them betrayed me."

"Well that's just great!" Michelle stomped to the other side of the room. "Go ahead! Walk out on our relationship if it makes you happy."

"Are you going to tell me she was the only one you had sex with besides me?"

"Of course she was." Michelle's expression of outrage didn't alter — except for the tiny crinkle at the corners of both eyes.

Hot anger surged through Rayann and her vision blurred for a split second. "You've lied to me all along, haven't you? You knew I'd hate it, so you lied and lied!"

Michelle's eyes grew big with tears. "No!" She stumbled for words. "I was afraid — I thought you might — oh Ray, you can't go!" She burst into tears.

Rayann's anger evaporated and she fought an overwhelming impulse to comfort Michelle.

"I can't believe it happened, I never meant it to. It just happened. Lori . . . Lori wanted to. She hadn't ever been with a woman." Even in tears Michelle was beautiful.

Rayann fought the appeal of Michelle's pleading eyes. It seemed cruelly unfair that somehow Michelle was more upset and in need of sympathy and pity than Rayann

15

was. Her voice was hard and rough as she said, "Don't pretend you made the sacrifice on behalf of recruiting someone new to the Lesbian Nation. Blaming the other woman is an old, old line, Michelle. She wasn't the only one. You know it and I know it."

"It was a mistake." Michelle took a step toward her, but Rayann stepped back.

"I can't forget. I can't forgive you for bringing her here and doing it in our bed. And I can't go on pretending there's a reason to stay with you." *Except for monetary reasons — lots of monetary reasons.* Rayann knew she couldn't accept a future together based on money — accepting that their past had been was going to be hard enough.

Michelle tossed her long blonde hair. Rayann remembered all the times she had pulled that hair up over her stomach while — *No, it's over.* "Don't take away what we have because I made a mistake in judgment."

"What do *we* have? An occasional evening together? Doing the laundry? This place is yours and I'm the temporary belonging." Rayann sat down on the bed. What had they ever had that was equally theirs? What had there been that wasn't mostly Michelle's?

"Darling, you were never a belonging, you know that."

"A convenience then, like a built-in toaster. Handy to have around because you knew I'd be here. If there was no one else, you knew I'd be here for you." Rayann's voice shook. "I think I hate you."

"Never hate me," Michelle whispered, and her lips went to Rayann's clenched hand.

"Don't." At the touch of Michelle's lips three years of loving and wanting and having washed through Rayann's senses.

"Darling, I love you. We're so good together. Don't let anything come between us."

"It was so good because I could count on it — and you. I trusted you. And I'm not the one who has let something . . . lots of somethings come between us."

"I'll make it up to you."

Rayann's body began to swell with the familiar

wanting. "You can't make it up to me. The damage is done."

"You want me to touch you, I can tell, and I know just how. You can't walk away from that."

"Yes, I can." Rayann summoned all her will, stood up, and opened the suitcase. She gathered a handful of polo shirts. Her knees were nearly liquid, but she kept going. She knew how easy it would be to say to herself, *Just once more, one last time.*

"Go ahead then," Michelle whispered. "Go ahead and try to walk way."

"Why do you want me around?" Bewildered, Rayann stopped with an armload of clothes to look at Michelle. "Every time you do anything new I'll wonder who taught it to you. Don't you see? There's no magic left for me."

Michelle laughed. Rayann heard the edge of bitterness in it. "You've always been an incurable romantic."

"Well, I think you found the cure. You'll have to put another notch in whatever doctors notch when they make someone well." Rayann paused. Her throat went tight with anger and tears. "Thanks. Thanks so much."

"Can't we be adult about this?" Michelle asked. She pushed away from the wall, hands in her back pockets, and walked toward Rayann. Michelle's shirt pulled tight across breasts Rayann had caressed hundreds of times.

"If being adult means I shouldn't feel as if you lied to me —"

"Only to keep from hurting you —"

"And that I shouldn't believe love and trust are inseparable —"

"Oh, grow up, Rayann!"

"I have! Damn you! I aged fifty years when I saw you on top of her."

"Oh shit. Let's not do this, okay? Go ahead, hate me if it makes you feel better." Michelle turned her back.

Rayann looked at that beautiful back and sketched a mental picture of karate-chopping the hell out of Michelle. The image twisted: anger turned to passion and their bodies were melted together, straining and climaxing.

She broke out of her frozen stance, breathing hard.

17

*How easy to forget about the lies and the other lovers . . .
How easy to live one day at a time. At least I'd have
Michelle instead of no one.*

Deep inside, Rayann balked. She thought of her
mother suddenly, and knew that while she'd defend being
a lesbian to the death, standing in line for Michelle was
something she couldn't defend. She knew that if she gave
in, Michelle would take it as permission to go on having
affairs. And she would become the equivalent of a kept
woman, the number one wife, the steady mistress, the
head bimbo. She wouldn't be able to face herself in the
mirror.

"You're not very good at playing the martyr," she said
to Michelle's back. "I'm going to pack now."

Michelle turned, her hair a shining cape.

How easy to just reach out and touch it one last time.

"Where are you going?"

"What does that matter to you? Lori and all the
others like her will comfort you in your hour of need, I'm
sure." Rayann found her loafers under the bed and then
added a half a dozen pairs of socks to the suitcase.

"I lied to you because I knew you'd be childish about
it. But I've never said I love you to anyone but you."

"Next you'll be saying that love means never having
to say you're sorry. Don't stoop to clichés or I might start
thinking you never did have any class."

Maybe you're right," Michelle hissed. "I loved you."

Rayann drew in a sharp, aching breath. *Okay, it's
over. Bette, if you're up there, please don't let me cry.*

Michelle watched her in stony silence as Rayann
carried the suitcase out of the bedroom. She filled her
backpack with some of her wood tools, then realized she
couldn't carry them all. She didn't want to leave them,
and she didn't want to leave her computer which had
been under the bed for almost two years now. And there
were the half-started projects and a few pieces of her
early work Rayann hated but wouldn't part with for the
world. She almost cried when she saw her first creation
— a whittled ashtray she'd made for her father, who

hadn't smoked. There were two armloads of mailing tubes full of rolled posters she had designed — before Michelle.

The books, and albums and the rest of her clothes she'd have to leave, for now. She picked up the suitcase and slung the backpack over one shoulder. She held her head up. "I'll send for my things," she said. *I'm the emancipated Judy Holliday, but I've got no William Holden on my arm.* But to believe Michelle's lies, Rayann reminded herself, would be naive.

"I could have some movers take them to your mother's house. That's where you're headed, isn't it?" Michelle spoke spitefully and Rayann winced.

"I'm *not* going home to Mother," Rayann said stoutly. *But that's exactly what you were going to do.* "Not that it's any concern of yours."

"Aren't you forgetting this?" Michelle was holding Rayann's last anniversary present.

Rayann looked at the sixteen-inch square of mahogany. It was so thin that light shone dimly through it, making the design dance in red and orange. The carving was her finest work — suggestive of a woman's form, stretched and taut, hair flowing outward to form the textured pattern of the beveled edges. Michelle had hung it in the front window where it glowed in the setting sun. "I meant it for you. You can keep it as a sample of your patronage of the arts."

Michelle remained where she was, clutching the mahogany square. Rayann opened the front door and without a backward glance struggled down the steps outside the apartment. She didn't hear the door slam — her ears seemed as numb as the rest of her — but she knew it had been slammed because the stairs shook and the ground rocked as she walked unsteadily away.

2
Finding a Niche

Rayann wanted to sit down on her suitcase and cry. The cold fog bit into her exposed hands and face while she began to sweat under her jacket. When she finally made it to the Muni station she just wanted to get on the next train and let it take her somewhere as long as somewhere was not here.

After Michelle's scathing remarks, Rayann would not go back to her mother's. *I won't play Alice Cramden or Ethel Mertz.* She thought about calling Judy, but Dedric and Judy had enough strays in and out of their apartment. Rayann at least had credit cards — there must be an inexpensive hotel somewhere in the city. She laughed to herself even as she considered the idea. Not in San Francisco.

Judy, then, or back to the bar. Maybe she would run into someone who would be willing to put her up, just for a few nights. Even as she considered it, Rayann felt a sharp stab of embarrassment and fear. Everyone would know she'd left Michelle. And which ones would know why — which of her friends had been with Michelle? Would she go into the bar and find out, from the looks and whispers, that she was the last to know? She couldn't face anyone. Not until she proved she didn't need Michelle, or her mother, or *anyone*. She was just fine on her own. When a train bound for Embarcadero came along she got on it.

Muni to BART. From Embarcadero to the Richmond/ Daly City line. Her ears rang as the train glided down the Transbay tube and under the bay. Something inside her head began to pound, but she couldn't tell if it was fear or the pressure of the water. The pounding eased only slightly as the train rose above ground in West Oakland. At the station she looked across at the train that had pulled in heading for the city. Women in tennis shoes sprinted for the closing doors and clung to the too-high overhead bars as the other train pulled out. Rayann envied them their jobs. She was mercifully numb as the train skimmed smoothly along through more dark tunnels and bright stations. When they got to the end of the line she took the next train out, bound for Fremont.

Her first priority was a place to live and a way to pay for it. Don't forget, she told herself, you always have your education — at least that's what the campus recruiters had promised. Her attention was captured by a billboard hyping a new apartment complex with all the amenities the single life could possibly want, including, apparently, a scantily clad woman on a sailboat. The billboard wasn't particularly well designed so the text didn't catch her eye; she couldn't afford a place like that anyway. But she was riveted by the sails puffed out to the straining point — like the woman's bikini top — leaping bravely ahead of the wind. If she were a sailboat, she'd say there hadn't been any wind in her life for a long time.

Sure, she'd had a few ideas for wood pieces. She'd had a commission and sold another piece to an interior decorator, but inertia had slowly claimed her. She'd barely found enough energy to crawl to her teaching job, not that it paid much. Her self-image as an artist had become almost non-existent while she had bent and molded herself around Michelle. The loss of her artistic drive hadn't been apparent until now. *I will get it back. She congratulated herself for having established two priorities.*

That momentous decision left her complacent for quite a while, and she hardly realized the train was pulling into Fremont station. End of the line. Again. She took the Daly City line out of Fremont. Between San Leandro and Coliseum, Rayann decided on a third priority. She wasn't sure how or when or who, but somehow she would show herself and her friends — and Michelle — that Michelle's infidelities had not been because Rayann was lacking in any way. She needed to find a new lover. She would show them all that Rayann was fine.

At Fruitvale, Rayann realized the train was going to take her back through San Francisco, back to Civic Center where she would normally exit. She couldn't go back, wouldn't go back, not until she knew what she was going to do, how she was going to survive. The doors slid open at the next station and Rayann stepped off, her suitcase feeling twice as heavy as when she had got on. The door chime sounded and the train pulled away in a quiet hum of electric efficiency.

Rayann was depressed and empty and the station was freezing. *Isn't this the part where I should contemplate suicide? Maybe throw myself in front of a train. Does it hurt? I should have read* Anna Karenina.

Another train pulled in and the rush of frigid air and swirl of people around her made her dizzy and nauseous. Food. She was hungry. Maybe there was a place to eat nearby. *Near where?* She looked up a the signs and realized she was in Oakland's Lake Merritt station. Maybe there was a motel nearby where she could leave her suitcase and go in search of food, and in search of a job, a place to live and self-esteem while she was at it. Did she have enough money for a motel? She looked in her wallet and sighed. She could charge it. But the bill would go to their — Michelle's address. Michelle might pay it again. How many times had Michelle reassured her the money didn't matter, that she loved Rayann, and what Michelle had was Rayann's as well? Rayann had believed that, too.

She'd see if there really was a lake in Oakland. As a native San Franciscan she'd always thought Lake Merritt had been made up by the Oakland Chamber of Commerce. The rowing championships they held every year were probably hoaxes. Maybe she'd throw herself into Lake Merritt — if it really existed.

There was no lake in sight as she climbed the steps out of the station. The water on the wind was all creeping fog. Laney College loomed out of the gray curtain, then the Oakland Museum. She walked past the Calvin Simmons Theater only to find she couldn't cross the next street. *Where is Oakland?* Was she anywhere near Lake Merritt? Exasperated and more than a little frightened, she sat down on her suitcase and hoped for inspiration.

The fog lifted in a sweep of wind and a burst of sunlight, leaving her blinking. She tried to get her bearings in the hazy late-morning light. Fog clung to the hills but she could make out the tall buildings in Oakland's business district at least eight blocks to the east. The skyline was a pale imitation of the city's magnificence. And there was no sign of a lake anywhere. *I knew it — they made it up.* She decided her best bet was to look for some food in the business district.

Her mouth tasted of a bad night's sleep, and as she walked she looked for a place to eat. The first coffee shop she passed was too crowded — she might have to talk to someone. The next was too empty. She wanted to be anonymous. So she walked on, frequently switching the suitcase from side to side, and ignored the ache on both calves where the suitcase kept bumping her. She walked through Oakland's Japantown where the aroma of sizzling garlic and roasting ginger made her stomach growl. But none of the restaurants were open yet.

Blocks later she finally found a McDonald's. *Anonymity in styrofoam.* She ordered an Egg McMuffin only to be told she was too late for breakfast. The Chicken McNuggets she ate instead made her feel queasy so she kept walking, hoping the exertion would make her feel better so she could start thinking about what to do.

She struggled up Broadway, past another BART station at 12th Street and City Center, then another at 19th. All she could see further up the street were car lots and businesses with formidable wrought iron gates across the entrances. She wandered slowly back to City Center. She looked at Christmas decorations and stared at the displays in shop windows. *I should have gone back to Mom's.* The thought depressed her further.

She watched a fountain bubble into a small pool that had only a few coins in it. She stared into the water then dug in her backpack for her change. She examined the coins — not a feminine symbol in sight. She was not about to give up her lucky Susan B. Anthony dollar. Finally, she chose a dime because FDR was on it and he had at least been married to a terrific woman. She took a deep breath and balanced the dime on her thumbnail tucked under her index finger. *Okay, I'm listening.* She flipped it out as far into the pool as it would go.

Nothing magical happened, of course, but the fountain reminded her of her ambition to find the supposed lake in Oakland. She had to ask three bustling commuters before a tired-looking woman gave an irritated gesture toward the south. She had only gone a block when she stopped to switch sides with the suitcase and glanced at one of the shops. It wasn't a shop at all — the sign said, "Women's Center of Oakland." Of course! Rayann heaved a sigh of relief. They would have housing and shelter referrals. *This should have been my first stop.*

The black woman at the desk gave Rayann an odd look as Rayann set her suitcase down. The coffee she poured Rayann was hot and sweet, and Rayann mumbled a request for housing referrals as she warmed her hands on the cup.

"Are you running from someone who hurt you?" The woman's gaze swept over the suitcase. She shifted her weight, opening up her stance, which encouraged honesty from Rayann.

Tears stung her eyes, and Rayann didn't know if the woman believed her when she said, "No, someone just doesn't love me anymore." Rayann wanted to be cuddled and comforted on the woman's ample bosom.

"This won't make sense to you, but I'm relieved. All the shelters are overflowing. But we do have some listings of women who are renting rooms in their houses. That might be just what you need." She showed Rayann where the housing referrals were, and explained how to decipher the codes on the cards.

An older woman came in as Rayann bent over the stack of cards. She shut out the enthusiastic conversation the two women had about events they'd attended. If she understood the codes right, the first card said there was a lovely room in a Lake Merritt Victorian, with kitchen privileges. Rent, which Rayann thought she might be able to raise as a cash advance on a credit card, included utilities. The preferred applicant would be a "LFNSNP17V." She referred to the codes — a lesbian feminist no pets nonsmoker with a child to share day-care responsibilities no alcohol vegetarian.

Vegetarian living would be good for her, no doubt, but maybe there would be one where she didn't need a child. The next listing preferred another smoker or nonsmoker who wouldn't complain. The next one she could afford preferred someone who had been through a twelve-step program for mutual support and would agree to no meat, no eggs, no alcohol, no drugs, no overnight guests, no loud music. The next card said anyone who even knew what a twelve-step program was need not apply.

Rayann sighed. She could live alcohol-free, pet-free,

maybe even meat-free, but she was allergic to cats and dogs, though she loved them, which ruled out the studio above the veterinarian's practice. Nor did she feel up to the rigors of separatist living. She'd be turned away at the door as soon as they saw the Gucci emblem on her suitcase. Still, the rent was cheap. Maybe she could say she stole her suitcase from a men's store. *No, that won't work. Some of my polo shirts have little alligators on them.*

"Finding anything?"

Rayann started. The older woman was leaning over her shoulder. Her hair, falling forward in curls and waves of black and silver, hid her expression.

"Not much."

"I came in to add this to the stack," the woman said. She handed Rayann another card and Rayann took it, then realized she was staring. The woman turned away, saying, "Well, Nance, keep up the good work. I wish I could leave a big fat check with you."

"You paid your pledge, Louisa, so don't worry about it. We get by, as always."

Rayann looked at the card Louisa had given her. A room and kitchen privileges at a reasonable rent. The rent could be partially offset by some hours worked in the bookstore downstairs. Her heart leapt. Louisa hadn't bothered with codes. Firm, bold handwriting stated she was looking for an independent woman, preferably one who wanted to work in the bookstore, which required knowledge of literature and simple arithmetic, in that order.

"Hey," Rayann said loudly. The woman, almost out the door, turned back to her. "I took a year of accounting. I know my alphabet." She smiled giddily. "I was an art major, but I roomed with an English major for two years before she switched to psych. But I read books all the time." She finished her short resumé on a note of hope.

"An increasingly rare pastime," the woman said wryly. As the watery sunlight illuminated her face, Rayann realized she was much older than Rayann had thought.

26

"I'm Louisa Thatcher," she said. She crossed the room quickly, and firmly shook Rayann's hand.

"I'm Rayann. Rayann Germaine."

"Scandinavian?"

Rayann shook her head. "My father was Ray and my mom's name is Ann."

"Oh, a parent splice. Well, it's pretty," Louisa said. She put her hands in the pockets of her denim jacket. "You could have been BobLou or JerryEllie, I suppose." Dark brown eyes studied Rayann, taking in the suitcase and backpack. "I'm guessing you'd like to start right away."

"Yes," Rayann said. She held her breath.

"Okay."

"You mean it?" Realizing she sounded like a child who expected the grown-up to back out of a promise, Rayann tried to put lots of assurance into the way she picked up her suitcase, but her aching arms made her wince.

"I could go home for my car and come back for you," Louisa said. "It's several blocks."

"No, I'm fine," Rayann protested. She couldn't start out looking like a weakling. She tried to give Louisa a carefree smile and then thanked Nancy. "When I can, I'll be back with a big fat check."

"Promises, promises." Nancy waved her away.

Two blocks of pitted sidewalks later, Rayann saw a body of water across the busy boulevard they had arrived at. It was a large patch of smooth darkness between the glass and concrete buildings of downtown and the hills scattered with houses and apartment buildings.

"Is that Lake Merritt?" Rayann set down her suitcase as Louisa stopped to answer.

The older woman nodded. "It's man-made. I like to walk the perimeter about once a week — three and a quarter miles. The path runs the top of the concrete walls, and through the park. It's a nice walk but I sure wouldn't do it after dark."

The lake's surface was broken only by the ripple of a passing scull, its occupant stroking powerfully southward.

Rayann said, "And here I thought Lake Merritt was a real lake. I looked for it all morning."

"It's not exactly a fake lake," Louisa said. She smiled. "It's more of a pseudo-lake. And it's filthy."

Rayann protested when Louisa picked up her suitcase. "I can carry it."

"You probably can. So can I. It's not far now."

They walked in silence again, leaving the lake's calm behind. Rayann heard sirens in the distance mixed with the hum of the freeway and honking cars. Traffic clogged the four-way stops as people left the buildings for lunch. Rayann stole an occasional sideways glance at her guide, but saw nothing more than a high-cheekboned profile and a straight nose accentuated by the plentiful hair swept back by an occasional puff of wind.

They left the high rises behind, then passed smaller office buildings until finally, after a senior citizens residence, they entered a neighborhood with two-story houses, most of which appeared to have been converted to law or medical offices. Louisa, whose pace left Rayann slightly breathless, turned from the street and rapidly climbed steps in front of a house. It was built with a porch ten steps off the street. *Protection against floods from the concrete-encased lake?* Rayann gave a silent laugh. The porch would be perfect for catching breezes on a sultry night, but sultry nights only happened in the Bay Area once every century or so. The railings, she noted, needed a refresher coat of white paint.

Louisa led the way across the porch, unlocked the metal gate, then the door, and Rayann entered a softly lit interior. Bells tinkled as the door closed. "Just in time to open up, Louisa said. We open late on Wednesdays and Thursdays, and stay open late on Fridays and Saturdays. We'll work out a schedule — I'm assuming you want to work in the store."

Rayann nodded. The smell of books drew her inside. She loved the smell — new books with fresh paper and the sharp aroma of ink, and old books reminding her of musty wood. Sometimes she had forgotten all sense of time and missed beloved art classes because the stacks at the Cal Berkeley Libraries had seduced her with their knowledge-of-the-ages headiness. She inhaled deeply, aware of sensations again. Her feet ached. Like damp cedar, the smell of the books was incense to her brain, soothing her ragged spirit.

Louisa unlocked another door in the middle of the far wall of the bookstore's main room. Rayann followed her slowly, feeling a little dizzy. *Or is it relief?*

The door opened on a stairwell with a very bright light at the top. Rayann blinked several times as her eyes adjusted. She studied Louisa, who was shrugging out of her jacket, revealing a pale blue workshirt left unbuttoned to show a plain white turtleneck. The two layers of shirts were tucked into the slender waist of blue jeans. Yes, the hair was dark, with strands of silver, and the shoulder-length salt-and-pepper was caught back with filigree combs.

Their eyes met as the older woman looked Rayann up and down. Her deep brown eyes seemed to examine Rayann in microscopic detail. Rayann became acutely aware of her rumpled clothing and hair. She thought of Michelle suddenly, for the first time in hours, and a stab of pain must have showed.

"Are you all right?"

"Sure," Rayann said, after she had swallowed. The living room was sparsely furnished with antiques Rayann vaguely appreciated. She moved to the rocker, setting down her backpack while Louisa carried the suitcase into the room to the left of the short hallway. The carvings, which looked handcrafted to Rayann, dated the rocker at the mid-1800s, or, at the very least, a good copy of a rocker from that era. "This piece is lovely," she said.

"A garage sale bargain. Would you like some lunch?"

"What if customers come in?"

"I'll hear the bell and go down." Louisa smiled and Rayann felt as if she had asked a silly question. "You look starved."

Of all the possible expressions on her face, Rayann would not have thought hunger would be foremost. Nevertheless, she gratefully slid into a chair at the kitchen table, absorbing the green and white speckled linoleum and yellow-avocado tones of the appliances. The gleaming chrome toaster and bread box reminded Rayann of decorating books she'd studied, circa 1965. She wondered if the kitchen had looked the same for the last twenty-five years or if Louisa had deliberately decorated it for the Sixties feel.

Rayann's feet and calves throbbed with relief. She watched Louisa skillfully crack eggs open with one hand and toss the shells into the trash can. The eggs sizzled in the iron skillet and the cozy kitchen filled with the aroma of butter and ground black pepper. Rayann's stomach growled. It was unfathomable to her that she was comforted by the smell of frying eggs.

Louisa turned from the stove and caught Rayann staring. She cocked an eyebrow. Rayann said the first thing that came into her head. "You look like a Louisa somehow."

"Do I?" Louisa didn't seem pleased. "I've never thought of myself as a Louisa. Lou is okay, but I've always wished I were named Eleanor. As in 'of the Aquitaine.'" She put a steaming plate in front of Rayann, who didn't hesitate taking her first bite.

"Delicious," Rayann said, her mouth half full. She swallowed. "Somehow I don't think of Eleanor making scrambled eggs."

Louisa smiled wryly. "I'll bet Eleanor Roosevelt made great scrambled eggs."

Rayann was further distracted wondering if Eleanor Roosevelt had ever made scrambled eggs for Lorena Hickok in some stolen moment they had had together. She opened her mouth to speculate, then closed it again. Louisa seemed very reasonable. She *had* been at the women's center, but she *hadn't* put anything about wanting to rent her room to a lesbian. One just never knew. She concentrated on her eggs and then the crusty buttered toast Louisa offered.

"These are really wonderful," Rayann said after a few

minutes, indicating the eggs. "I didn't know how hungry I was."

"Thanks." Louisa smiled and took her plate to the sink. "You don't have to tell me why you were hungry and tired and searching for Lake Merritt."

"I was thinking." Rayann felt a stab of pain as she remembered the vision of Michelle, her face hidden by the other woman's thighs. "Wondering where I was going to end up. Thanks for renting me your room."

"Don't mention it. Believe me, you'll feel as if you've earned it." Louisa went to the large wooden block and drew out a long, serrated knife. Turning, she came back to the table. The blade glinted.

This is it, Rayann thought. *This is where she slices me up and makes me into pies. Sweeney Louisa.* She giggled. Her heart pounded.

Louisa reached past Rayann to a basket on the table. "This banana bread is fresh — do you want a slice?"

"No thanks," she choked out.

"What's so funny?" Louisa carved a slice of bread, put the knife down and picked up a raisin that had fallen on the table, popping it into her mouth.

"Too many *Friday the Thirteenth* movies. Even the commercials give me nightmares. Too many women chopped up."

Louisa gave a warm, husky laugh. *"Part Thirty-Nine: Louisa Takes Lake Merritt."* She brandished the knife, then wiped it on a tea towel and returned it to its slot in the knife block.

Rayann laughed, and after a moment was unable to catch her breath.

"Hey," Louisa said, still smiling. "That joke doesn't . . . ah, merit that kind of response."

Rayann laughed harder. She looked up through the tears rapidly filling her eyes to find Louisa staring at her with an intense brown gaze.

Louisa said in a quiet, persuasive voice, "You'll feel better if you let go."

* * * * *

She flailed and crashed to the floor. *What in the . . .*

She wasn't at home. Rubbing her knees, she realized she'd slept in a T-shirt she didn't recognize, in a sprawling room furnished with twin beds. *The shirt must be Louisa's. Who is Louisa? Why . . .*

The past two days rushed back like a reel of film on ultra-high speed. Michelle, the other woman's body arching, her mother, BART trains, the fountain, the lake, Louisa, scrambled eggs. And finally the tears soaking into Louisa's shirt. She remembered pain mixed with the comfort of brushed cotton against her hot forehead and cheeks.

"You'll be okay, you'll see. Trust me, you'll be all right," Louisa had said over and over. She had left Rayann to cry and fall asleep in her new bedroom while she tended to business downstairs. *I must have been exhausted to have slept so long.*

Her body had urgent needs. She crept to the door, opened it slowly, and listened. Voices were barely audible from downstairs. From the light she would guess the time was late morning. She had slept another night through but she didn't feel rested. *Not after that dream.* The floor creaked beneath her feet as she found the bathroom. She remembered Louisa leading her there and mopping her face with a damp cloth. The cloth was still there. It inadequately addressed the need to feel clean, so Rayann went back to her room, opened her suitcase and collected some clothes, then returned to the bathroom and removed the T-shirt she'd slept in. She stared at herself in the mirror, remembering her vow to find another lover. *Who would be interested in someone who looks like she's been kicked in the teeth?*

A door closed below her with a tinkle of bells. Then she heard the stairwell door open and close and a quick step come up the staircase.

"Are you up?" Louisa called.

"Yes," Rayann answered, glad of the robe hanging on the back of the bathroom door. She kept her gaze fixed on Louisa's shoulders, unable, for the moment, to meet the deep brown eyes she remembered as penetrating.

"It sounded as if you fell out of bed," Louisa said.

"I did," Rayann admitted, and laughed. "I'm not used to twins . . ." The laughter faded.

"No, I don't suppose you are," Louisa said, her expression unchanged. "You have a shower and I'll make some lunch."

Blissfully Rayann turned the hot water up till she felt her skin tingle and come alive. She slid into her clean clothes, feeling stronger and more awake. She used the blow dryer which hung from a hook next to the mirror. Fortunately her hair was thick enough to stay neat. Unfortunately it was still mouse-brown. But she looked like a human being again. She might even start feeling like a real person sometime soon. She padded barefoot from the bathroom and heard voices from downstairs, then the tinkle of bells. Again, Louisa's steps were quick and firm as she hurried up to the living quarters.

"You look as if you're going to make it," Louisa said, assessing Rayann as she had the night before with a piercing gaze.

"Did you think I wouldn't?"

"I had moments of doubt," Louisa said, and she released Rayann from her brown stare. "When I first saw you I thought you were a ghost. But a good night's sleep will cure a great many ailments."

"I think I'll probably need a few more," Rayann said. The memory of waking in Michelle's arms after a good night's sleep suddenly stabbed at her. She couldn't meet Louisa's eyes again — they were too intense — so she studied instead an excellent reproduction of Edward Hopper's *Nighthawks* that hung over the low étagère that held the television and stereo. The clean lines and clear colors of the painting suited Louisa's air of independence and solitude.

"You must be starved. Do you eat ham?"

"Sure." Rayann found herself agreeing to ham and swiss with lettuce, no mayo, extra mustard, chips on the side and a large glass of apple juice. They ate in silence.

33

By the time Rayann finished her sandwich, she felt fortified.

"You run a good restaurant, Louisa," she said, wondering how she would repay Louisa for her generosity.

"I've had practice. When my son was in high school it felt like I spent all day making food which disappeared the moment it was made. You are undemanding and far more polite by comparison."

Rayann filed away the information that Louisa had a son. "*I've* had practice. I spent my high school years learning the finer points of etiquette and deportment for girls. At fancy dinner parties, which I attend frequently — one every twenty years or so — I know which fork is for what food." She smiled and added wryly, "Now if only fork-choosing was a marketable skill."

Louisa returned her smile, then reached across the table to take Rayann's hand, turning it palm up. "I'm not doubting your fork-choosing ability, but your hands say you don't spend all your time at dinner parties. These callouses aren't just for show, are they?"

Rayann nervously withdrew her hand from Louisa's warm touch. She thought her hands unattractive, with nails down to the quick and scars from splinters. Michelle had been after her lately to get a manicure.

"No, I would definitely say they weren't for show," Rayann said quickly, trying to turn her mind away from Michelle by studying Louisa's hands. Long fingers, square at the tips, adorned by short, serviceable, glossy nails.

"Well, I know it wasn't quite what I had in mind when I said help around the store, but I have a carpentry project, and I've been putting it off because I didn't know anyone I could trust to do it right."

"How do you know you can trust me? And that I'll do it right?"

Louisa shrugged one shoulder. "I just do."

There was a long silence while Rayann attempted to read Louisa's expression. Deep laugh lines were embedded around her mouth and eyes, and her long, straight nose added to the angular planes of a lean face. There was strength in the set of her jaw and a suggestion that she'd had to be strong. Her eyes were unreadable yet familiar. Rayann searched her memory for those eyes. "What do you need?" Rayann asked at last.

Louisa blinked and let out a breath as if she had been holding it until Rayann answered. "Do you know anything about carpentry?" she asked as if she was already dismissing the possibility.

"Now we're entering my area of expertise," Rayann said. "I'm as happy putting up shelves as I would be shelving books. I'm not a carpenter, but I do know my way around wood. I've restored antiques, and I know how wood fits into itself and how to find the grain angle for maximum strength." She swallowed the last of her apple juice. "I'm an artist. I used to do computer-aided graphic design. I work in woods. I teach an adult ed class in carving," she finished abruptly, wondering if Louisa thought Rayann would have been better off sticking with the computers.

"Can you really build and reinforce shelves?" Louisa asked eagerly.

"I picked up extra money in college putting up shelves in frat and sorority bedrooms. Two dollars a shelf plus materials," she reminisced. "I did great business right at the start of each semester." The years at Cal were a pleasant memory. She'd been independent of her mother, and had supported herself before Michelle gave her financial freedom that now appeared to have had a high price. *I'll have to start calling them "the good ol' days."*

"This is almost too good to be true," Louisa said. She smiled widely. "There's a set of shelves that need to be replaced." Louisa glanced down. "I don't really know how to go about it, and I've been getting out of shape for that sort of thing."

"You could have fooled me," Rayann said impulsively. Louisa was neither slender nor fleshy. Her waist appeared trim, especially in contrast to her broad shoulders and generous bust.

Louisa looked up at her again, crow's feet at each temple deepening as she smiled. "If you tackle the shelving project I'd waive the rent — that's what I was going to use the rent money for. Once the big project is done, you could help me shelve the used books. I'm way behind. I'm not ready for the Christmas rush. Not that the Christmas rush is all that different from the rest of the year. There aren't too many customers." Louisa frowned as if she had just realized Rayann might find the absence of customers a problem. "But the regulars are pretty interesting."

"I don't think I could cope with crowds right now. Maybe later," Rayann said.

"You'd have all the books in the world you'd want to read."

"I love reading. And books."

"And a wide selection of magazines. But I don't stock *People*," Louisa added, frowning again.

"I hate *People*."

"You'd be cooped up with me all day."

"I've already accepted the room. And I'll accept all the work you throw my way." She smiled and saw her relief mirrored in Louisa's eyes.

3

The Old Veneer

Rayann's superficial impressions of the bookstore from the day before deepened as she followed Louisa down the stairs into the shop. She inhaled the smell of new paper and ink and recognized the subtle spice of older books.

Louisa gestured with one arm, taking in the whole store. "Look around." She went to the cash register and unlocked it, reaching under the bill tray for checks. "I'm going to work on the bank deposit, such as it is."

Rayann began her exploration to the left of the door, which was directly across from the cash register, and worked her way slowly clockwise around the store. One table held best-selling fiction, stacked in tiers, and one held best-selling nonfiction. Shelves from Rayann's knees to more than twice her height were labeled "Fiction" with titles filed alphabetically by author. Rayann checked for her favorite lesbian authors. They weren't there. But vintage editions of many classics promised eye-pleasing typography with full color plates and illustrations for the reader's enjoyment. She stepped around the sliding ladder, an elegant construction she'd only seen in movies. She visualized Betty Grable perched on it, skirt split to modestly display million-dollar legs. She pushed it along its track. It needed oil.

The stairwell to the upper floor was encased by a wall which divided the store almost in two. Behind it the ceiling dropped to a normal eight-foot height. Rayann slowly perused nonfiction sections of Cooking, Travel, Sports, How-Tos, and Self-Help. *A curry cookbook. Once I got my cooking tools, I could pay Louisa back with some gourmet meals.* It was a pleasant thought, something to look forward to. Under the Women's section there weren't any books published by the small women's presses, with one or two exceptions, nor were any of the books specifically titled to attract the lesbian reader. Still, the collection of nineteenth-century feminist writings was amazingly diverse, and many of the editions here were also vintage. Rayann caressed a collection of Olive Schreiner's essays and short fiction, then studied briefly the health manual for "Ladies of Leisure and Ladies Who Go Out to Work." There were many modern feminist titles — some used copies of out-of-print classics from the nineteen-sixties and seventies — certainly as many feminist titles as some of the gay and lesbian bookstores she'd been to. Although she hadn't been expecting to find *Sapphistry*, at least she wasn't confronted by penis postcards and stud photos when she turned a corner.

The store was well-equipped for general interest, but it looked as if Rayann would have to go elsewhere if she wanted the latest lesbian books. She stole a glance at Louisa, who was bent over some papers. Most of what she owned at Michelle's were books. How would she move them, and what would Louisa's reaction be if she saw *Lesbian Bedtime Stories* and *Beyond Stonewall*?

The bells on the door tinkled and two elderly women came in. They were outfitted in tweed overcoats, thick stockings, sturdy gloves and hats — not caps, hats. Two very proper ladies.

"I'm so glad you came in today," Louisa greeted them. "I just received the copy of the Ken Follett you wanted, and I want you to meet the woman who's renting my spare room. She's going to get the Poetry Corner back in shape."

Rayann walked to the counter and shook hands properly with the Misses Greta and Hazel Schoernsson, who lived in the retirement complex up the street.

"How lovely you're here to keep Louisa company," Hazel said as Louisa went in search of their book.

"She's been alone five or six years." Greta opened her purse.

"Seven years," Hazel said adamantly. "Since Christina's unfortunate accident, may she rest in peace."

"Whatever you say," Greta said. "I know better than to argue with your memory."

Greta spoke with a straight face, but Rayann found herself grinning at the look of suspicion that Hazel gave Greta. Greta blinked innocently. Louisa emerged from a room behind the counter, book in hand. Greta paid while Hazel tucked it into her mesh satchel.

"We were wondering if you thought we would like Tom Clancy," Greta asked.

Louisa smiled again and shrugged. "He's not LeCarré, but you might."

"Yes," Hazel broke in, "but doesn't Clancy glorify military weaponry and extol a jingoistic approach to American foreign policy?"

Rayann blinked, trying to sort through Hazel's statement.

Louisa laughed and said, "I think Clancy may not be the writer for you."

"If only there were more spies like George Smiley,"

Greta said, shaking her head sadly. "With his fine existential sense . . ."

Rayann was out of her league. Louisa and the Misses Schoernsson discussed several authors Rayann had heard of, but none she had actually read. She'd never been interested in intrigue and espionage — boys' games weren't her taste. Realizing the other women wouldn't miss her, she wandered over to Fiction and drew an old copy of *A Room of One's Own* out of the extensive Virginia Woolf collection and opened it, savoring the old-fashioned type and the gilt-edged pages. She replaced it and glanced around her. The store felt safe and comfortable.

For the first time, she noticed the large needlepoint sampler stretched over a colonial-style frame which hung above the door. The fabric was elaborately worked with the letters of the alphabet in blue, numbers zero through nine in mauve, all framing an open book stitched in ecru and beige with black letters. The book pages read: "The Common Reader." Rayann glanced at the cash register and saw a sign: "Make checks payable to The Common Reader." Well, it certainly was an appropriate name and explained why there were several copies each of *The Common Reader* and *The Common Reader II* along with all Virginia Woolf's other books on the shelves.

An older man, evidently well-known to the Misses Schoernsson, walked in and immediately entered the discussion. Louisa left them and joined Rayann in front of Fiction U–Z.

"Every Friday they meet here to argue," Louisa said. "They're all three staunch liberals and have decided they're better off hiding out here than talking politics at Merritt Park — that's the retirement center. Apparently they were all run out of the rec room during a debate at the last election." Louisa gestured at the trio, whose conversation was growing more animated by the minute. "They really started trouble by suggesting that this year the huge nativity scene in front of the retirement center should be put in the chapel where religious symbols belong, not out where non-Christian people have to look at it. Apparently they've been called anti-Christs and told they might be happier elsewhere. It blew over when one of the male residents was seen buying condoms."

Rayann laughed. "I suppose it's like living in a small town," she said. She'd never actually wondered what retirement centers were like.

"Hazel said it was a juicy scandal that lasted four or five days. But they still spend a lot of time here because they don't seem to fit in there. I've been wanting to put in a few chairs for them in the Poetry Corner."

"Why haven't you?" Rayann asked, looking over at the shelves. The books were tightly packed.

"It needs to be fixed first. Go ahead," Louisa said, leading the way to a particularly tight shelf. "Pull out a book — the Dickinson collection would be a good start — and you'll be well on your way in your first project. The books are the only thing holding those shelves up. I've already bought replacements, but I just didn't think I could undertake the entire project."

Rayann peered closer. "Oh, I see."

"There was a water leak last winter — or was it the winter before? Well, anyway, the wall is probably all right, but the books and shelves are ruined."

The bells tinkled and Rayann was left to examine the shelves in the rear corner of the store. Louisa was right. The books were ruined, and the particle board shelves — not a good choice by the original carpenter — had warped and split in places. Rayann suspected the wall behind them was not in good shape either. One good tug on Emily Dickinson would bring everything tumbling down. *Emily, did you ever suspect you'd be such a pillar of strength?* Rayann left well enough alone. Tomorrow she would make a fresh start on the project.

She was engrossed with watching customers until mid-afternoon, when Louisa taught her the simple inventory and cash register procedures. As the day grew later the customers grew younger. It appeared that college students came because they could find used copies of lesser-known works. Rayann suggested a computer might be helpful with the inventory. Louisa laughed the idea off, saying there wasn't enough turnover to bother. During a lull, Rayann said, "By the way, the teaching job I mentioned is three hours on Tuesday afternoons until Christmas."

"No problem," Louisa said. "I can cope by myself for a few short hours." She was almost smiling.

"Oh, I'm sure you can," Rayann said quickly, not sure if Louisa was teasing. Her expression was so hard to decipher. "Is it all right if I go upstairs and make a few phone calls? Not long distance. Just to the city."

The smile deepened. "Don't worry about it. I knew someone would be missing you."

"Yeah," Rayann said. "Just not very much."

After the little scene she'd made at the bar, word was probably going around about "marital strife between her and Michelle. Rayann wondered how many of her friends knew she had been — what was the Old English word? Cuckolded? She shuddered. But she could trust Judy. Judy would have told her if she'd known. At least Rayann thought so. She dialed Judy's home number and was greeted by the answering machine. A blast of Talking Heads segued into Dedric, Judy's lover, saying, "At the beep you can talk your head off."

Rayann left a brief message, saying she'd moved to Oakland and apologizing for her absence. She knew that Michelle had come between the friendship she and Judy had shared through and since college. She knew she hadn't found time for Judy because Michelle had been more important, though she didn't like people who used friends as fill-ins between lovers — and it seemed she was guilty of doing just that. She continued, "I know it's been a long time. Listen, call me and we'll talk. You don't even have to be the therapist. We'll talk about you for a change." She read off her new phone number and then paused. "Please do call me, Jude." She couldn't think of anything more to say.

While she had her courage, she called Michelle and got the answering machine, as she hoped she would. She left a succinct message saying she would pick up her belongings tomorrow. She could probably borrow Louisa's car, and she wished she didn't have to. She'd sold her own car to finance materials — she could use Michelle's anytime she wanted, right? She'd had a lot of wood blocks and finished pieces when she'd moved into Michelle's, but over the past three years her collection had shrunk. Michelle had urged her to work with the wood blocks Rayann already had before she started anything new. She hadn't felt right buying anything while the ironwood still served as an end table. Every inspiration she'd sketched out had been suited to lighter, softer woods. Rayann realized that she had been frustrated and trapped, and never realized it. *How could I be so stupid?* Michelle could keep the ironwood forever — *I never want to see it again.* Her computer was stored under the bed, and there were albums and books. The purple robe was hers, even though Michelle wore it more often. *Good God.* She angrily wiped tears away. She would not cry again.

The next morning, Rayann's first thought was of Michelle, which upset her since she'd spent so much time the night before deciding she would not think about her. But she couldn't help herself. More asleep than awake, she could almost feel the warmth of Michelle's breath against her ear as she whispered love and passion to her. *Hold me, baby, I'm . . .* Despite the cold, Rayann threw the covers back and sat up, holding her head in her hands. Almost choking with bitterness, she thought she now knew why Michelle had always called her "baby" when they made love — so she wouldn't accidentally say the wrong name.

Now that's what I call starting the day out on a positive note. I'm going to have to work on the looking-forward attitude I talked myself into last night.

Shivering, she dressed and tried to anticipate the day. It wasn't that hard. The evening had been surprisingly pleasant. After dinner, she and Louisa had agreed on a work schedule and house rules, such as how to hang damp towels and the amount of coffee that went into the basket filter — intimate little rules that would make life hell if they both didn't follow them. They found they both thought anyone leaving the cap off the toothpaste was uncouth.

Louisa had also offered to include groceries in the price of rent. Rayann protested. Since Louisa was waiving the rent while Rayann worked on the shelves, Louisa was getting the worst of the deal. But Louisa laughed it off and had her way, saying a well-fed laborer would labor well. Over drinks, Rayann opened up a little and told Louisa stories about her life, up to and including college. She alluded to her lesbianism, but hadn't used the L-word itself, which drew no comment from Louisa. Louisa mentioned her son and grandson, but mostly they had talked about books and movies. Louisa had groaned when Rayann hailed "good old movies" like *All About Eve, Anastasia* and *Bus Stop* — movies Louisa said she'd seen in the theater during their first release.

Rayann stared out the kitchen window as she ate a bowl of cereal. Fog wrapped the house in quiet, and an occasional drip of water from the window sills broke the silence. Cereal bowl rinsed and drying in the dish rack — in accordance with the house rules — she went down to examine the shelving project. Alone in the bookstore for the first time, she resisted the temptation to linger over the books. There would be plenty of long, lonely evenings for reading. *Thinking positive again already!* As she crouched in the Poetry Corner she heard water running upstairs and Louisa's light tread moving from the bathroom to the kitchen.

The Poetry Corner was going to take some effort. Rayann carefully removed everything that could be removed without prying or toppling the infrastructure. As she set down the last stack she became aware of Louisa watching her.

"I thought I'd get an early start," she said, feeling as if she were a guest caught in the wrong part of the house.

"I didn't realize you were an early riser. I thought

maybe you'd reconsidered," Louisa said. A look of anxiety faded away.

"No. I'd tell you. I don't run from things . . . not usually." She looked at her feet, then back at Louisa, who smiled.

"You don't have to start that today. There's lots of time."

"My mother would say time was a-wasting." *Oh my God, I've started quoting Mother. I knew it would happen some day.*

"There is plenty of time. A time to every purpose."

"No time like the present. Your turn," Rayann said with challenge in her voice.

Louisa smiled. "Okay, ummm, time . . . 'The strongest warriors are Time and Patience.' That's three quotes. Add a fourth, you can call it a gallon."

Rayann groaned. "It's too early for Groucho Marx! Let's see — 'Do not squander Time, for that's the stuff life is made of.'"

"Okay." Louisa's expression was a mixture of laughter and stubbornness. "You want to play hard ball. Well, I'll say 'Time is issued to spinster ladies in long white ribbons.' Top that."

Rayann wrinkled her nose. "I've never liked the word spinster. It has such bad connotations."

"There's nothing wrong with the word," Louisa said, moving away and taking a philosophical tone. "It's the meaning people give it. Spinster is often synonymous with unloved or unlovable. I think Woolf meant something different. Louisa May Alcott — for whom I was named, by the way — certainly meant something different. Her spinsters usually weren't alone by chance but by choice. She was an ardent advocate of women's health and independence."

"Really? I thought she espoused women-in-their-place themes." She had wondered why there were so many Alcott books.

"Heavens no," Louisa said. "She herself hated *Little Women*, but it paid the mortgage. The sequels, which are more feminist, are not as well known, and her works for adults are quite radical for Victorian-era novels."

"I'll have to read them," Rayann said, turning back to the shelves. "I had no idea."

Louisa laughed, and went over to the sales counter. "Don't read them just to please me. My friend Danny says I never know when to stop selling books."

Rayann realized that she did want to please Louisa. It was probably because Louisa had not met her while Rayann was at her best, and she wished that circumstance were otherwise. Louisa was an interesting woman, and Rayann would like to have her respect. A knock interrupted Rayann's thoughts.

Louisa glanced at the clock over the cash register. "Good lord, it's after opening." She hurried to unlock the front door.

Why on earth am I sweating? Maybe it's just from moving these books.

She raided Louisa's garage-slash-storage shed for tools. She spread them on the lawn and hosed them off.

"Did you find what you needed?" Louisa asked as Rayann came through the front door.

"Mostly. I couldn't find a saw, but they're not terribly expensive. Can I buy one when I get the wood?"

"Certainly. The laborer needs her tools. Do you think you'll be able to salvage any of the wood? I know the books are lost."

"I can't see enough of it to tell yet." Rayann frowned. "I'll try, but you could be looking at all new materials. It's hard to say." She was surprised when Louisa laughed.

"You sound just like Paulette — the plumber who came to fix the water leak. So serious."

Rayann smiled. "Well, this is a job, isn't it? I should be careful how I spend your money."

"True, but it's hard to take you seriously with those lumps in your pockets. What are they?"

Rayann pulled out the tape measure and a variety of sockets for which she'd been unable to find a socket wrench. "This and that. I'll get them sorted out. By the way, do you have an old towel?"

"As in, I shouldn't expect to see it again?"

It was Rayann's turn to laugh. "Oh, you'll see it. You just won't want to touch it."

Towel in hand, she went back outside and dried the tools, stacking them in the toolbox. The task completed, she congratulated herself for having accomplished something useful without even once thinking about — *Well, it was nice while it lasted.* Sighing, she went back inside, toolbox in hand.

Louisa looked up from her ledger. Her smile froze, then slowly thawed, becoming simply forced.

"Have I done something wrong?" Rayann asked.

Louisa shook her head. "I'd forgotten Chris's toolbox was in there," she said. She cleared her throat. "Glad to see it's still in good shape."

After an awkward silence, Rayann said, "Well, I'll get started on the shelves." She remembered Hazel Schoernsson mentioning a Christina, but Rayann didn't know who she was.

Louisa nodded and refocused her attention on the ledger.

Despite her earlier efforts, there were still a lot of books wedged in place, all of which were bloated from water and had fused to one another after they dried. She hooked the hammer behind Emily Dickinson and pulled. Nothing loosened except her grip on the hammer. She tugged, but nothing budged. *Sorry, Emily, but it's got to be done.* She felt like a dentist as she wedged the crowbar behind the book and pulled. It shifted.

Rayann fell on her rear with a cry of alarm as the remaining books, then the shelves, peeled away from the rotted Sheetrock, and toppled toward her. She scrambled back but something heavy — most likely *The Complete E.E. Cummings* — landed on her shin. She sat up and looked at the ruin as a layer of mildewed Sheetrock dust settled over the entire scene.

She started to laugh but suddenly very strong, masculine arms were around her. Her self-defense training went instinctively into action as she shoved the man back and rolled away. She came up crouched, crowbar in one hand. "I can get up by myself," she said fiercely.

"Jesus Christ, are you trying to break my neck, too?" He steadied himself and glared down at her. "Who the hell are you? Good lord, look what you've done. Are you nuts?" He glared at Rayann and the mess, then brushed futilely at a dusty handprint on the sleeve of his suit jacket.

"What's it to you?" Rayann demanded, equaling him in belligerence if not in height. She didn't like to be touched by strangers, least of all men, particularly men in three-piece suits who looked as if they thought women were helpless. She clutched the crowbar. Behind him Rayann saw a little boy watching them with his mouth open. The boy looked familiar — which was strange because she knew absolutely no children.

"What in the — Oh, I see Emily did the trick," Louisa said, appearing behind the man. "Teddy, have you introduced yourself to my new assistant and tenant?"

"No," he muttered, glaring at Rayann. "I suppose she can clean this up. I'll come by after work and put up some new shelves." Rayann's annoyance migrated to anger.

Louisa laughed, her eyes resting on Rayann. "Dear, you've been saying that for a year at least. Rayann's in the middle of putting up the new shelves. She started, quite appropriately, by dismantling the old ones." She walked to the wall and peered at it, then prodded the fallen Sheetrock with a loafer-shod foot. "Rayann, do you know anything about Sheetrock?"

Ignoring the man, who now also seemed familiar, Rayann turned to Louisa. "Enough to know that it's got to be replaced. And the project will take a little longer than an evening to do properly."

Louisa shuddered as she peered into the hole left in the wall. "I hate to think what's behind there. Well," she continued, turning back to the sandy-haired man, "to what do I owe this honor?" She stepped over the rubble as if it were an everyday occurrence and hugged him, then bent to the little boy who submitted with good grace to her embrace.

"Tucker's going to the dentist so I thought we'd drop by on the way." To Rayann's surprise he smiled. The smile clicked. Of course, she thought. Several pictures of him and the little boy were upstairs in the curios cabinet. "I had no idea it was a construction zone." He shot a glance at Rayann that seemed teasing on the surface but guarded hostility.

Rayann wiped her hands on the back of her pants, and then reached out to shake hands. "I'm Rayann Germaine," she said sweetly. She couldn't afford to antagonize Louisa's son. He was older than she thought he'd be. Louisa had either been in her teens when she had him or was older than she appeared. *She's so attractive for her age.* The thought came to Rayann involuntarily.

He squeezed her hand briefly. "Ted Thatcher. And this is Tucker." The little boy peered at her from behind his father's legs.

"Do you have time for a cup of coffee?" Louisa took his answer for granted as she headed for the stairs, followed by son and grandson.

As the door closed Rayann heard him say, "Are you sure she knows what she's doing? Why on earth did you get a renter?"

Louisa's laughing answer, before it faded out of Rayann's hearing was, "Dear, it was your idea, remember?"

Rayann's pique dissipated as she set about separating books from Sheetrock and usable wood from rotten planks. She ignored the flash of attraction she had felt for Louisa. *After all, you've got a broken heart and you don't even know if she's gay. But then who was Christina?* Rayann shook her head fiercely to clear it. *None of your business, that's who. You're just starting to feel lonely.* Not much of the wood was usable. It wasn't long before Louisa's son and grandson left and Louisa returned to survey the work in progress.

"The older I get the more dependent he thinks I should be," Louisa said suddenly. "Have you ever been convicted of a major crime?"

Rayann blinked. "I've never even been arrested. Some of my more radical friends are disgusted with me."

Louisa laughed. "They'd love me, then." She laughed again at Rayann's shocked expression. "War protest. It wasn't fun at the time but somehow so very important. I lost my job because of it and we were pretty hard up for a while." Louisa paused. "Anyway, Teddy's a lawyer and he's going to ask a friend at the police department to see if you have a rap sheet."

Rayann dusted her hands on her backside but they only got dustier. "I'm not sure I like that. I mean, I don't work for him."

Louisa said, "You're filthy," and she swatted at Rayann's behind, creating a cloud of dust. "No, you don't, but once he knows you're not a hardened criminal he might be willing to part with his ladder, sawhorses and electric saw for a few weeks."

"A lawyer who owns sawhorses?" Rayann asked skeptically.

"Teddy will surprise you. Besides, he bought most of the equipment when he first promised to do the shelves. He might even give you a hand."

Over my dead body. Rayann decided she'd have the new Sheetrock and shelves up in record time.

After lunch, she cleared away the debris, and pried the remaining Sheetrock from the wood beams. They were real 2x4s, dating the house to pre-fiberglass insulation days. It was an exterior wall, so Louisa agreed with Rayann that she should pack it with fireproof insulation before replacing the Sheetrock.

Rayann loaded the debris in the back of the El Camino to take to a dumpster. El Caminos were such useful car/trucks. One of Rayann's first crushes had been on her gym teacher — of course — who had driven an El Camino and had been able to load up an entire softball team's equipment in the back and include two, or maybe just one lucky passenger in the front. Rayann worked up a sweat moving the books, remembering one ride when she'd been squeezed between Miss Smith and Rita "Tomboy" Barker and nearly fainted. Breathing hard, but pleased, she slammed the tailgate.

"Don't you want to see my license?" Rayann looked at the car keys Louisa tossed to her. Louisa raised both eyebrows with a glance that plainly said she hadn't considered it necessary. "I think you're far too trusting."

"Just don't break the car. She ain't pretty, but she's all I got."

A half an hour later Rayann was standing on the tailgate of the car, keenly aware of the construction workers watching her. When she'd driven up they'd told her she could throw her trash in one of the dumpsters — and pointed to the tallest of the group lining the site.

Daunted, but stubborn, she lifted ruined books and heaved them up and over her head. They went over the side and dropped to the bottom with a satisfying crash. It hurt to throw away books, but they were ruined — and they did make a lovely sound. She forgot about the construction workers watching her as her body found a lift-shove-push rhythm. Once the books were gone she tackled the ruined lumber. She threw the pieces overhand, listening to them ricochet and ping off the dumpster walls. She practiced putting a spin on them, and the overhead motion reminded her of the tennis she'd cultivated in high school. Boos from the workers broke her concentration. She looked up and saw a figure headed her way.

A smiling brown woman looked up at her from under a fluorescent orange hard hat. "Hang on a moment and I'll make it easier," she said, walking past Rayann. She disappeared around the dumpster, and then the side began to lower. Eventually the side of the dumpster was level with Rayann's knees. *Typical men — they weren't going to tell me it lowered.* Rayann hopped down from the tailgate and pulled the largest piece of Sheetrock toward her. Two gloved hands joined hers and Rayann looked up in surprise.

"They're all after your body, and if I don't get you out of here I won't be responsible," the woman said. Black eyes glinted with laughter over high cheekbones that hinted at Native American ancestry.

"I appreciate it. Thanks for lowering the side, too," Rayann said, slightly out of breath. They worked companionably and in a matter of minutes had completely cleared the back of the car. "Thanks again," Rayann said as the woman slammed the tailgate.

"De nada. I'm Zoraida." She took off her hard hat and wiped her face with the bandanna tied around her neck.

"Rayann."

"Rayann." Zoraida trilled the R. "Very pretty." More trilling, and Rayann became acutely aware of the honest appraisal she was receiving. There was a prolonged silence during which Rayann could think of nothing to say. Then Zoraida said, "Would you like to have a beer sometime?"

Suddenly Rayann felt a glow. *She thinks I'm attractive. I'll be darned. Coupledom didn't ruin me completely. For heaven's sake, say something!* "When?" she asked. *Wow, you really bowled her over with that snappy come-back. For someone who made finding a new lover a priority, you're not being very aggressive.* But there was something about Zoraida that told Rayann she wouldn't need to be aggressive, even if it were her style.

"Whenever you think you can handle it — or me," Zoraida said. She tossed her head and put the hard hat on at a jaunty angle. "We're only on the third floor and there's fourteen more to go. I'll be here whenever you're . . . thirsty."

Speechless, Rayann watched Zoraida as she walked away. Suddenly Zoraida turned, walking backwards. "I lied when I said they were all after your body. I don't know about them, but I certainly am." She turned forward again and sauntered into the site. Rayann drove back to Louisa's, a two million megawatt smile on her face.

Later, showered and grim, Rayann was ready. She knew that Michelle should be back at work on another 72-hour shift, but she might have taken time off to guard her precious possessions while Rayann removed her own. Girded for battle, Rayann thought her jeans and sweatshirt looked tough. All she needed now was a pair of six-shooters, and Zoraida's hard hat. The recollection that Zoraida had found her attractive eased the ache inside a little.

She went down to the store. "I thought I'd go and get my things," she told Louisa in as firm a voice as she could manage.

"Need company?"

"No, I have to do this myself. Thank you for loaning me the car. I wish I'd never sold mine."

"Why did you?"

"There were things I needed . . . and I didn't feel as if . . . she should pay for them." *There, another chance for her to admit she's gay. She has to be.*

"Now, of course, you wish you'd let her," Louisa said, with a smile.

"I'm not sure," Rayann said seriously. "I never thought of her as a meal ticket." She met Louisa's gaze, for once, and said, "I was never looking for a sugar daddy. Mommy. Whatever." She stopped, realizing how silly it sounded.

Louisa laughed. "It's funny how the concept of sugar mommies don't pop up much in literature."

Rayann made a joking response as she left the store, her suspicions about Louisa's sexuality still unconfirmed. *Of course, what was she supposed to say? "I used to be a sugar mommy? I once had a sugar mommy?" Get real, Rayann. She'll tell you when she's comfortable.*

The drive, in early afternoon, was only slowed by the

usual backup on the Bay Bridge. Her first stop was at her mother's office. Armed with one of Louisa's business cards, she parked in a loading zone, and transferred empty boxes from the cab to the truck bed, hoping the parking monitors would think she was delivering something and cut her some slack. She hurried into the Transamerica Tower and took the express to the seventy-third floor. She swallowed rapidly as her ears popped twice on the way up.

Her mother's new office had moved further away from the reception area. Rayann was aware this was an increase in status, but was a little peeved when an officious young woman in a suit offered to help her find her "party." She looked as if she thought Rayann had wandered in off the street. Rayann wished she had a six-shooter handy. *Take me to your leader,* she'd say. Instead, she explained she had something for Ann Germaine. The robot replied that "Ms. Germaine wasn't available," and that she would give anything Rayann might like to leave to her.

"I'm her daughter," Rayann said bluntly, but she smiled when the robot became a human being.

"Sorry, her office is this way. She's really not in, but you'd be surprised how many people try to butt their way in to see her."

Rayann forgave the woman when she saw her mother's office, complete with the words "Creative Director" under her name. She hadn't known her mother was now the head of Creative. From her days in graphic design, Rayann knew the creative director of any ad agency was only a few steps removed from God.

She put Louisa's card on her mother's desk, and wrote a note explaining that she was living and working at the address on the card. Then she wrote, "Sorry about yesterday. Give me a little time and then I'll probably be interested in any *pro bono* you know about."

Feeling better about the world in general, Rayann returned to Louisa's El Camino, which did not sport a parking ticket, and drove back through the Financial District to the South of Market area where Michelle's apartment was. The parking space was empty, so Michelle was not home. She could make this short and sweet.

She cleared the bookshelves, then packed her albums, the rest of her clothes, videotapes and her favorite coffee mug. One boxful was the cooking equipment she had paid for and the bottle of authentic basalmic vinegar Michelle had recently bought her as a surprise gift. *I wonder if it was a guilt offering, like when the unfaithful husband suddenly brings home flowers to the little missus. Should that have tipped me off?* From under the bed she drew her Macintosh in its padded case, and two large boxes of diskettes. Finally, she dismantled her stereo components: receiver, speakers, turntable. The equalizer and CD player were Michelle's. From the back of the closet she found the tubes of her posters and her dusty but still serviceable portfolio case.

Everything, without any piling or squeezing, fit in the back of the El Camino and Rayann realized how little she could call her own. It wasn't that she put great stock in possessions, but surely an almost thirty-year-old woman should have more to her name than an odd collection of wood and a bottle of basalmic vinegar.

She stared at the ironwood block, knee-high and eighteen-inches square. It represented a creative failure, but had cost a fortune. She had piled Michelle's stuff unceremoniously on the floor, finding a pair of her own earrings in the process. It took all her strength to leverage the block onto the sofa, then onto her shoulder. She nearly fell down the stairs with it, which probably would have killed her, but finally it was in the back of the El Camino, mostly unscathed.

Her last task was gathering and wrapping the chess pieces she'd carved, all female pieces with meticulous design work on the base of each figure. she could probably sell the set, but she had always liked it too much to consider parting with it.

A quarter hour later she was on the Bay Bridge with the sun dropping behind the Financial District skyline. Another half hour and she turned up the streets to The Common Reader.

* * * * *

"Do you need some help?" Louisa left her stool behind the counter as Rayann nosily entered carrying her suitcases. Rayann declined. "Are you . . . well, ask if you want some help. The back door would be faster." Louisa went back to her perch. There were various stacks of invoices on the counter.

Rayann unloaded her clothes into the dressers, then took the outside backstairs down to the car. Her back and legs ached from the afternoon's exertions. She filled her arms, then plodded stoically up the stairs, through the back porch, into her bedroom. She stacked everything in the huge walk-in closet. She piled more clothes on the other bed. She set her Macintosh case in the corner where she could get to it if she felt some sort of creative urge — which she rather doubted would happen. She hadn't used her Mac since she'd typed Michelle's last paper. She hadn't used it for herself since she'd given up her job. *Stop sniveling! You didn't have to give up your job. You just wanted to be available when Michelle was available. For all the good it did.*

"Looks like you're making yourself comfortable. You need some space, though," Louisa said from the doorway.

"It'll all fit when I get organized," Rayann said. She wiped her shirt sleeve across her sweaty forehead. "If you lived in a newer house the room would probably be half this size, but as it is there's plenty of closet space and shelves. And I love the wardrobe and all its nooks and crannies."

"So do I," Louisa said. "Well, I'm glad you're making yourself at home."

Rayann smiled and wondered if she had imagined Louisa's fleeting expression of wistfulness. "I brought some videotapes from my collection. Maybe there are a few movies you haven't seen. They're in here." Suddenly her heart began to pound. Would Louisa recognize the significance of *Lianna* and *By Design?* Had she ever heard of *Two in Twenty?*

Louisa bent over the box and read the titles. "Do you

56

know I've never seen *Star Wars?* Hard to believe it's been out since the mid-seventies. Wait until Tucker finds out you have it."

"I have *Empire* and *Jedi*, too," she said, calming herself. *For goodness sake, get a grip. There's no reason to suddenly feel naked.*

Louisa looked up from the box. "I was going to start some dinner. You must be starved."

"I am. But I want to finish moving everything in. I'll worry about organization tomorrow."

"It's a casserole so you can microwave some when you're ready. Mind you, I'm not very good with the fool thing except for heating coffee, so you're on your own."

"Why do you have one, then?"

"Teddy thought I should have one. So just help yourself."

Rayann focused on a stack of clothing to hide the rush of tears at Louisa's persistent kindness. "Thanks, Louisa. I appreciate it. You've being very good to me."

"Goodness has nothing to do with it," Louisa quipped as she left the room. "I'm not losing a bedroom so much as gaining an indentured servant."

Rayann went back to moving. If she stopped she'd drop. The last load was the stereo components. She stacked them up and then decided she was too tired to carry them upstairs to her room — there was no space for them anyway.

"I don't think these will fit in my room," she said to Louisa as she went through the back door into the bookstore. "And you have a nice stereo in the living room already. I don't know why I took them except they're mine."

"Enough reason. It's been a quiet evening for a Friday." Louisa stood up and stretched. They were the same height, but Louisa seemed taller somehow. "Would you mind if we set them up down here — oh, for heaven's sake put them down. You look done in. The casserole's very good, by the way, if I do say so myself." Louisa unloaded the components from Rayann's arms.

Rayann shook her arms and swayed slightly.

57

"Casserole sounds like ambrosia right now. I'm really tired."

"I knew you shouldn't have tackled Emily today." She stared at Rayann's arms.

Rayann smiled. "It sounds as if we were playing football." Rayann rolled her shoulders forward and back, then winced. She felt the intensity of Louisa's gaze on her face. "What did you want to do with the stereo?"

"I'd love to set it up down here. And play something nicer than what that old radio will tune in. All I need is a table of some sort."

"I have the perfect solution," Rayann said. She ran out to the garage with the last bit of her energy, and struggled back to the bookstore with the ironwood block she had been going to hide with the camping equipment.

"Are you nuts?" Louisa hurried to the door and pulled half the block's weight onto her own arms, which seemed more than up to the task. "You're going to destroy your back. What on earth is this?"

"Ironwood."

"Feels like it." Together, they set the block upright in a corner near the register. Louisa stared down at the block. "What were you going to do with it?"

"I don't remember now." Rayann set the receiver on top of the block, the turntable on top of the receiver and the speakers to either side. "I saw something, someone, stretching and . . . reaching . . . and it's gone now."

Louisa put her hand on Rayann's shoulder. "Well, as soon as you want to start on it, I'll find something else to hold the stereo up. In the meantime I think it looks nice."

"Probably the world's most expensive stereo table," Rayann said wryly. Louisa's touch sent a warm flush through her shoulder, and she recalled a similar flush when Zoraida had been so outrageous earlier. *A perfectly normal response for someone on the rebound.* Still her shoulder felt cold when Louisa withdrew.

She untangled the cables and plugged the pieces together. When she was done she felt settled. It was always the same when she moved. She felt as if she were home once the stereo was put together. At Michelle's there had been foreign components and it hadn't felt like hers anymore. Not exactly *theirs* either.

"It gets AM, doesn't it?" Louisa peered at the knobs and buttons. "I'm a real baseball fan. If you don't like baseball already you'll have to learn, I'm afraid."

Rayann frowned and held back a giggle — relief and exhaustion played tag with her rapidly fogging brain. "I don't know. Aren't there . . . two leagues or something? Because the A's never play the Giants except when they did in the Series. They should play more often. It would save money, wouldn't it, because they could take public transportation to the games." She fluttered her eyelashes for good measure.

Louisa looked away and Rayann could see her rolling her eyes. Then she shook her head and gave a patient sigh. "I follow the A's, and they're in the American League. You may have heard of them. My friend Danny and I go to a couple of games every year."

"The American League. Hmmm. So you're basically a supporter of the DH rule. Don't you think it takes away some of the strategy in the use of middle relievers? But then I can't blame you for liking the A's. They're a real class act. One of the best cheap thrills in the world is watching the ninth-inning relief strike out three in a row. It would take something away from the mystique if the pitchers batted. But then again, some pitchers can lay down a bunt that hugs the third base line like —"

"You big faker," Louisa said. She grinned. "I bet you know the starting lineup and their lifetime averages."

"I'm San Francisco born and bred, but I have always liked the A's," Rayann said as she found the plug-in and turned the receiver on. "Ever since BillyBall." Static, then she tuned to a station that played the quiet new age music she loved. A soothing piano melody wrapped around her.

"Lovely," Louisa said. "I like that station, too. You know, I think we're going to get along just fine."

Rayann forced a smile, trying to fight the memory of similar music, the fireplace, Michelle and lovemaking. "As

59

long as you agree that the best thing the A's could do is get a right fielder with class." Louisa protested and they argued good-naturedly. It was very comfortable.

That night, unable to sleep, Rayann went into the living room and turned on the lamp next to Louisa's easy chair. She hoped she wasn't disturbing Louisa, but the strangeness of her room had suddenly overwhelmed her. The magazine she picked up held her interest for a few minutes, but after a while she let her head fall against one of the chair's wings and found her eyes in line with the photographs that crowded the curios cabinet. Ted Thatcher looked out at her frequently, as did Louisa.

Interested in these younger images of Louisa, Rayann got up to study them. The earliest photos appeared to be of Teddy alone. They were dated by his age in months, then years old. When he was five or so, Louisa suddenly appeared in the pictures too. She smiled radiantly at the camera. Rayann studied the lines of the smile; they would later become the laugh lines on the Louisa she knew.

Teddy's high school graduation photo revealed a boy who hadn't quite grown into his knees and elbows hugging a mother who still beamed at the camera. He looked as geeky in his picture as Rayann did in her senior portrait — the clothes said he had been only a few classes ahead of her. Then his college graduation photo. Rayann held them side by side for a long time. Louisa still smiled at the camera but it was — controlled. Teddy, who had shared his mother's smile in the past, was almost, but not quite, glowering at the camera.

Rayann went over the photos again and decided that Louisa's radiance was not directed at the camera, but at the person holding the camera. Someone who had taken the photographs, but never appeared in them. And in all those pictures there was no sign of the man who had supplied some vital genetic material in Teddy's creation. There was the sudden change in Louisa's expressiveness which had taken place while Teddy was in college but her eyes were always the same — dark and intense.

There was no Christina in any of the pictures, unless she had been holding the camera. Nor were there any pictures of the friend Danny that Louisa mentioned frequently. After a long span of time not covered by any photographs until Tucker was born, Louisa appeared again, a mere shadow of the woman Rayann knew. Hazel had said Christina's death had been seven years ago. Tucker was seven. Rayann's artistic instinct told her she was looking at the face of grief when she studied Louisa holding baby Tucker. The later pictures showed the grief eased away, to be replaced by the vitality Louisa gave off in her every movement.

A creak of the floorboards made Rayann jump. She spun around, flushing with guilt.

"You have a strange kind of insomnia," Louisa said drily. Her hair was loose around the shoulders of her maroon flannel pajamas.

"I'm sorry — how rude of me." With fumbling hands she put the last photos she'd been holding back where she'd gotten them. "I couldn't sleep and I was looking at the pictures. They're so well done." That was true, even if it wasn't the real reason she'd been staring at them. *And just what is the real reason?*

"Chris was good with a camera. I always got red eyes and bleached out foreheads." Louisa remained where she was, leaning against the wall next to her bedroom door.

"I don't see a picture of Chris," Rayann said. *Please tell me what I want to know.*

"She hated having her picture taken. The few pictures I had of her I put away after she died."

Rayann looked at Louisa, whose face had grown wistful, and blurted out, "Was she your lover?" Louisa nodded, eyebrows lifted. "I didn't know you were gay."

"Didn't you? I'm sorry, I thought it was obvious after the way we met."

Rayann's skin prickled with a sudden cold sweat. *Well, now you know. What's it to you?* "No, it isn't obvious, except you didn't object to what I said about Michelle and . . . and sugar mommies."

Louisa laughed. "I'm sorry — I wasn't being deliberately obtuse. It's a part of me, but not the biggest part of me."

What is the biggest part of you? Your store, your son, what? Rayann's feet reminded her she was getting cold. She faked a yawn and said, "I didn't mean to pry, really."

"De nada," Louisa said. "You'll catch cold though if you don't put on some slippers."

"I'm ready to sleep now," Rayann answered. Remembering Zoraida, she smiled, a little of the megawatt voltage Zoraida had given her zinging through her body. "Goodnight."

Louisa looked at her quizzically, then answered in her low voice, "Goodnight."

4

Finding the Grain

Rayann insisted on doing the dishes after Louisa made breakfast in the mornings. "It's the least I can do," she said firmly.

"I'm not a fool," Louisa said, smiling. "You may do the dishes as often as you like. I'm going to go fiddle with the invoices again and then flip a coin to see who gets paid this month."

Rayann finished the chore and folded the dishtowel on the counter, then went to find her tennis shoes. Though her sides and arms and legs ached from her continuing work on the Poetry Corner, she wanted to finish the shelving project to prove her abilities to Louisa's skeptical son. She would show him, and herself for that matter, that she did know what she was doing.

Her first trip to the lumberyard had been for insulation, Sheetrock and nails, sealing tape, finishing nails and sheets of paneling. The days had flowed one after another as a series of rainstorms cleared the winter air and left the atmosphere exhilarating. Louisa took advantage of the crisp sunshine in between storms to walk around Lake Merritt. Rayann made yet another trip to the hardware store in the pouring rain for waterproof tarps to protect the floors from her muddy footprints as she tromped in and out through the back door to the garage for supplies. Teddy had dropped off tools and sawhorses while she had been in the city teaching her wood sculpting class. Louisa reported that he'd been impressed by the amount of work already completed.

Clad every day in her comfortable tennis shoes and her most worn-out jeans, Rayann went to work. She was going to impress the socks off of one Ted Thatcher, and his mother, though Louisa had already said she was impressed. Not one shelf was going to be even a quarter bubble off center. Every support would be plumbed perfectly. The shelves themselves, cut from sturdy, cured pine, would be sealed against water and lacquered so the books would slide easily on and off. The shelves would be standing long after the house had fallen down.

During the following week she left the project long enough for her class, only to discover that just three of her students had braved the sodden weather. She met Judy for dinner and told her the long, sad story. Judy had put away her therapist persona and listened supportively without once saying, "And how did that make you feel?"

Eight days after she began the project, Rayann emerged from her bedroom in the jeans and sweatshirt she reserved for painting and lacquering. Louisa looked up from her breakfast and broke into laughter. "You look like Jackson Pollack's sister!"

Rayann laughed as well. "When the jeans get too stiff to move around in, I'm going to prop them up in a corner and maybe someone will give me a grant to further develop them into a complete art showing."

She went out to the garage for varnishing supplies. Laden with the awkward buckets and cans, she ran back to the house through the rain, hurrying because the brushes were threatening to fall. She backed against the barely open door into the bookstore. It didn't budge, so she gave the door a good shove only to find someone opening it from the other side. She stumbled through the door and everything she was carrying slid through her arms to the floor.

"You seem to make a habit of this," Teddy said as he bent to help her.

"You shouldn't stand behind doors. It's not safe," Rayann snapped.

"You should know better," Louisa said.

Teddy glanced at his mother as if puzzled, then at Rayann. "I thought I'd see how everything was coming along."

"I'm almost done." Rayann stood up again. She knew she was being brusque, but something about him made her feel foolish.

"So I see." He set down cans of varnish next to the sawhorses.

"This is messy work for a suit. Varnish doesn't wash out," Rayann said.

"The judge will understand," he said. He smiled and Rayann realized his eyes were very similar to his mother's. Louisa's were more penetrating and yet more welcoming, somehow. Rayann still couldn't figure out whose eyes Louisa's reminded her of.

"I didn't work myself to the bone to put you through Boalt Hall for you to show up in court smelling like a construction zone," Louisa said. Her manner was teasing and lovingly indulgent, something that Rayann had never seen.

Teddy rolled his eyes and glanced at Rayann. "This is where the two-jobs-at-once story starts. Every time it gets worse."

"It does not," Louisa protested. "And every word's true."

"In the next version she'll be saying she took in laundry."

"I almost did when the fees were due." Louisa tossed her head at her son, eyes snapping with mock-offense.

"I know, Mom." He stepped over crumpled tarps to hug Louisa. "And I'll always be grateful. In fact, I stopped by to find out if you would be available for dinner tonight."

Arm in arm, mother and son drifted toward the door, arguing over a restaurant which would please them and not bore Tucker to distraction. Teddy wanted to try a new French restaurant, but Louisa resisted because Tucker wouldn't like it.

"I'll watch him," Rayann heard herself saying.

They both turned to her. Teddy said, with a grin, "You don't know what you're offering to do."

"I'm sincere. Really. He can watch videotapes and I can make us dinner. We'll put out the Christmas decorations down here if he gets really bored. I always liked doing that when I was a kid."

"Ray, that's very sweet of you," Louisa said. "And Tucker is not the hellion his father makes him out to be."

"You don't live with him, Mom." He looked at Rayann. "It is very nice of you. Now I can take my best gal out somewhere swank instead of McDonald's." He smiled again and this time Rayann was able to smile back. Maybe he was starting to like her. Somehow that was important.

The evening went well. Rayann made pork and beans and *Star Wars* kept Tucker occupied while she finished lacquering the last of the shelves. When she opened the first box labeled "Xmas Stuff," he could hardly wait to help. They twined garland around the sliding ladder and gift wrapped the front door. He supervised Rayann's stringing of garland swags from wall to wall, then passed up ornaments to her to hang from the garland. The end result was bright and festive. They added more touches upstairs, then, after Tucker promised not to tell, Rayann drove him to Fenton's for "mondo" ice cream sundaes, as Tucker called them.

When Teddy and Louisa came home Tucker was sound asleep. Rayann hoped no one figured out he was in a sugar coma. Teddy lifted him gently to his shoulder and kissed Louisa goodnight. They watched him move carefully down the back stairs and lay Tucker, still sound asleep, in the car. He waved and they both waved back.

"Did you have a good time?" Rayann stood back to let Louisa close the door.

"Very nice." Louisa looked at Rayann in the semi-darkness of the back porch. "Thank you. It's been a long time since I've gone to such a quiet restaurant. I knew what to do with all the forks." In the dark Rayann could see Louisa's teasing smile — lips curved just slightly, eyes bright with laughter. "Even if it was just with my son."

"Tucker was fine," Rayann said. "We went to Fenton's." She had not intended to tell Louisa that, but there was something about Louisa which encouraged openness.

"You'll be his friend for life," Louisa said.

Rayann turned back to the kitchen though she didn't really want to leave the dim porch. But they couldn't just stand in the darkness and talk. It was too intimate. She remembered something very prosaic she needed to ask Louisa. "Are you any good removing splinters?"

"Like most mothers, I'm a wizard at minor surgery. Let me get a needle." Louisa returned in a few moments with a needle, cotton balls and peroxide. "The reading light is the strongest."

"I can usually fish them out, but this one is awkward." The splinter had lodged in her palm, then broke off.

"Sit down on the floor in front of my chair." Louisa settled herself in her easy chair, then put on her reading glasses. She tsk'ed in a motherly way when she saw the splinter. Steadying Rayann's hand against her knee, she quickly and efficiently fished out the splinter with the needle. "Nasty thing."

"Teach me to sand more carefully."

"This will sting," Louisa warned as she doused the cotton with peroxide and dabbed lightly at the wound. When Rayann didn't protest she held the cotton firmly down, letting the peroxide soak in.

"Oh, yeah, that stings now," Rayann said, taking a deep breath.

Louisa lifted the cotton and blew on Rayann's palm. The sting instantly subsided and Rayann was aware that she was tingling all over. The back of her hand braced against Louisa's knee felt warm while her palm was cool from Louisa's breath.

"I'll go put a bandaid on it," Rayann said. By the time she'd managed to get one plastered on she felt normal again. *Normal, that's what it is. I haven't been . . . active for a while. I understand having dreams about sex. But maybe I should look up Zoraida.*

"I guess I'll call it a night," Rayann called from the bathroom. "I can barely keep my eyes open." Not quite true, but she suddenly craved . . . solitude. She wanted to be alone.

She was awakened by a knock on her door. She opened her eyes groggily, groaning a response to the knock. She sun was shining. She hadn't slept this late in days.

Louisa looked in, grinning. "The morning is off to a wonderful start. The sun has come out and I've just been downstairs. You didn't tell me the shelves were done! And the decorations have never looked so swank."

Rayann sat up, holding the sheets over her preferred sleeping attire — nothing at all — and smiled shyly. "I wanted to surprise you."

"I am appropriately surprised. How does bacon and eggs sound as a celebratory feast?" They ate breakfast sitting on the floor in front of the gleaming new shelves.

"You've unlocked a demon," Louisa said, glancing at Rayann. "Now I have the let's-do-it-today bug."

"Uh-oh. What exactly does that mean?" Rayann mopped up the last of the delectable, disgusting goo of her eggs with the last bite of her English muffin.

"They just look so bare." Louisa looked wistful now.

Rayann gave a forebearing sigh. "Where are the books?"

"Oh, no hurry," Louisa said, with a patient sigh.

"If there was no hurry you wouldn't have brought it up."

Louisa got up and lifted the curtain to the room leading off from behind the counter. "The poetry books are in the far corner. I'll just do the breakfast dishes while you get oriented." She dashed away, scooping up their plates and cups as she went.

Rayann peeked behind the curtain. "Oh, my God," she whispered. She leaned back toward the open door to the stairwell. "I'm not doing this by myself!" She heard Louisa laughing. There were boxes and boxes of new books stacked on each other and behind them boxes and boxes of used books. She slowly negotiated the carefully preserved path about one foot wide that ran the length of the room. Six boxes marked **P** sat in the far corner. Under used copies of Longfellow, Wordsworth, Shelley, Yeats, and more, she discovered, to her surprise, a copy of Renée Vivien's *Muse of the Violets*. She wondered if Louisa knew she had poetry by lesbians in these boxes.

Louisa's attitude toward matters lesbian had Rayann puzzled. She'd freely told Rayann how many years she and Christina had been together, the different places they'd lived and other factual details. There was reticence about the emotional quality of their relationship, though, but perhaps Louisa still hurt from losing Christina so pointlessly in an auto accident. And the bookstore contained no books by lesbians, except, she now discovered, this forgotten volume by Renée Vivien. There was a closeted aspect to Louisa's life that was disconcerting for such an independent woman. But that was Louisa's business, not hers.

She hoisted the first box. The muscles that had developed during the shelving project came in handy. She dropped the box to the floor in front of the shelves and it promptly split its sides. Sighing, she went to the foot of the stairs. "Alphabetically or by time period," she hollered.

"Alphabetically. You and I are probably the only people who'd understand why Theocritus and Dylan Thomas were at opposite ends." Louisa came to the top of the stairs and looked down. "I'll be right down, I promise."

"Promises, promises," Rayann muttered. She went back for the second box.

In the midst of sorting she remembered her stereo and flipped it on. She knew the piece right away — Suzanne Cianni's *Velocity of Love*. The pensive piano melody seemed appropriate to arranging poetry. The doorbell tinkled and Louisa appeared as if by magic. She grinned at Rayann, saying, "I'll just see to the customers and then I promise I'll help. At least they're all priced."

"As if that's the hard part," Rayann said sarcastically. She grumbled to herself when Louisa just laughed. Lost in concentration, Rayann didn't realize someone was watching her until the floorboards creaked. She looked up with a start.

"I told you we would startle her," Greta Schoernsson said.

"We've come to see how everything looks," Hazel said.

"What do you think?" Rayann smiled up at them.

"Very sturdy," Hazel said. "They show pride of workmanship. I'm sorry, workwomanship."

"Indeed," Greta said. "Would you like some help, my dear?"

"Oh no, that's all right," Rayann said. She raised her voice and looked toward the cash register. "Louisa will be helping out any moment now." She heard Louisa's low chuckle.

"We're quite able to help," Hazel said. "We may be old but we can read."

"That's not what I meant —"

"Of course not," Greta said. "Hazel, she just doesn't want to impose."

"We could sit at that table over there and if you brought us the A's we could get them in order while you did the B's. Many hands make light work." Hazel went to the table and Rayann realized that if she didn't accept their offer Hazel, at least, would be offended.

Greta shrugged her shoulders and whispered to Rayann, "you may as well give in. I've been giving in for sixty years or more." Greta seated herself opposite Hazel. Rayann grinned, handing the accumulated A's to Hazel who began rapidly alphabetizing.

"Perhaps if you brought me the U's through the Z's, I could do those. We'll meet up in the middle," Greta said.

"Sounds like a good plan," Rayann said.

Aside from occasional customers and the stereo, the store had a library's hushed atmosphere. Hazel rarely spoke, while Greta hummed quietly. Louisa shelved the books Rayann delivered from the sorters' hands. Rayann found herself smiling at Greta each time she retrieved Greta's completed stack. Greta was much slower than Hazel because she stopped to examine the books and read the jackets. Rayann was dumbfounded, however, when she saw Greta slip a slender volume into her satchel. She need only have asked, and Rayann was sure Louisa would have given it to her.

The incident bothered her after the Misses Schoernsson left for lunch and Rayann wondered what exactly had intrigued Greta. Puzzled, she dismissed the incident and finished up the last of the M's. Miraculously, working from both ends had landed them perfectly in the middle.

Louisa stood behind her and applauded as the last book slipped into place. "Poetry on sale at *The Common Reader* again!"

"And what about all the other books in the storeroom?"

"Ouch!" Louisa winced. "That was really mean of you. I've been trying to forget about them."

"Some of them are new," Rayann said. "Didn't you have to pay for them?"

"Not exactly. Some distributors will wait six months before they get nasty."

"But you can't sell them if they sit in the storeroom. And if you don't sell them you can't pay for them."

"That's very true. I'm trapped by your flawless logic." Louisa nodded with guileless sincerity.

Rayann realized she had been had. "I suppose they need to be organized."

"Yes, I guess that would help," Louisa said. "But it could wait until Monday."

"I think it will wait until Monday."

"You're so much fun to tease," Louisa said.

Rayann winced. Louisa's words were an echo of Michelle's, but in an entirely different context. "Well," she managed, "since people are already drawing up their Christmas lists, perhaps I'll start tomorrow."

"It can wait until Monday," Louisa said firmly. "You're too easy to manipulate, you know."

"I know," Rayann said, her chest going tight. "I'll have to work on my resistance."

Louisa put her hand on Rayann's arm. "Do that. Life will treat you better. I won't, but life will."

Rayann smiled slightly. "Well, if this is as bad as you're going to treat me, I think I can take it."

"I make no promises," Louisa said, her arched eyebrow bringing a flush to Rayann's cheeks. "No promises of any kind."

* * * * *

Rayann sliced open a box of Harlequin romances and put them in the rack designed specifically for them. They wouldn't last long because the women from the retirement center positively devoured them. Rayann knew how they felt — she could do with a "good read" herself. She wasn't desperate enough to read pulp heterosexual romances, but when she'd been growing up she had been an addict. She hadn't read them in years — not since she'd discovered the Lace Place Tea Room and Bar, in fact.

She could still remember being in the car with her mother. Looking out the window while they waited at a stoplight, she had commented on the odd name. "How can anything be a tea room and a bar?"

"It's not a place where decent women go, Rayann," her mother had said, and then changed the subject.

Her first lover had taken her there and Rayann had made the vital link to the world of wonderful, delightfully indecent — to use her mother's phrase — women.

Rayann sighed and stretched, then sliced the box so it would fold flat and carried it out to the garage to add to the growing stack for recycling. She should really borrow the car and head over to Mama Bear's and stock up on some new books. Every book she had was so dog-eared from rereading that the thrill, so to speak, was gone. But every time Rayann thought of going she was sure she'd end up asking Louisa why she didn't stock books for lesbians, which was none of her business. *The Renée Vivien!* The one book in the store with lesbian themes would be a joy to rediscover. Rayann ran back from the garage and went to find it.

Except *Muse of the Violets* wasn't there. Not under V, not under R, not even under M. It was so slim — Rayann riffled through the books, then slowly neatened the shelves. Where could it have gotten to? She glanced at the table where Greta and Hazel had been sorting and recalled suddenly the volume she had seen Greta take. It had been the right size and color. Rayann began to smile. Greta did not strike her as an aficionada of French Romantic poetry. And that left only one reason why Greta had wanted the book — because it was by a lesbian and about lesbian passion and love.

She hugged the secret to herself. It didn't matter whether Greta had wanted it out of curiosity or because she was a lesbian. Rayann felt just as good as she had when she found out about Eleanor Roosevelt or Martina Navratilova. It made her feel a part of a vital society of women who loved women.

One day, when she felt particularly brave, she was going to ask Greta what she had thought of Renée Vivien. Rayann hoped Greta, like herself, shivered when she read, "My clever fingers linger with the shudders / Of your flesh under your soft petaled gown."

The door chimes tinkled. Rayann jumped and peered around the bookshelves to see who was there. Louisa came in, breathing hard, wiping her brow with her sleeve. Dampness soaked her sweatshirt which clung to her back and sides. She pulled out the combs which had held her hair up off her shoulders. Rayann hadn't really realized before how slender Louisa's neck was, with feathery silver hair right at the hairline. As Louisa shook her hair down, Rayann decided the overall effect was scrumptious.

Stop that. Stop that right now. Just knock it off. No more.

"I'm drenched," Louisa said. "Oh my. I'm getting too old for the whole lake."

"What makes you say that?"

"I'm wiped out. I don't know why I'm so exhausted."

"You've only been gone an hour. Usually it takes you sixty-five minutes."

"Really?" Louisa looked at the clock. "Goodness. No wonder I'm tired. I'll give myself a heart attack." She pulled her sweatshirt over her head, revealing a weathered A's T-shirt.

Rayann suddenly realized she couldn't have said anything if she wanted to. Her heart had jumped into her throat and wasn't allowing any room for her windpipe to function. On top of that her palms started to sweat, which was nothing but trouble because once her palms started getting damp, then other parts started getting damp. She finally managed to suck in a breath, but only after she stopped tracing the "A" on Louisa's chest with her eyes. *She's old enough to be your mother, remember? She has a friend, Danny, remember? She's not interested in you, remember? What's wrong with you?*

"You know what I think I deserve?" Louisa scrubbed her face with the sweatshirt. When Rayann didn't answer, she looked up. Rayann shook her head. "Since I selected so able an assistant, I might play hooky for the rest of the afternoon. I could use a glass of wine, a good book and a long soak in a bubble bath."

If she'd had any breath, Rayann would have groaned. Instead she nodded her head. *Like an idiot. Like a fool. Like a teenager.* Someone somewhere inside her was screaming. Alarms were going off in her head.

"See you later," Louisa said, after giving Rayann an odd look. She hurried up the stairs, humming.

Too long without sex. That must be it. That surely accounts for everything. It's the logical explanation. Makes perfect sense. Yep. Right. Sure.

Rayann found her lungs were working again. After a moment she peeked down the front of her shirt. She wasn't exactly Twiggy but Louisa certainly had plenty in common with Jane Russell. She sighed, disgusted with herself. *Do you possibly think you could get your mind out of Junior High?* This is just normal, she told herself. *My libido is in full gear and it's just natural. If only I'd gotten Zoraida's phone number.*

Louisa held out the phone. Rayann looked up from the huge box of dictionaries she had unearthed. "For me?" She took the phone not knowing what to expect.

"You *are* alive," Judy said.

"Of course. So are you, it seems."

"I thought you promised to keep in touch."

"It hasn't been that long," Rayann said. "Don't exaggerate."

"You're no fun anymore, you know that? Only kidding.

Listen, I'm calling because I promised Jilly I'd remind you about the Post-Thanksgiving Pre-Winter Solstice Holiday party. You haven't missed one yet."

"I hadn't forgotten, but I'm not sure —"

"I knew it. You don't feel up to it," Judy accused.

"Well, I don't."

"You *have* to go. Don't you think I don't know it'll be hard for you? But as your informal therapist —"

"Extremely informal. I know how low your test scores were —"

"It would be good for you to see your friends. Your friends would like to see you."

"But you *know* who else I'll see."

"So what? I don't want to be cruel, but I don't think Michelle will even know you're in the room. She's been burning the candle at both ends."

"Lovely. Meanwhile I don't even have a wick."

Judy laughed politely. "You need some practice at gay banter. Pun intended. Bring a date."

"A date? You must be joking."

"Would I joke about something like that?" Judy sounded very offended. "If it weren't for a certain cop in my life, who is armed twenty-four hours a day, by the way —"

"Sounds kinky —"

"I'd go with you myself. I could fix you up —"

"No thank you," Rayann enunciated with deliberate clarity. "I'd rather go alone."

"Okay, but don't say I didn't warn you. Why don't you bring the woman who answered the phone? I'd like to meet the owner of that voice."

Rayann dropped her voice. "I told you she has a son older than me."

"What's that got to do with it? She has a nice voice. It's positively Garboesque." Judy sighed. "Well, Dedric and I will make sure you don't sit all night. We'll dance your feet off."

"That isn't necessary," Rayann protested weakly.

"The offer will remain open."

When Rayann hung up the phone she realized Louisa

was watching her. "My best friend was reminding me about our annual holiday festivities. She said I should bring a date but I don't know anyone," Rayann said before she could stop herself. *Oh God, it sounds like I'm asking her.* "Well, I did meet somebody recently I could ask." *A red herring, my kingdom for a red herring.* "About this box of dictionaries."

"Oh, those. I suppose we could give them to a school or something."

"Why?"

"I don't really sell a lot of reference books."

"Why did you order two boxes of forty each of *Webster's New Collegiate Dictionary?*" Rayann held out the packing slip.

"I didn't order them." Louisa frowned.

"Why didn't you send them back?"

"*I'm* not paying to send them back. The sleazy distributor's rep made up the order and then tried to convince me to pay for them at big discounts. He was the ultimate Herb Tarlick." Louisa paused. "You do know who Herb Tarlick is, don't you?"

Rayann pursed her lips again. "I'm *not* a child. I saw 'WKRP in Cincinnati' when it was first on television, not to mention reruns. I had a crush on Bailey Quarters," Rayann added, as proof she did know what she was talking about. "Anyway, you said the rep made up the order," she prompted.

"Then the distributor went bankrupt and so there's no one to send them back to."

"When did they go bankrupt?"

"About a year ago, more than that."

"You mean I've gone through almost a year of boxes?"

"Yes," Louisa said. "And a fine job you're doing, too." She smiled innocently.

Rayann started a sarcastic come-back, but was silenced by a sudden flash of creativity. "Hold the phone. Alert the media. I have an idea."

"I told you, I sell about two dictionaries a year. They're already a little out of date."

"I know just what to do," Rayann said, clutching her

head as if it would explode. "Leave everything to me." The more she thought about it, the more sure she was her idea would work. It felt terrific to have a creative urge — any kind of urge that didn't center below her waist — again.

"I don't like the sound of that," Louisa said, frowning.

"Do you like the sound of change in the cash register?" It had been bothering Rayann that there weren't very many customers. Louisa seemed to spend a lot of time sorting through invoices.

"Yes, but I'm not out to compete with Waldenbooks. I don't need to make a fortune. The house is paid for." Louisa stopped abruptly and turned her face slightly away. "Chris's insurance took care of the mortgage. I just need to pay for the books and for food and utilities. And now a new furnace, which makes me glad I still have you." She smiled at Rayann.

"But I'm working all my rent," Rayann said urgently. "I haven't brought in any cash at all. There must be some first editions you're longing to buy."

"I don't want you to feel beholden that way —"

"It's just an inexpensive and simple promotion scheme," Rayann said. "The labor will be cheap," she said, indicating herself, "and the fixed costs — printing — are easily offset by the expected increase in revenues."

"Printing?"

"For the flyers."

"Oh, of course." Louisa frowned. "For the flyers. Silly me for not knowing."

"I'll take care of everything," Rayann said. "You get final copy approval." She grinned. "And what's so wonderful about this ingenious holiday promotion scheme is that the customers still get value because books are precious and they're going to get a dictionary free."

"Of course. Just what I thought," Louisa said, shaking her head.

"I'm going to leave these books here for now, and go up to my room for a while. I need to be alone." She did her best Garbo impression, but her voice did not have the same timbre as Louisa's, or Garbo's for that matter.

Louisa frowned. "Is that part of the scheme?"

"Yes," Rayann said, putting her hand to her forehead. "All geniuses must rest after being brilliant."

"Pooh," Louisa said. "I've heard that one before."

Communing with her Macintosh, Rayann hummed "it's a gay world after all" under her breath. She felt glorious and alive as she played with her software, importing some scanned pictures of ribboned packages from Clip Art, cropping out the Santa she didn't want, then placing her text. She ran downstairs for paper, then cranked a sheet into her printer. Louisa appeared in the bedroom doorway.

"I didn't realize you had a computer," she said.

"Not *a* computer. A Macintosh," Rayann said haughtily. "There's a difference."

"Sorry, I didn't know. What are you doing?"

"Come look." Hauteur gone, Rayann patted the bed and sat down. Louisa examined the flyer. "It'll look better printed out on laser. And I don't care for how big this type is, relative to the offer type. The graphic is fine, though."

"Where did you learn to do this?" Louisa turned to look at Rayann.

"I learned art design in college and Macintosh desktop programs on my own. I was getting pretty good at it. The marketing people at the bank were sorry to see me go, I think."

"Why did you go?"

"To become a serious artist and a lesbian housewife."

"Now I remember," Louisa said, her smile gentle. "We're all entitled to one little mistake in judgment."

"Have you made any?" Rayann stared at the flyer but when Louisa didn't answer right away, she looked up.

Louisa was staring at her intently, then broke the

intensity with a slight smile. "One . . . or two. This seems very artistic to me," she went on, indicating the flyer.

Rayann smiled wryly. "Thank you for saying so, but it's not. It's Design One-A basics."

"I couldn't do it. A lot of people couldn't do it. It's certainly special." Louisa studied the flyer again. "It's attractive to look at and I keep reading the name of the bookstore over and over. How did you do that?"

Rayann leaned over and pointed out the different text positions and how they worked together to move the eye to the name of the bookstore. She became aware that she wanted to rub her cheek against Louisa's soft chambray shirt and sat up again. *Judy was right. I need a date. Fast.*

"I don't see how you'll have any problems finding a job in the business world if you wanted," Louisa said. "After I've completely burned you out."

For some reason Rayann's heart decided to beat triple-time. "I have three years without a work history to explain. It makes companies suspicious."

"But you can start over, when you're ready. Don't sell yourself short." Louisa stood up. Rayann looked up at her. She seemed so tall — perhaps because her legs were so long. "I think this idea of yours will work. Isn't a twenty-dollar minimum too high?"

"I think it's low, but a good place to start. That's about one hardcover and one paperback to get a free hardcover dictionary. It's pretty cheap, really."

"You're not going to go around and put them on people's cars, are you? I hate that. It's annoying and wasteful."

"No, I'm going to leave copies with receptionists in the offices within a three-block radius. If that works, I'll go out to four blocks."

"No holiday is complete without books," Louisa read, "the perfect gift. We can help you find just the right book for everyone on your list." She handed the flyer back to Rayann. "I like it. And I'm going to get my storeroom back in the bargain."

"Let me fix the text sizes and I'll print it again," Rayann said. "It only takes a second."

Louisa leaned over her, watching the screen as Rayann manipulated the text. "That's amazing," Louisa said. "I did an abortion-rights flyer once, twenty years ago at least, and I used rub-off lettering. I kept getting the exclamation points stuck to my elbows and nothing would line up. I never dreamed you'd be able to do all this by yourself. It's how Gutenberg must have felt when he realized he had the power to print anything he wanted."

Rayann kept her eyes on the screen, aware of the cameo pendant Louisa was fond of wearing swinging next to her ear as Louisa bent over. The cameo usually nestled at the top of Louisa's breasts and Rayann thought she could feel a glow of warmth brushing her ear as the cameo swung by. The door chimes sounded downstairs and Rayann found herself thinking it was just in the nick of time.

She concentrated on her flyer, humming Bonnie Raitt's "Nick of Time," then copied the file to a floppy disk and labeled it. She puttered for a long time and when she went downstairs again, she was able to breathe normally.

Rayann was worried about the impending party at the Lace Place, and her dateless state. *What happened to that vow of finding a fun and carefree lover to prove to everyone you weren't hurt in the least?* She watched Louisa climb the library ladder — which moved on well-greased wheels again — for a book a customer wanted. *She certainly has a nice — I need a date.* But there was no way she would ask Louisa to go. Everyone would get the wrong idea.

When Rayann went to get the flyer printed and copies made, she found herself driving by the construction site where she'd dumped the first batch of lumber and ruined books. It looked as if they had added a few more floors. *This is desperate, the absolute rock bottom.* She parked and wondered how she could locate Zoraida. She started the car up to dive away, then turned it off again. She listened to "Born To Be Wild" on the radio, trying to find enough courage to get out of the car — that all-important first step to asking Zoraida for a date. She had never known how to pick up women. *I should call Michelle and ask for advice.*

A knock on the car window startled her out of her thoughts. Zoraida was on the other side, smiling, her breath coming out in white puffs. Rayann rolled down the window.

"I wondered if you'd be back," Zoraida said.

"I, umm." *I'm so articulate.*

"Want to have a beer?"

Rayann nodded and was still nodding when she found her voice. "Okay."

"Follow me, then."

Rayann watched Zoraida get into a black 4x4 truck, and then followed it to a bar a few blocks away. She tried to sink into obscurity in one of the booths as Zoraida went to the bar for the beers. Rayann sat on her hands to combat the urge to bite her nails.

It was most definitely not a gay bar. Zoraida's black leather jacket and muddy boots drew stares as she gracefully carried two bottles of Corona and frosted pilsner glasses back to their booth with a swagger that defied anyone to say anything.

"So, what brought you my way again?"

"I, umm." *Maybe I should practice in front of a mirror.*

"Yes, well, I am glad to see you." Zoraida tipped her head to one side and smiled seductively. "Very glad."

She has nice lips. Not as nice as Lou— stop that! I'm glad to see you too, I umm, was wondering if you'd like to go to a party Saturday night?" What a stunningly subtle lead-in.

"Whose party?"

"It's at the Lace Place Tea Room and Bar." *Stop nodding. She'll think you're one of those tigers in the back window of people's cars.*

"I've been there." Zoraida smiled and sipped her beer.

"I am glad to hear you've been there, too. I was beginning to worry."

"About what?"

"That you were looking for initiation."

"I don't under— Oh. No, I umm, don't need to be initiated." Rayann took a large swallow of beer. *I'm so suave she thinks I'm straight and looking for my first woman.*

"You just don't seem very sure of yourself. It's kind of sweet."

Sweet? "I guess I'm not. I'm getting over someone."

"She leave you?" Zoraida's eyes swept over Rayann's face, then her hands.

Rayann shifted under the intimate glance. "She was sleeping around. A lot."

"You do not appear to be the type of woman who is willing to share someone you love. If she didn't know that, she was a fool." Zoraida raised her full eyebrows over the brilliant black eyes that danced with energy.

"That's what I keep telling myself."

"So, the one who slept around, is she going to be at this party?"

Rayann ducked her head and nodded.

"It's okay. I just like to know the score. I can make you forget she's there."

Rayann glanced up and smiled provocatively. At least she hoped it was provocative — she hadn't flirted in a long time. "I'd like to see you try." *And she's not the only one I'd like you to drive out of my mind.*

"Are you daring me?" Zoraida grinned and tossed back her thick black hair. "I love a challenge."

"I can see you do," Rayann said. "I just want you to know I'm not looking for . . ."

"Every woman is looking for something," Zoraida interrupted. Rayann watched her mouth form the words. "Some are just not interested in games. Like you."

"Do I look that boring?"

"Not boring, honey. You do not look boring." Zoraida finished her beer and leaned back, her open jacket framing a muscular, firm body. "I think you are one of those women who love passion but not quite as much as you crave love."

Rayann blushed. She was staring at Zoraida's chest and Zoraida knew she was staring. "Don't you think a woman can have both? Passion and love? Can't they be the same thing?"

"If she wants to wait for it. But while you're waiting . . ." Zoraida reached across the table and ran her finger over Rayann's wrist. "Passion can certainly be a pleasant way to pass the time."

Rayann put her hand over Zoraida's. "Only if it's not confused with love and nobody gets hurt."

Zoraida withdrew her hand and raised her beer with a wink. "This could be the beginning of a beautiful friendship, shhweetheart."

Rayann returned to The Common Reader flushed and feeling feverish. Zoraida had suggested a practice session before the party, but Rayann had managed to collect her wits and refuse. Zoraida's aggressiveness frightened her a little, but she didn't think she was getting into anything she couldn't handle. But Louisa expected her for dinner, and Rayann had never been able to relax enough with a stranger to hop into bed after a few minutes conversation. *Another tip I should have asked Michelle about.* Zoraida, no matter how charming, was still a stranger. Nevertheless, Zoraida had fanned her urges. *And Smokey Bear says they're already at the high fire risk level, so watch out, campers, for those lit matches.* She tried to be cool, but Rayann was feeling a bit like a forest fire when she showed Louisa the flyers printed on astrobright "Really Red" paper.

"You can see them a mile away," Louisa said.

Rayann couldn't tell if she liked them. "That's the point. When someone's looking for the store they'll recognize the flyer from the street and not be afraid to come on in. And it's certainly Christmassy."

"I can see you'll have to be the marketing manager. I would have never thought of that. Or saying 'While quantities last' and putting down an expiration date."

"You can't forget the mice type."

"Mice?"

"The fine print," Rayann said. "I'll start making the rounds tomorrow morning so people will have them before they spend all their Christmas money. I hope this works."

"So do I. I can't believe I'm going to have the storeroom back. Oh," Louisa said, "I almost forgot." She reached under the counter and came up reading a piece of paper. "Judy called and said she'd call again tonight and that you weren't to forget about the party."

"She'll be happy to know I've got a hot date."

"That's good. Sounds like time is healing wounds." Louisa put her hands on the flyers. "Should I go ahead and tape some of these up in the windows?"

"Never too early to build business," Rayann said easily, though she studied Louisa's hand, thinking it seemed gentler than Zoraida's. Maybe she should have given in — she had a feeling that an hour with Zoraida would be more than memorable and might bank the flames that scorched her thighs at this very moment.

"Rayann?"

"Oh, sorry, what did you say?"

"Could you hand me the tape?" Louisa said. "Oh, and could you take this book over to the Schoernsson's? They both have colds, the poor things. Greta sounded miserable, and they've read everything they have."

"Sure. I'll just go put these in the back and then run it over." Rayann stacked up the boxes of flyers, then hurried down the street to the retirement complex, yet another Ken Follett tucked under her arm.

She identified herself to the guard, and found their apartment number on the directory inside the door. When she knocked, a feeble voice called, "Come in, please."

The apartment had a mini-kitchen and a small living room. A voice led her to the bedroom door where both ladies, propped up with lots of pillows in identical full-size beds, were clad in complementary bed jackets — Greta in peach and Hazel in blue. A pitcher of water, cups, reading glasses and a box of tissues cluttered the bed stand that separated the beds. Otherwise the room was as neat as a pin and smelled faintly of cough drops.

"Oh, my dear, thank you so much," Greta said. "I was getting desperate."

"She's been fidg'ding since last night, when she finished this a'd gave it to me," Hazel said, hindered by completely stopped-up sinuses. She waved a blue-veined hand at the book in her lap. Rayann gave the book to Greta and retrieved a box of tissues that had slipped partially under Greta's bed.

"I'd wondered where that had gotten to, thank you so —" Greta said, breaking off to sneeze twice. She collapsed back on her pillows, out of breath.

"Are you sure you're both all right? Isn't there a doctor?" Rayann thought both ladies were far too pale, but then again they had extraordinarily fair skin.

"There is Estelle Betts, a perfectly lovely nurse, who said she'd stop up to check on us later today. We can have dinner on trays, too," Hazel said. "Please don't worry."

"Well, maybe I can make some tea while I'm here." Rayann immediately went to make it when both women perked up and looked very thankful, though they assured her she shouldn't bother. Rayann found mugs and tea bags, then saw that there was a cut lemon and a jar of honey on the counter, used probably for tea earlier in the day. Rayann added liberal amounts of both to the mugs and brought them back to the bedroom.

Greta had risen and was plumping Hazel's pillows. Hazel settled against them again, looking up at Greta with tenderness that surprised Rayann. She put the mugs down, and plumped Greta's pillows as she got back in bed.

"Very nice," Hazel said, sipping slowly.

Greta cleared her throat after a few sips. "I'm so glad you're here," she said slowly, "because my conscience has been bothering me a bit and Hazel was sure, after you put up the shelves, well, she thought you wouldn't be upset . . ."

Rayann smiled encouragingly. She had a feeling she

knew what Greta was leading up to. Greta opened the small drawer in the bedside table and drew out *The Muse of the Violets.*

Rayann's smile broadened. "I hope you enjoyed it," she said. "It has very moving moments."

"We both enjoyed it," Greta said. "When I saw it I wanted to read it and then I just couldn't bring myself to buy it, not in front of Louisa."

"She would not have minded," Rayann said. "But what does that have to do with my putting up the shelves?"

"You reminded me of Greta moving arou'd in her mother's kitchen when we were both very much younger." Hazel sipped her tea and blotted her nose with a fresh tissue.

"I'm afraid I don't understand," Rayann said. "I thought you were sisters. You look very much alike."

"We're cousins," Greta said. "We both have the Swedish Schoernsson look, but we're really only related because our grandmothers were half-sisters. Still, it has been useful over the past fifty years to appear as sisters."

"It was certainly helpful when we immigrated." Hazel sipped her tea again and Greta's lips curved into a gentle smile.

The hair stood up on the back of Rayann's neck. "You immigrated to be together, didn't you?"

"We ran away on the eve of my wedding," Greta said. Her pale blue eyes, almost an exact match of Hazel's, softened with remembrance. "Because Hazel said she would cease to live if I married."

"As I recall, I said I was planning to leave immediately after the wedding to join missionaries going to Africa." Hazel stared into her tea. Rayann had a hard time envisioning practical Hazel threatening anything so outrageous.

"And I said the climate would kill you and you said you didn't care."

"I wouldn't have, knowing you were truly married."

"How long had you been in love?" Rayann asked. She

was enthralled by the longevity of their caring for each other. They communicated silently as to who should answer Rayann's question.

"Two weeks," Greta said. "Hazel was sent to our house by her mother to help with my trousseau. We hadn't seen each other since we were girls."

"I wouldn't agree to marry the silly boy my parents had chosen for me and they sent me to Greta's wedding hoping the excitement and glamour would make me envious."

Greta continued, when Hazel stopped, "Instead she fell in love with me."

"How did you know? In just two weeks? I'm completely fascinated." Rayann handed Greta another tissue when she sneezed again.

"As I said, she had a way of moving around in her mother's kitchen. You reminded me of her when you were sawing the shelves. She looked as if she could do anything. Her hair kept falling out of its net but she never noticed. I watched her for hours because she didn't seem to realize I was even there."

"I was concentrating on my intended as a good Christian girl should. Every time I saw Hazel I had to remind myself I was getting married in a few days and she would no longer be there, making me laugh and long to stay in the kitchen all night talking."

"Why were you getting married?"

"Because it was expected. He was decent enough. Don't snort, dear, I know you disliked him, but he was a decent man. I would have been happy just living at home but he offered for me and lickety-split I was putting up preserves and sewing sheets. I was glad when my mother said my cousin Hazel was coming to help because the preparation was such a lot of work."

"And instead of helping she courted you?" Rayann pictured an old-fashioned kitchen with two maidens in long gowns who stole glances at one another as they sewed before an open fire. She blinked back unbidden tears.

"You make it sound too cerebral," Hazel said. "As

more guests arrived we were forced to share Greta's bed and one night I . . . convinced her my love was sincere. Back then it wasn't uncommon at all for women to share beds — here we have to pretend Greta sleeps over there all the time or the church people who own the place would probably show us the door."

To Rayann's delight, Greta blushed. "She said she hated the man I was marrying because he wouldn't know how to make me happy because he was a man. I was hurt and said I was sure he would be a good mate and what did she mean by saying he wouldn't love me the right way?"

"So I showed her." Hazel shrugged. "By morning she was convinced."

Rayann put her hands to her own blushing cheeks. "How incredibly romantic!"

"I didn't know it could be so . . . quiet," Greta said, her blush returning.

"I know what you mean," Rayann said.

"As I knew you would." Hazel set her cup down. "We haven't told our story to very many people. Most of them have passed over. We just went on living our life together."

"When all the wonderful things were happening years ago I wanted to come out, but Hazel — you have probably noticed she's the practical one — wanted to know just who we were supposed to come out to? We knew who and what we were."

"And I knew there were the young people. This closet issue was really their struggle. Your struggle."

"It's a struggle for everyone, but I guess we all struggle in different ways." Rayann gathered their empty cups. "I'm so happy you told me because now I'm more sure than ever that women like us have always existed."

She made a second dose of tea for both women and told them to call her if they needed anything at all, or if she could pick up groceries. On her way out of the building she stopped at the nurses' station at the personal care ward and gave Estelle Betts the phone number of the bookstore, asking her to call if Hazel and Greta wanted anything. They were all bound together now in a larger family — sisters in the best sense. Hugging *Muse of the Violets* to her chest, Rayann hurried back to the bookstore.

5

True to Her Grain

It's a mental condition. Or just a normal response to suddenly being single. Rayann tried to find solid rationalizations to explain the uncontrollable bursts of lust that had washed over her all morning, leaving her wrung out and decidedly damp.

It was bad enough when it happened at the bookstore. It was downright uncomfortable though Louisa had not, by look or touch, indicated any sexual interest in Rayann. But when Rayann left the bookstore to deliver the first of the holiday flyers, the feeling of wanting to *be* with another woman was so strong it practically walked beside her. At a minimum, it was wearing her underwear.

It's just a normal thing. Stop dawdling. As she began the fourth floor in the City Center building, Rayann pulled another handful of flyers from her backpack. She took a deep breath, hoping this receptionist would be different from the previous ones she'd talked to on floors two and three.

She wasn't. She had quite possibly the most erotic notch in her collar bone that Rayann had ever seen. A delicate, old-fashioned cameo — not unlike Louisa's — nestled right in the notch.

"Can I help you?" A faint Gaelic lilt. Rayann's knees went wobbly.

Oh, yes, you can help me. I bet I could help you, too. "Hi. I'm from The Common Reader Bookstore, just a few blocks over on Alice, and we're having a special on dictionaries for the holidays. This flyer explains all about it."

"I didn't know there was a genuine bookstore this close," the woman said, the lilt making the words fall like poetry on Rayann's ears. Her throat was smooth, slender and looked softer than silk. "B. Dalton's is just round the corner but they're not very friendly. Half the time they don't have what I want. Can I have a few more of these — there are a couple of other people I think would be interested." A faint spray of freckles broke the pale pink flush of her skin.

"Sure. Feel free to make copies. Our supply of dictionaries *is* limited, so tell everyone to hurry." Rayann couldn't help it — her right eye winked at the woman all by itself.

The woman smiled innocently and said, "Thanks for stopping by." Rayann escaped.

The receptionist was not there in the next office and Rayann heaved a sigh of relief. Maybe she could get in and out without . . . no such luck. A tall, sleek, panther-like woman appeared from around one corner, moving silently toward Rayann on black high heels.

Rayann breathed in with the rhythm of the woman's steps, her eyes moving slowly from instep to ankle, then the long, long journey up legs that stretched from San Francisco to St. Louis, encased in black stockings that whispered as thigh brushed thigh.

Oh no — don't think about her thighs! Too late. Heart pounding, Rayann delivered her spiel, left the flyer and ran for it. She leaned against the wall in the corridor. *If only most receptionists weren't women. And I know that it's an abomination that companies hire attractive women to be receptionists.* Furthermore, Rayann told herself sternly, ogling women like this was . . . patriarchal, and not to be encouraged. *Get a grip.*

Chin up, she went resolutely into the next office. This receptionist did not have an angel-food-cake kind of beauty — no fluff, mousse or acrylic nails in sight. She was a dyke. Rayann almost rocked from the shudder that traveled from the pit of her stomach to her toes and then sent sparks through each fold and wrinkle of her labia — the sensation destroyed what little was left of her composure.

Piercing black eyes looked out of a tanned face unembellished by makeup and framed by two small pink triangle earrings. The face led to a throat hidden behind a turtleneck. A gray pullover tightened around a trim waist and left Rayann's imagination to fill in the . . . curves in between. Curves vividly sketched by her mind's eye, Rayann's imagination then tackled the tight black jeans which did not leave much to the imagination. *I'll faint if she turns around.*

"Uh . . ." Rayann managed to get through her description again. The woman took the flyer, smiling, displaying the most sensuous laugh lines around a full-lipped mouth that Rayann had ever seen. A flash of memory showed her another mouth, other laugh lines, the sight of which, only this morning, had also left her speechless.

She found the women's restroom and splashed water on her face. *I'm getting a thing for older women. And*

*younger women. And women my age. And women in suits
and heels and turtlenecks and jeans.* She leaned her
forehead on the cool mirror. She would never be able to
tell Louisa just how exhausting this flyer delivery
business was. She had another fifteen floors to go.

The agony of the day — and the night that followed
— seemed worth it. The week was exhilarating as
customers bearing flyers converged on the store. Rayann
was glad for the diversion during working hours. The
evenings with Louisa spent watching a movie or quietly
reading were intimate enough.

When the time came to get ready for the party, she
was grateful for her date with Zoraida. Zoraida, she was
certain, would completely distract her. As she rinsed
shampoo out of her hair, Rayann realized that thoughts of
Michelle weren't the problem. The problem was the
overwhelming urge to wear Louisa's bathrobe hanging on
the back of the bathroom door. The thick maroon chenille
smelled like Louisa.

"You look festive," Louisa said when Rayann finally
appeared.

"Everything is at least three years old." Rayann, not
wanting to wear anything Michelle would recognize as
something she had paid for, had changed four times,
fruitlessly trying to find an outfit that said "I look good
but I didn't fuss." And it was ultimately important that
Louisa not get the wrong idea about anything. *Just what
idea do I want her to get?* If she knew the answer to that
question, she might stop jumping every time Louisa came
within two feet of her.

"You're supposed to say thank you," Louisa said, "not
run yourself down." She studied Rayann over the top of
her reading glasses. Rayann realized that Louisa, too, was
dressed up — her jeans had a razor-sharp crease in them
and instead of her usual button-down workshirt, she wore
a white cotton blouse with the collar open, nesting the
cameo. Gold earrings glinted in Louisa's small earlobes.
Louisa's denim jacket was slung over the chair near the
door. Rayann swallowed with difficulty as she considered
the overall effect.

"Thank you, then," Rayann said at last. She sat down, feeling nervous. Her black corduroy slacks were neatly pressed and so was the white shirt she wore under the forest green pullover. "You look like you're going out too."

"Surprise tickets to the Beach Blanket Babylon revue from Danny. The midnight show."

"Maybe I'll get to meet her, finally." The doorbell at the bookstore entrance rang and Rayann went to the window.

"Must be yours," Louisa said. "Danny'd come round to the back."

Rayann saw the familiar black 4x4 out the window. "Yes, it's my date. Have fun at the theater," she said and she hurried down the stairs through the bookstore. Her heart was beating hard and fast, and she had the sensation that she was escaping to something less frightening — but when she saw Zoraida's black jeans, black T-shirt and black leather jacket and boots, she wasn't so sure.

"Rayann!" Jilly swept around the end of the bar to hug Rayann. As bartender, she wore felt antlers that quivered. "Gosh, it's good to see you. You look terrific as always, better'n the last time I saw you."

Rayann started to say the sweater was three years old, but said instead, "Thank you. Those antlers are adorable."

Jilly giggled. "I know. It's hard to believe an old butch like me would want to wear something adorable, but I'm going to hate taking them off on December twenty-sixth." She glanced at Zoraida. "You're a familiar face, but I don't know your name."

"Zoraida," she said, shaking hands firmly. Golden hoops flashed against her black hair and Rayann was aware that women were turning to stare at Zoraida's dark, exotic looks. Out of construction gear Zoraida was every bit as powerful and confident.

"Spiced rum and coke, right?" Jilly nodded as Zoraida

agreed, and then said to Rayann, "Your usual Tanqueray?"

Fixed with drinks, Rayann and Zoraida found two empty stools side by side. "You look like an outlaw tonight," Rayann said.

"Different from muddy boots?" Zoraida held out one foot.

Rayann glanced down at the supple leather boot that encased a surprisingly small foot. "Quite different." *Stunning conversation already?*

"I love to dance," Zoraida said. "These are, believe it or not, my dancing boots from college. I was a dance major."

"I was an art major. What happened to dance?"

"You mean why did I give up the humdrum life of a dancer for the glamour and excitement of construction?"

"That's not exactly what I meant." Rayann sipped her drink.

"Dance gave me up. I dropped out. I managed to get the construction job because the contractor didn't meet their minority quota for federal jobs. I fulfill three counts — woman, Mexican-American and Native American."

"I'd noticed."

"Which part? I certainly hope you noticed the woman part."

"I did. Under a fluorescent hard hat."

"Orange or yellow?"

"Orange, I think."

"Ah. I look good in orange."

"You do." *I can't stand much more of this.*

"Enough chitchat," Zoraida said.

Rayann laughed. "That's exactly what I was thinking."

"I'll bet you weren't thinking what I was going to say next."

"Which was?"

"What's your favorite form of foreplay?"

Rayann blushed. She couldn't help it. She was aware that Zoraida was attracting attention with her vitality.

She knew that several women nearby had heard the question and were now waiting to hear the answer. "No, I was not thinking about that."

Zoraida leaned toward her, putting one hand on Rayann's cheek. She whispered in her ear, "Excuse me but there is a woman who just came in. She is blonde and she is staring at you. Should I let her know I have a firm grip on you?" Her lips nuzzled at Rayann's neck, then her chin, before she leaned back and said, more loudly, "You should start thinking about it. I'll want an answer later, *mi novita.*"

Rayann didn't dare look. It was probably Michelle. "I remember in eighth grade Spanish class I called my best friend my *novia*. Our book said *novia* meant best friend or sweetheart, and *amiga* was just friend. The teacher teased me about it for a long time and said girls didn't call other girls their *novias*."

"She is coming this way, *novia*, and now I think I should be kissed — just for effect, you understand."

Rayann self-consciously leaned over to kiss Zoraida on the ear and found herself kissing her lips instead. It was not a difficult task. Zoraida caught Rayann's lower lip in her teeth as the kiss ended.

"Oh, *novita*, she has gone away," Zoraida said sadly. "No brunette, sorry."

"You said there was a blonde!"

"I lied. Punish me with another kiss," Zoraida pleaded. She sounded penitent, but her eyes were dancing.

"Maybe later when I tell you about my favorite form of foreplay," Rayann said.

"Hello, Rayann."

Every nerve in Rayann's body prickled at the smooth, familiar voice. She turned. "Hello, Michelle." She knew it was her imagination that all talk in the bar ceased as if they were in an E.F. Hutton commercial.

They stared at each other. Then Michelle smiled coolly. "Are you afraid to introduce me to your friend?"

"This is Zoraida."

"It's always a pleasure to meet someone new."

"Enchanted," Zoraida said, giving her attention to her drink.

"You have to meet Laura," Michelle said. She pushed her hair back in the gesture Rayann had seen a hundred times and had found alluring every time — until now. "She's here somewhere."

"I thought her name was Lori," Rayann said.

"Laura is different from Lori," Michelle said.

Rayann smiled serenely. "I'll be sure not to use the wrong name. Perhaps if you gave me a list I could keep them straight. At least the top twenty or so."

"You never knew how to be bitchy, darling."

"Merry Christmas to you too."

Zoraida put down her drink. "Dance with me, *novia,*" she said, propelling Rayann to the dance floor. Once her muscular arms were around Rayann, holding her tight, she whispered, "*Novia,* she is all looks and no substance."

"I can't agree. I was with her for three years. She can be funny and thoughtful and she's usually good-hearted."

"That's the first time I've heard it called that. She hurt you and so I hate her already. When I say 'spin out' step back and do one turn and step back in. Got it? Spin out."

Rayann twirled out and back to Teresa Trull's "Shady Glen." They didn't talk about Michelle again and after a while Rayann forgot about her and gave in to the exhilaration of dancing under Zoraida's guidance. It felt just fine to let Zoraida lead. When the music slowed and Zoraida's lead pulled Rayann close to sway hip to hip, Rayann didn't object. The heat from Zoraida's body increased the heat within and Rayann felt their bodies fuse together.

"You two should get a room," someone whispered in her ear.

Rayann's eyes flew open and Zoraida released her. "Judy!" She hugged Judy, then Dedric, and they left the dance floor, searching for a table. Rayann introduced Zoraida when they all settled in.

"It's about time you got here," Rayann said.

"You look as if you're glad you came," Judy answered.

"She hasn't done that yet," Zoraida put in. Judy laughed and Rayann hoped she wasn't blushing.

"Not armed tonight, are you?" Rayann still had a hard time believing Dedric was a cop.

"It's just cleverly hidden," Dedric said.

"She has to carry it. Department policy." Judy made a face. Their club sodas arrived and Rayann saw them glance at each other and touch glasses in a private moment.

"You two look as if you have a long history," Zoraida said.

"Eight years," Judy breathed.

"Eight and a half," Dedric added. "It would be nine years if she hadn't taken so long to make up her mind about whether it was permanent or not."

"You kept me in bed for four months. You hardly gave me enough oxygen to think. You were such a beginner," Judy said, smirking. "It took forever for you to get it right."

"You'll pay for that remark, my ball and chain. You make me sound like the femme in this relationship." Dedric gave Judy a cool, unamused look, but her lips quirked when Judy stuck her tongue out at her.

"Then you're the butch," Zoraida said, arching her eyebrows.

"She's both," Judy said. "And neither."

Rayann sipped her drink. She knew next to nothing about what butch and femme were supposed to mean. She wasn't aware that any of her past lovers — not that there were enough for a valid statistical sample — fit either category. She didn't know which group she fit into either, and she wasn't sure she wanted to be categorized anyway.

The conversation was interrupted when Tina Turner's "Merry Christmas Baby" came on the jukebox and Rayann and Judy got up to dance. Rayann was a little surprised when Dedric and Zoraida didn't follow suit. Instead, they scooched their chairs closer together and talked to each other. Within a few minutes they seemed to be laughing a good deal.

"What's that all about?" Rayann inclined her head toward Dedric and Zoraida.

Judy glanced over. "Oh, I think they share some of the same views on life. Being tough, butch. You know."

Rayann smiled as if she understood. When she was coming out, butch/femme had been passé, or so she had thought. Maybe it was back in style. But what made Dedric and Zoraida seem butch to Judy? Frankly, Rayann hadn't thought of either of them with that particular adjective — only as direct, aggressive and strong women. Was that what butch meant?

"How's business?"

Judy grimaced. "How's teaching?"

"That bad?" As the students dwindled to two a week, then one, then none, Rayann had vaguely worried about the class failing. On the last day it had been a relief. She knew she wasn't cut out to be an instructor. She didn't have the gift of seeing inside her student's heads for their hidden talents, nor did she have enough self-assurance to criticize other people's work — even though someone long ago had said criticism was easier than craft. Michelle had thought teaching a good idea, which was probably another reason why Rayann's enthusiasm had taken a nosedive about two months ago.

The song ended and Judy said, "Women must be getting healthier, or poorer, because my client base is shrinking. I might start wishing I'd stuck with English."

Zoraida met her at the edge of the dance floor. "You're not finished yet, *novia*." She pulled Rayann to her for a slow dance.

If she's being butch, then I like it, Rayann thought. Certainly Zoraida's approach was different from Michelle's, but then all women were different. Zoraida rocked Rayann in her arms, moving slowly and sensuously. *Oh, I like it.* When Rayann traced her lips over Zoraida's chin and throat, Zoraida's hands slid lower, to Rayann's hips,

100

increasing the pressure of her thigh between Rayann's legs.

"You're a good dancer," Rayann murmured into Zoraida's ear.

"I don't know that I'd call this dancing." Zoraida's voice was husky, her breath warm as it whispered past Rayann's ear.

They were almost motionless. Zoraida's hands slid under the back of Rayann's sweater. Rayann could feel the zipper of Zoraida's jacket pressing against her. She could sense the outline of fabric under the jacket, not thick enough to hide the swell and tautness of Zoraida's breasts. Melting, Rayann put her forehead on Zoraida's shoulder.

The song ended and the floor lights went up slightly. Rayann pushed herself away from Zoraida, holding her by the forearms for steadiness. She didn't know if Zoraida had been aware of how aroused Rayann had become; she glanced at Zoraida and saw the answer there, a mirror of the desire they shared.

"*Novia*," Zoraida whispered, "come home with me. We have to finish this dance in a more appropriate place."

Rayann closed her eyes with a shudder. She opened her mouth to say yes — the word was almost out of her mouth. She opened her eyes again, and over Zoraida's shoulder she saw Louisa.

She blinked. Louisa was still there. Now Louisa was looking their way. Then Rayann saw a leather-clad arm around Louisa's shoulders.

"*Novia?*"

Rayann forced her attention back to Zoraida. She'd been about to say something, but whatever it was had completely escaped her. "I'm sorry, I saw someone I knew." Rayann glanced at Louisa again. Louisa raised her eyebrows and smiled.

Zoraida turned to look in the direction Rayann was indicating, and as the next song began, she herded Rayann off the dance floor. "Who? Which one? Not the blonde bitch again?"

"No. The tall woman, with the black and silver hair — over there in the denim jacket, next to the woman wearing the leather jacket."

"You mean the woman next to the butch in the bomber jacket?"

"Yes. That's the woman I work for," Rayann said.

Zoraida looked at Rayann for a long moment. "I thought it was the one who broke your heart," she said slowly.

"Why would you think that?"

"Because of the expression on your face. Never mind."

"Michelle didn't break my heart," Rayann said. She was confused.

"So, the woman you work for, is it all work?"

"Of course!"

"Why of course! She's very . . . riveting for her age."

"She and the woman she's with are a couple," Rayann said.

"And that's why it's all work?"

"No, that's not what I meant . . . I'm not, I mean —"

"That's not what your face told me when you first saw her."

Rayann was aghast. Zoraida had gotten the completely wrong idea. "After the way you danced with me, what expression would you expect me to have?"

"One that I was responsible for." Zoraida put her hands in her back pockets, her expression one of studied nonchalance.

"What's it to you, anyway? You said no strings, remember."

Zoraida smiled at that and shook her head, looking at the floor. "I did say that, didn't I? It's my motto. It's just . . . I like to know the score."

"I'm free," Rayann said stubbornly.

"Free to come home with me tonight?" Zoraida moved closer again and Rayann's body reminded her of the wonderful sensations Zoraida had engendered.

"I didn't think I'd see you again this evening," Louisa said. She had crossed the dance floor to where Rayann

102

and Zoraida stood. "But at least you can meet Danny finally."

"So you're Rayann. It's a pleasure," Danny put her arm around Rayann, giving her a bruisingly enthusiastic hug. Her arms felt as tough as oak. "Where're you all sitting?"

"What a surprise," Rayann managed. "I thought you were going to a midnight show."

"It's a ways till midnight," Louisa said. "Danny and Jill go way back so she had to put in an appearance. I've only been here a couple of times, but it's a nice place." She looked at Zoraida, one eyebrow lifted slightly.

Rayann, completely bemused, performed introductions. She found herself introducing Louisa and Danny to Judy and Dedric and sat helpless while everyone scuffled for two more chairs. *Okay, now we're all sitting down. What am I going to do?*

Rayann donned a veneer of rationality. She joked, aware of Zoraida's arm against hers, just as Dedric's was against Judy's. She studied, when she could, the spare, hardened features of Danny's face, noticing how different she seemed from Louisa. Zoraida had immediately called Danny a butch — was it the leather jacket? Zoraida wore a leather jacket. Did that make Zoraida butch? Judy seemed to think so. If Danny and Zoraida and Dedric were all butch, did that make Judy and Louisa and herself all femme?

It's beside the point. No, she answered herself. It's important. If I don't figure this out I may never figure Louisa out. *Which is what I want to do.*

Rayann hoped no one else noticed her shaking hands. She wanted to go home with Zoraida. She wanted to have a fantastic, mind-blowing night of sex. She needed to — it was the only solution to the insane, unstoppable, inappropriate infatuation she'd developed for the woman she saw every morning, every night and most times in between, the woman right over there who was sitting next to a full-fledged butch who looked as if she'd stepped out of a golden oldie lesbian paperback. In fact, Danny looked

103

as if she could beat the daylights out of anyone at the table — with the possible exception of Dedric — but it wasn't the threat of Danny's physical presence that made Rayann think twice about any half-baked ideas she had about herself and Louisa. It was the unmistakable signs of a longtime friendship and respect between Danny and Louisa. She would not, could not, be responsible for endangering it. If she tried she was no better than Michelle.

"Honey, something tells me you have a light." A brunette in her mid-forties, in a short red skirt and tight blouse, stopped next to Danny. Danny turned and the woman leaned over, cigarette between her index and middle fingers. The blouse fell forward, affording everyone a view of what lay under it — Danny with the best view of all. Rayann watched as Danny deftly flipped open her lighter, sparked it with a negligent flip of one thumb and held the flame under the cigarette the brunette slowly inserted between her lips. The brunette steadied Danny's hand and the view down the front of her blouse swelled and receded as the brunette inhaled once, then again, then stood up.

"Thanks, lover."

"Don't mention it." Danny watched the woman walk away, a faint smile of satisfaction playing around her mouth.

Rayann shot a look at Louisa. Louisa was studying her drink. Rayann was enraged — how could Danny do such a thing, something so . . . so *intimate* right in front of Louisa?

Dedric said to Danny, "Was it good for you?"

Danny laughed. "I haven't lit another woman's cigarette in years. It really takes me back."

"Sometimes I miss smoking," Dedric said. Then she laughed and glanced slyly at Judy. "Just about every night."

"Everybody I know who's quit says they really miss smoking after dinner," Zoraida said.

"I was not thinking about after *dinner*." Dedric grinned as Judy playfully slapped at her.

The banter went on, eddying around Rayann's ears. She didn't contribute much. When Zoraida asked her to dance, Rayann was aware of Louisa's gaze on them. She slowly shook her head. "I'm tired," she said feebly.

Zoraida's eyes flashed, startling Rayann. Zoraida turned her head for a moment then asked Dedric to dance. They disappeared in the mass of bodies on the dance floor, each moving in a similar assured step.

Louisa looked at her watch and gave Danny a shake. "Come on, we've still got to find a parking place near the theater. Beach Blanket Babylon is *always* crowded."

"Okay. Give me time for a smoke outside, and then we'll hightail it." Danny strode to the door, her walk defiant, daring anyone to get in her way.

"Well, it was certainly a pleasure to meet the woman with the Greta Garbo voice," Judy said. "Rayann was positively secretive about you."

"Was she?"

"I don't like to gossip," Rayann said quickly, "unlike my ex-roommate." Judy threw an ice cube at her; Rayann threw it back.

Louisa smiled as she stood up. "I know better than to get caught in the middle of a long-standing feud." To Rayann's surprise and utter shock, Louisa fished an ice cube out of her drink and actually threw it at Rayann. "See you tomorrow, Ray."

Rayann was stunned. She watched Louisa join Danny at the door and then they left, arm in arm.

"They look like old friends," Judy said.

"They're a couple."

"Oh?" Judy's eyebrows went up under her bangs and she shrugged. "Well, I'm sure they have a lot in common — age, history."

"Is that important?"

Judy's eyebrows came down and she studied Rayann with a frighteningly intense analytical gaze that Rayann had never seen before. "It's a factor," Judy said, finally. "Ray, are you —"

"Miss me?" Dedric dropped a breathless kiss on Judy's forehead. "Good lord, she's worn me out."

Zoraida, similarly breathless, collapsed into her chair. "I think it is the other way around."

Everything seemed to go back to the way it was before Louisa and Danny had arrived. Somebody took the two empty chairs to their table, and it could have been as if they'd never been there. Except that Rayann had a frightened, aching truth lodged like shrapnel in her heart. The pain kept her in her seat, drove her through a couple of extra gin and tonics. It kept her from going home with Zoraida. Zoraida took it well, said "maybe next time," and left Rayann at the bookstore door with the impression that Zoraida knew exactly what had caused Rayann's cold feet. Rayann wished Zoraida would explain it to her.

She dozed off sometime around daybreak, aware that Louisa was not home yet, and aware that it was no business of hers where Louisa spent her nights — aware too that searing visions of how and where Rayann wanted Louisa to spend her nights would make her life a living hell until somehow she got over it.

6
Inlay

Rayann regretted not going home with Zoraida. She regretted it every morning when Louisa, still damp from her shower, skin glowing from the hot water, came out of the bathroom in her robe. She regretted it when Danny dropped in for a cup of coffee and she and Louisa talked what amounted to a foreign language, about places and people and events Rayann could hardly follow.

She lived with her regrets because of the things she didn't regret — leaving Michelle, striking out on her own. One sketchpad was already filled with images that might some day become something more concrete. She was on speaking terms with her mother — had even found herself inviting her mother to stop by the bookstore anytime. Everything would, in fact, be perfect if only her body would behave itself when Louisa was around.

Using up all her spare energy, Rayann threw herself into working on Christmas gifts for her mother and Louisa, and keeping the shelves restocked. She certainly had no regrets about making the flyer, or even about what a swoon she'd been in when she delivered them. The bookstore was crawling with customers who agreed that books *were* the perfect gift and who delighted in the personal help they received. By the end of the following week the eighty dictionaries were gone. In the flurry of business Louisa had reorganized the tables into For Him, For Her, For Kids and For That Special Someone. Rayann watched happily as customers sought out Louisa's advice and left the store contented.

"I never would have believed we'd have this much business," Louisa said in the first lull of the week. "I'm not sure I want to work this hard."

"Well, then I'll give you an incentive." Rayann crooked her finger, adopting the light teasing attitude she'd found she could sustain around Louisa. Louisa followed her into the storeroom.

Rayann spun around and held out her arms. The bare light cast Rayann's shadow against one wall. She made a shadow rabbit. "What do you think?" The room was empty save for the card table Rayann had unearthed.

"Oh, my God," Louisa murmured, and then she shook her head. "It hasn't been like this since Christina . . ."

Rayann made another shadow rabbit scurry across the wall. "It needs painting but when I'm done what are we going to do with the space?" She segued from shadow-rabbiting to antler-dancing. She felt giddy.

"I want to expand the store and put shelves and tables in here," Louisa said, "but I can't think what exactly to move where. And if I'm going to have customers going in and out, I'll have to move the cash register and counter elsewhere. But again, I don't know where to."

"Where will we put the deliveries?"

"In the anteroom." Louisa turned with a huge grin when she saw Rayann's shadow on the wall. "What on earth are you doing?"

"Antler-dancing. It's the right time of the year." Rayann stopped, breathing hard. "What the heck is the anteroom?"

"Walk this way," Louisa said.

If I could walk that way I wouldn't need the talcum powder, Rayann thought, watching Louisa's legs whisper against one another. *No more antler-dancing. It makes me silly.* Rayann followed Louisa across the store to a door Rayann had assumed led to the outside but was locked for safety. She was wrong. Louisa unlocked it and stood aside.

"There're only a few boxes in here, but they're very old. A collection of books Chris bought at an estate sale and never got around to sorting."

Rayann hauled them out one by one. She sneezed twice from the dust and mercilessly stomped on a spider that meandered groggily out of one of the boxes. "Hope there aren't any more of those," she said, sniffling. She took the tissue Louisa proffered and felt less bleary after she blew her nose. "You know, I think once these are taken care of, you're right about using this cubbyhole for deliveries. It's about the right size to keep us from getting lazy."

Louisa's smile didn't quite reach her eyes. "Or sentimental." A customer entered and Louisa looked over her shoulder. "She has a flyer — duty calls."

Rayann heard Louisa explain that the dictionaries were gone but that the flyer still entitled the woman to twenty-five percent off the price of the hardcover best-seller of her choice. Kneeling, Rayann set about sorting and pricing the books.

"How come whenever I see you you're picking something up?"

Startled, Rayann looked up. Teddy was leaning against a set of shelves watching her with a look of amused indulgence.

Rayann smiled. She knew more about him now, and even taking into account Louisa's natural prejudice, he didn't sound all that bad for a man. As a single father with a demanding career, he seemed to be doing a good job raising his son after Tucker's mother had departed with another man for parts unknown. "You really shouldn't sneak up on people like that."

"And then you lecture me, just like my mother."

"I do not lecture you," Rayann protested. "I'm right, though."

"I know. I snuck up on you to be mean. Would you care for some help?"

"No, but thanks. I'm almost done."

"The shelves look really good, by the way."

"Thanks again."

To Rayann's surprise he lingered, talking about how her structure was greatly superior and stronger to the one he'd been planning to put up. Rayann found herself liking him, a little.

"Listen, while Mom's busy," he said, after glancing over his shoulder "can you tell me what she might want for Christmas?"

Rayann thought for a second. "Well, she said she liked the Paul Winter tape I played so I was thinking of getting her his *Sunsinger* album."

"I didn't know she liked Paul Winter," Teddy said. "She's always been a classical music lover."

"We listen to all sorts of stuff, actually. She also likes k.d. lang." At Teddy's uncomprehending look, Rayann went on, "She's a country singer. K period, D period, L-A-N-G. Louisa said she reminds her of Patsy Cline."

Teddy pulled a small notebook from his pocket and scribbled. "Country? I'd have never known. Do you have any idea what size sweater she wears?"

Rayann took his pencil and notebook, smiling. She'd taken notes when she'd done laundry before deciding to make Louisa's gift. They wore the same size — except Louisa's bra was two sizes larger than Rayann's. She jotted down sweater, slacks, and shirt sizes, then handed the notebook back.

"Gee, thanks. This is great. I always have to ask her and then she guesses what I'm getting her, which is no fun whatsoever."

"What are you two whispering about?" Louisa loomed over them.

Teddy got up to hug Louisa. "We were whispering about your Christmas present."

Louisa smiled with what Rayann thought was relief. "What are you getting me?"

"No hints, not this year."

"You're no fun. I'll just torture the secret out of Rayann."

"These lips are sealed," Rayann said. She went back to categorizing and pricing the books and imagined some of the ways Louisa might be able to torture her. Like wearing that turquoise shirt with the high collar. And putting her hair up in those filigree combs . . .

After she filed the volume of Yeats, Rayann caressed *The Muse of the Violets*. She knew what she would do with the storeroom, but then again, this wasn't her shop. *And I'd better stop saying things like "Where are we going to store deliveries" and acting as if this is my place.* But since she was indulging in druthers, if she had the storeroom to herself, she'd turn the whole area into a women's book area, including books by and about lesbians, women's spirituality, and women's health. There were all sorts of topics Louisa's current space just didn't allow for. She'd make The Common Reader famous in the East Bay for women's literature. *In your dreams.*

"Ray, we're going to go up and have some coffee — you'll be okay?"

Rayann waved to Louisa in response and took up a position behind the counter. She did admire Louisa for keeping such a close relationship with her son. It was something her own mother had not achieved, but lately

Rayann had been willing to place a little more blame at her own door than she had in the past. She looked forward to better times.

When Louisa returned, Rayann went back to examining the books. "Some of these will have to be thrown away. Mildew."

As Louisa took the book their fingertips touched. Rayann promptly dropped everything she was holding. "Goodness there's been a lot of static electricity today," she said, all in a rush. She bent to get the book, hiding her face. *Yeah, right.*

Within a few days Rayann was glad that her overwhelming and sudden crush on Louisa hadn't lasted. There was just one little problem: the crush had mutated into a gigantic infatuation which felt deep and serious. But of course it had to be infatuation because nothing would ever happen between them. She was sure that at times, from the indulgent way Louisa treated her, she must seem like a child to Louisa. Or the daughter-she-never-had. They listened to k.d. lang and Louisa heard Patsy Cline; Rayann heard k.d. lang. Rayann wasn't sure she'd know Patsy Cline if Patsy Cline walked up and kissed her. There was just so much she didn't know about Louisa and her history.

Louisa glanced up and caught Rayann staring. At that distance her eyes looked black. Rayann smiled and turned to help the woman she'd noticed browsing in a lost sort of way. "Can I help you find something?"

"You have such an incredible variety I don't know where to start." The customer, sporting an irrepressible smile, scratched her head. "I just need some ideas." She had strong, broad hips, and moved from table to table in comfortable tennis shoes and sweats.

"Who's left on your list?" Rayann suggested books for parents, step-parents and several friends. Watching Louisa had taught Rayann confidence in dealing with customers, and how to ask the right questions to help them make a good choice.

"This is great," the customer said, a few minutes later. "Everyone's covered, except me. I'm out of things to read, which drives me nuts. I'm looking for something entertaining and romantic." Rayann started to point out several authors but the woman interrupted her with a shy look. "No, not those. You don't seem to have . . . the kind I'm looking for. But I thought maybe you could tell me if there's a woman's bookstore around here." There was a slight emphasis on "you."

"I understand." Rayann met the woman's gaze honestly. *Someday these cryptic conversations won't be necessary.* "You're right. We don't carry any . . . of those books, but I could draw you a map to Mama Bear's."

The woman bit her lower lip and stared shyly at her shoes. "If you get off work sometime soon you could come with me. Save you making me the map." She looked up.

Rayann blushed. "I'm . . . I —" she floundered. "I'm flattered, but I'm not really free." *You are so!*

"Well, it was worth a try." The woman gave Rayann a cheeky smile. "I'll bet you could recommend some good books, though."

Rayann wrote down several titles. "I recommend them all."

"I haven't read any of these. Thanks a lot. I really appreciate it." She went her way, moving gracefully around the tables. She was the last customer of the day, and when she left, Louisa turned the door sign to "Closed." She turned back to Rayann with a knowing smirk. "Smooth operator."

"What'd I do?"

Louisa aimed a thumb after the departing customer. "She told me to tell you her phone number is on the check. She made up a plausible story about you letting her know when a book comes in, but I know what she was up to." Louisa's eyes were shining with laughter.

"But I told her I wasn't really free at the moment," Rayann said. The more she blushed the more Louisa smirked.

"Zoraida might not take kindly to competition," Louisa said. Her voice had overtones that Rayann distinctly heard as maternal. *Why does she think Zoraida and I are serious? It was only one date. She's the one who didn't come home after the party.*

"Zoraida isn't . . . well, anyway," Rayann said, hoping not to discuss her love life any further, "it was a shame I had to send her someplace else to finish buying her books."

"Oh, why was that?" Louisa looked genuinely puzzled.

"She wanted something for lesbians."

"Oh." Louisa was silent for a few moments. Then she answered Rayann's unspoken question. "I can't, Ray. I know the small presses are very helpful and it would be pretty easy to stock up, but I couldn't possibly afford it. The steady customers might go elsewhere and they're the bread and butter of the store."

"It's your store. I just think — there's a market. And we're looking for a warm and friendly place to buy."

"I suppose. But I can't."

"The storeroom —"

"I can't. It's not —"

"I understand." Rayann smiled to hide her disappointment. Louisa's answer extended to more than just the books. "Let's forget I brought it up and have some dinner. I'm starved."

They watched the news and argued over the same political points they always argued over, agreeing in principle on sensitive topics such as abortion rights, U.S. meddling in Central America and the Middle East and the so-called war on drugs, but disagreeing on minor points and semantics. Ever since Rayann had started reading Louisa's back issues of *Zeta*, she had found herself much more informed on world affairs and could hold her own.

But when Louisa said good night, Rayann knew there was one argument she would never win. The storeroom would never become The Woman's Reader of her imagination. She didn't understand why, but she had to accept it. She crept down to the bookstore and copied the woman's phone number. *I'll call tomorrow.* She wouldn't have time tomorrow, the last shopping day before Christmas. *I'll call next week. Yeah, sure, and chocolate is not the lesbian national food.*

They caught the last hour of *Miracle on 34th Street.* Rayann sighed. "I wish this weren't colorized. I don't know why, but Maureen O'Hara's hair looks more red in black and white."

"Her legs are just as impressive," Louisa said. "I've always had a thing for women with great calves."

Rayann was startled. It was the first time Louisa had said anything of that nature. "They are, aren't they? Too bad she's so willing to give up her independence. She's raising Natalie Wood just fine all by herself."

"Mmm-hmm." Louisa's voice had a woolly sound and when Rayann glanced over she was not surprised to see Louisa's eyes were closed.

The minutes ticked by. Louisa didn't stir when the timer chimed. Rayann flicked the T.V. off with the remote and went to check some pies they had put in the oven. The apple mixture was bubbling and everything was a luscious golden brown. They looked almost too good to eat. She put them on the stove burners to cool, then switched the oven off and turned out the light. The kitchen and living room plunged into darkness. Stumbling over the coffee table, she turned the reading lamp on and went to wake Louisa up.

Louisa's expression was utterly relaxed; her expression lines were laugh lines only. Her pink-silver lips curved slightly in sleep. She looked almost unearthly in the dim light — although the streak of flour across one cheek made her seem more mortal. Rayann hated to disturb her. Leaning over, she gently shook one shoulder, enjoying the warmth and softness.

"Rayann?" Louisa's eyes fluttered open, unfocused.

115

Then her hands reached up, grasping Rayann's waist. "What are you doing?" The words weren't an invitation, but Louisa's hands gripped Rayann's waist and pulled Rayann down.

I don't care why. If I don't do this I'll go mad. Rayann stretched out next to Louisa on the sofa, her mouth finding Louisa's, tasting at last the smooth texture. She'd taken Louisa by surprise, but after a moment Louisa gasped, and gripped Rayann harder. Her mouth invited Rayann's exploration.

"Ray, are you sure?" Louisa whispered when Rayann finally released her mouth.

"Yes. I . . . want to."

Louisa sat up, then cupped Rayann's face. "What about the pies," she murmured.

Rayann laughed, and Louisa's finger traced her mouth. "I took them out. They're perfect," she said more quietly. Her heart hammered against her ribs.

"Good." Louisa's mouth captured Rayann's, and Rayann melted, twisted. Louisa was over her, her deliberate mouth moving from lips to forehead to chin and returning to Rayann's mouth, tasting deeply, then brushing with the softest press of lips. One hand unbuttoned Rayann's shirt, then the strong fingers slid inside. Rayann shuddered and reached for Louisa, wanting to feel her skin gliding under her fingertips.

Louisa caught Rayann's hand in her own, and held it down with gentle pressure. "Let me do this," Louisa said in her low voice. Her fingers claimed the tender flesh of Rayann's stomach, then slid upward, around to her back, dexterously unhooking Rayann's bra. Her lips came to Rayann's again as her hand moved under the bra, around Rayann's ribs and cupped the softness she had freed.

Rayann moaned through Louisa's kiss. *She is so sure — how does she know?* She felt the cool air on her newly bared breasts. They were swollen and aching, the chill tightening her already aroused nipples. Louisa's mouth left her lips and Rayann shuddered when her cold breast was covered with the warm softness of Louisa's lips.

Louisa teased Rayann's nipple with her tongue and

teeth. Rayann didn't realize her hips were arching up to Louisa until Louisa slipped one leg between Rayann's. Rayann rose to Louisa's thigh, aching for the feel of Louisa's skin against her own.

Louisa drew Rayann up long enough to remove Rayann's clothing from the waist up, leaving Rayann acutely aware of her own nakedness. Louisa turned her attention to Rayann's other breast and the buttons of her workshirt pressed into Rayann's bare stomach.

Rayann moved frantically against Louisa's thigh. She had never made love this way — never. With Michelle there had been long preliminaries, mutual rituals of foreplay that made them both ready for touching and stroking. They had undressed each other; undressing had been part of the ritual.

"Lou . . . oh." *I can't come this way. I can't* . . . But she did, arching up, grabbing Louisa, pulling her down as she spasmed, her nails digging into Louisa's back until her hips slowed. But even when the storm had passed, she continued to move against Louisa.

Louisa tenderly kissed Rayann's mouth, then asked, "Did you come?"

"Yes," Rayann gasped. "I didn't think I could, not like that."

Louisa pulled Rayann to her feet and guided her to the door of her bedroom. "Are you sure?"

"Yes. Yes."

Louisa pulled the bedclothes to the foot of the bed with one hand and drew Rayann down with the other. They shed their shoes and socks in a flurry of squirming, then Louisa was on top of Rayann again, her mouth seeking the taut points of Rayann's breasts again, hardened further by the cool sheet under Rayann's back.

Rayann ran her fingers through the black-silver hair. The black was coarse and thick, the silver silky and soft. She buried her face in the contrast, then held on to Louisa as she felt the buttons of her jeans opening. Those fingers — *so sure, so strong* — slid downward, inward, then cupped while Rayann gasped.

Louisa moved against Rayann, the friction of her

117

clothes against Rayann's bare skin bringing new heat between them. "Tell me what you like," Louisa said. Her hand was lazy and teasing between Rayann's legs.

"Let me get my jeans off," Rayann said. "So I can . . . so you can . . ." *So you can take me, so I can open up for you.* She had never longed for a woman's fingers to be inside her, not like this, not so much that she knew she was overflowing with proof.

She feels so good against me. Rayann twined her bare legs around Louisa's. The denim Louisa wore was sensuous against her hips, against her inner thighs. Then Louisa's fingers found her and Rayann showed Louisa what she wanted, rising, stretching, spreading herself on Louisa's fingers, shamelessly driving toward her own release.

"Like this?" Louisa spoke into Rayann's ear as she traced it with her tongue.

"Yes." Rayann struggled for breath. "Don't . . . don't stop."

"Never."

This can't be happening. But it is, it is. She's loving you, like this, giving you what you've wanted, what you've dreamed about almost since the day you met.

The first cry broke from Rayann and was caught by Louisa's mouth. The next flowed between them as Louisa kissed her deeply, straining against Rayann as Rayann froze, then collapsed, moaning at the loss she felt when Louisa's fingers slid away.

Louisa's wet hand came to Rayann's breasts, painted the wetness over them. Then Louisa's mouth tasted them again, and Rayann felt herself opening again, wanting again.

"Louisa, Louisa please," she begged. "Take off your clothes. I want to feel you against me." Rayann shuddered when Louisa's body moved away, and shuddered again when Louisa returned, soft, warm skin against her own.

She palmed the smooth planes of Louisa's back as Louisa straddled her waist, hair tickling Rayann's breasts, then lay fully atop her, knees falling between Rayann's. When Louisa rose again, she was kneeling between

Rayann's legs. Her kisses marked Rayann's shoulders, then her stomach.

"Do you like this, too?" Louisa's mouth moved lower. Her lips nuzzled above Rayann's dark triangle of hair.

"Yes." Rayann felt the cold claim her uncovered body, but her nerves devoted all attention to the hot spot, the inflamed center of passion, ignited by Louisa's seeking and teasing tongue.

The most incredible . . . Rayann covered her breasts with her hands, shaking as Louisa's mouth captured all of her, tongue diving and swirling, then teasing again. She gave herself over, took every sensation Louisa offered her, one building on the last until passion flared, then melted to sweetness.

Rayann closed her eyes to better concentrate on breathing. When she opened them again, she felt erotic wetness on her thigh, then she raised her thigh, giving it to Louisa, who moaned as she moved. Gathering courage, Rayann slid her hand down, her fingers curling, brushing against Louisa, becoming coated with Louisa's passion.

Louisa froze, then groaned. "Yes." Her hips moved faster, enclosing Rayann's fingers, then shuddering and jerking as she cried out. "Ray," she murmured, falling to the bed and gathering Rayann in her arms. "Thank you."

"My pleasure," Rayann murmured. "It's all been my pleasure." She kissed Louisa, then sat up to pull the covers over them. Louisa's arms were waiting when she stretched out again, and kisses consumed her mouth. Louisa's hand moved between her legs. "I don't think I can again," Rayann said, her voice raspy.

"Try," Louisa said. "Try."

7

Uncured

Rayann floated at the very edge of deciding to wake up. Over a period of several minutes she opened her eyes slightly. The light of day was harsh, but she persisted despite her body telling her to sink back into sleep. *Christmas morning — I feel as if I've opened all my presents already.* She could hear Louisa moving around in the kitchen, probably making a special tart for Tucker. Rayann wanted to call out to Louisa and ask her to come back to bed, but she was too satiated to exert herself yet. Better to lounge in bed for just a few more minutes.

It was not just any bed. Rayann had seen it when she'd done household chores, but she hadn't dared to study it before. Canopies weren't that rare, but the heavily carved posts were authentic Grecian design in what looked like fired olive wood — *that* was rare. Instead of lightweight netting or a swatch of decorative fabric, the posts supported a heavy tapestry with a medieval motif. She lay back, breathing in the scent of Louisa and the passion they had shared, and looked up at the scene above her.

A golden sun and silver moon occupied the top and bottom of the working, and in between, white symbols of the zodiac were arranged in a circle. Emerald-green runes were scattered against the royal purple background and Rayann wished she had paid more attention to Judy's hobby of mysticism during college. The borders were intricate golden leaves and red roses twined to form a briar. Overall, now that Rayann had had a chance to look at every part, it wasn't that medieval — the work itself was probably less than a hundred years old, but the design seemed of a far greater antiquity. It was beautiful, but somehow not what she would have expected Louisa to have above her bed. Still, in the dim natural light, the moon seemed to glow on its own accord. Rayann found it romantic, as romantic as her memories of last night. She had been right. Going to bed with Louisa had cured her of her infatuation. Her body was warm and replete. She wanted nothing more.

"Merry Christmas. Going to sleep all day?" Louisa, already dressed in faded jeans and an embroidered blue workshirt, appeared in the doorway.

"Merry Christmas. If I do it's because I'm exhausted. You're a real . . . taskmaster," Rayann said. She sat up.

Louisa smiled somewhat nervously, running one hand through the silver-black masses of hair that had not yet been lifted away from her shoulders with combs. The stove timer dinged in the awkward silence and Louisa hurriedly went to the kitchen, leaving Rayann clutching the sheets to her chest.

Breathe in. For God's sake, breathe in! When her

121

lungs finally obeyed, the light-headed feeling didn't go away. Actually, Rayann felt light-bodied, as if she could float. Her senses were fluttering — her stomach was nothing but butterfly wings tickling and teasing her heart.

If only I hadn't seen her hand. But she couldn't go through life asking potential lovers to hide their hands. She was cured of her infatuation for Louisa, to be sure. In its place she had come down with a four-letter word and the prognosis was terminal.

Goddamnit, I'm in love. Rayann groaned and threw herself back into the pillows. This could not be happening. A physical attraction for an older woman was one thing, but love — what could Rayann be thinking of? They enjoyed each other's company, but they had nothing else in common. So they liked books and baseball, but so did lots of people. Last night was just — it had to be just one of those mutual attraction things. Not love at all, but lust. That was it, lust.

The aroma of baked apple filled the bedroom, bringing too many memories of the previous night. Rayann, unable to consider being naked in front of Louisa again, found Louisa's robe, and went to her room. Heat flamed through her body when she saw her shirt and bra, abandoned last night in the living room, folded neatly on the bed. She stuffed them in the hamper, then quickly showered and dressed. As Rayann emerged from her bedroom, Louisa was adding two more slices of French toast to the stack waiting on the table. Rayann slid into her chair at the table. "I'm starved." *What an inane thing to say.*

"Ummm," Louisa said. "So am I. Must be the exercise."

Rayann put her fork down. "Louisa," she began slowly. "I — don't know what to say." *That's it — Bette Davis has just chosen someone else to be her fairy goddaughter.*

"Believe it or not, neither do I."

"I'm not sure why last night happened." *Liar.* Well, she had no idea why Louisa did it.

"Neither am I, but Ray, I've been thinking since I got up. Just because it happened doesn't mean we can't go on as before, does it? I'm sorry —"

"Please don't be. It was just fan—"

"You don't have to treat me with kid gloves. It just happened, and you should probably put it behind you. I mean we," Louisa said. "You have good friends and a life —"

"And so do you." *Danny. Oh, my God. I made her be unfaithful to Danny.* Deep down was the thought that she hadn't made Louisa do anything — it had been the other way around.

"Yes, but that's not important. I want you to know . . ." Louisa studied her plate. Rayann was glad Louisa's penetrating eyes were not focused on her. "I want you to know you don't . . . you're not obligated. To me."

Obligated? "I don't feel obligated." *I just feel like I want to do it again. And again.*

Louisa glanced up at her and Rayann felt the pierce of her gaze, then Louisa was staring at her plate again. "I'm glad. Look, I think it was just something we both needed."

"I understand," Rayann said. And she did. No strings, no ties, no repeats. In many ways, it resembled the offer Zoraida had made her. It had seemed an easy bargain with Zoraida — an equal contract, somehow. But this situation with Louisa wasn't easy. Nor did it feel equal. "Really, I do." She picked up her plate and carried it to the sink. "The pies look wonderful." She heard Louisa's sigh — relief, no doubt — behind her.

"Yes. Yes, they do."

There was a thundering series of bangs on the back door. A muffled voice called, "Hey, open up. Merry Christmas and all that but I'm freezing my butt off."

Danny. Rayann busied herself with the breakfast dishes and had both arms in suds when Danny came in through the back porch, laden with packages. She kept herself busy with the steaming water, hoping it would justify her flushed cheeks. *Danny, I'm sorry.* She would not for the world wish that last night hadn't happened. But it could not happen again.

She was aware that Louisa and Danny were speaking in low voices, but when she stole a glance at them,

123

Danny did not seem perturbed. When Danny put her arm around Louisa and hugged her, Rayann averted her eyes and scrubbed unmercifully at the already clean skillet. As she put the last dried dish away, Danny called, "Hey, Ray, don't spend Christmas on chores. Come join us."

Rayann sat in the rocker, and was mystified when Danny handed her a small wrapped box. "Danny — I didn't get you anything! You shouldn't have," Rayann protested, deeply embarrassed. She'd only met Danny once and after last night, it was too much.

"It's nothing, really. I love Christmas, I love giving presents," Danny said. She leaned forward, elbow set to one knee. Her gold-brown eyes held nothing but friendship as she regarded Rayann. "And you've been a godsend to Lou."

I can't believe I'm in this situation, wondering if she knows. Rayann looked at Louisa. Louisa seemed her usual self. Rayann opened the box nervously. Two simple pearl stud earrings glinted at her.

"Oh," Rayann breathed in. They were genuine — the pearls had an uneven pale pink sheen and lacked the pristine perfection of imitation pearls. "Danny, I can't accept these. You really shouldn't —"

"It's my pleasure," Danny broke in. "Besides, these are the Danielle earrings. Show them to Lou."

Rayann handed the jeweler's box to Louisa, who laughed when she saw them. Rayann looked back at Danny; she had missed the point somewhere.

"You are indeed honored," Louisa said, handing the box back. "Not everyone has received a pair of Danielle earrings. I myself have only two pairs."

"I don't get it," Rayann said.

Danny laughed. "Every year my brother gives me a pair of pierced earrings for my birthday. He addresses them to 'Danielle with love.' I must have told him a hundred times I don't wear earrings and I really prefer to be called Danny. So every year at Christmas I give them to a new friend who'd appreciate them." Her voice became gruff. "Makes me be sure I have at least one new friend each year."

"What was it last year — oh, sapphires," Louisa said. "And the year before it was diamond chips. You have to admit he's got taste."

Danny shrugged. "He has money. I haven't seen him in years and I guess it's sweet that he thinks of me. But if he saw me he'd look at me just the way he did when I told him I was a dyke, like I was part insect." Danny ran her hand through her short gray hair. "Hell, I just send a card for his birthday."

Rayann managed a smile. "Well, thank you. I am honored." *I guess I'm honored.* But the earrings only underlined how long Louisa and Danny had known each other, and just how briefly Rayann had known Louisa.

Danny handed a small envelope to Louisa. "I've been waiting about four months to give you this," she said.

Louisa opened it quickly and drew out a ticket. She gasped. "Is this opening day? Section one-twenty-one, row four — right over the dugout! Thank you!" Louisa threw her arms around Danny and hugged her.

"I kept the other one for myself, of course," Danny said, returning Louisa's hug.

Louisa released Danny and handed the ticket to Rayann to examine. An opening day ticket for the A's, prime seats no less. "You must know somebody," Rayann said to Danny.

"I'll never tell, but I didn't exactly pay the price on the ticket."

"Well, this seems like the time," Louisa said. She rose gracefully and disappeared into her room. Rayann was only too aware that she could *not* watch Louisa move. She wondered if the rumpled bedclothes would remind Louisa of the night before. But Louisa looked as serene as usual when she reappeared, two packages in hand. Rayann realized one was for her and she jumped to her feet and hurried into her room. Louisa's gift was not finished, but near enough.

When Rayann returned, Danny was opening a package that revealed a sweatshirt with an appliqued front. "Lou, it's stunning," Danny said as she lifted it from the box. Patches of purple and silver seemed to move in the light.

It was beautiful, Rayann thought, its bold colors suited Danny's strong features and whipcord body. Danny immediately stood up, pulled off her well-washed plain blue sweatshirt and tried on her new sweatshirt. Louisa stood up as well, turning Danny to face her. Her fingers slid under the collar of the white shirt Danny was wearing underneath and she settled it, pulling the points of the collar out. She took Danny by the shoulders and studied her at arm's length.

"I thought it would match your eyes," she said. "What do you think, Ray?"

"Perfect. It looks really good." It did match Danny's tawny eyes. But Rayann could hardly stand to watch Danny kiss Louisa with her thanks. It wasn't jealousy — it just hurt.

Louisa and Danny sat down again and Rayann accepted the wrapped box Louisa handed her, and, with a smile, handed her own offering to Louisa.

"You first." Louisa watched as Rayann fumbled with the red ribbon on the small silver-wrapped package.

Inside the box, nestled in green and red tissue paper was a strong silver chain. Rayann raised it and breathed, "Louisa, it's lovely," as an intricately etched silver phoenix emerged. The phoenix's wings were spread, and its tail was wrapped around a murky rose crystal the length of Rayann's little finger.

"This wonderful store has really exquisite pieces, and I thought the symbol of a phoenix was appropriate for you in this stage of your life — you're starting over, free as the wind, no one holding you back. I'm not sure what all crystals are good for, but it can't hurt." Louisa smiled.

"It really is beautiful. Thank you." Rayann slipped the chain over her head. Had she been naked the tip of the phoenix's tail would have rested between her breasts. She froze as Louisa reached over and lifted the pendant, admiring it again, and then let it fall gently back to Rayann's chest. Rayann managed to breathe out again.

"Sometimes I wish I wore jewelry," Danny said. "That is one stunning necklace."

"I'm overwhelmed," Rayann said. "A beautiful necklace

and pearl earrings." She directed a smile at Louisa, but was unable to meet Louisa's gaze, which she could feel focused on her. "Your turn to open your present."

Louisa slid away the ribbons on the package. *Her fingers are so sure — they could be so gentle, yet so demanding —* red warning lights flashed in front of Rayann's eyes. *Stop it, stop it!*

"Ray, wherever did you find them? I've looked, but there isn't much demand for wooden hair combs these days and I can't stand the plastic ones."

"Look on the back."

Louisa turned them over and studied the insignia. "It looks like an R inside of a G — of course. They're exquisite," Louisa said. "I can't believe you made them." She held them up under the light.

"I did, I promise. They're not finished."

Danny whistled when Louisa handed the combs to her. "You did all this fancy stuff? What kind of flower is that?"

"Lily-of-the-valley. I copied the shape from the combs Louisa wears all the time, then changed the flower carving."

"How can you see what you're doing? This is beyond me," Danny said, handing them back to Louisa.

"A magnifying glass," Rayann said. "But how Louisa can make these work is beyond me."

"You just grab a hunk of hair, twist, stab, wrap and shove. It's easy." Louisa demonstrated. The comb held its position, displaying a beautifully shaped ear. "What's not done?" Louisa untwisted the combs and held them under the light again.

"The edges. I was going to finish them last night, but . . . the pies . . ." Rayann's voice caught in her throat. It had not been pie-making that had stopped her. "Here, I can finish them now."

She sat at the kitchen table and dumped the contents of the pouch containing her smallest woodworking tools and set up her magnifying glass in its holder, glad to have something to put some distance between herself and Louisa. She felt as if she stood on the edge of an exquisite precipice. She wanted to jump but it scared the hell out of her. The comb edges were sharp and it took her only a few minutes to bevel the sides. Her skin prickled and she was aware that Louisa was behind her, leaning over.

"What kind of wood is it?"

"English walnut. You can see how the black tone is just faintly broken up with paler streaks. I could stain them to a consistent black finish, if you like, but I thought the unstained grain was a better match for your hair."

"Oh, no, don't stain them. Can I wear them today?"

"Of course. They're done now." Rayann handed them to Louisa with a flourish.

Danny said, "Well, I got more stops to make, but I wanted to spend the first Christmas cheer with you." She shrugged into her jacket.

When Louisa came back from walking Danny to her car Rayann busied herself putting away her tools and cleaning up the minute curls of wood. She wiped down the table for good measure and made small talk with Louisa as Louisa moved around in her bedroom. *She's making the bed.* Unwelcome and all-too-vivid memories washed over Rayann as she heard the rustle of sheets and blankets. The part of Rayann that knew which fork to use told her she ought to help make the bed. *Not a chance.*

Louisa's voice drifted back to the kitchen. "What are you going to do before you go to your mother's?"

"I'm going to have a pagan festival. Loud music and trash movies. You've probably noticed I'm not overly religious."

Louisa reappeared brushing her hair furiously. She had changed into a pair of gray slacks and turquoise sweater. "I noticed. I'm not exactly going to High Mass myself. But there's a big difference between being religious and being spiritual. I'd like to think I have the Christmas spirit all year . . . Christmas spirit the way Ghost of Christmas Present laid it on old Scrooge. Peace, goodwill, treating our Mother Earth well. The Mother

Earth part is me, not Dickens. Your flyer brought in a good deal more business than usual so the checks to Greenpeace and the Women's Center will be accordingly larger this year. Nancy will be thrilled."

"I'm glad," Rayann said. "I'm glad I did something good this year."

Louisa swept her hair back, then twisted the combs Rayann had given her. "I'm sure you've done something good every year. You don't strike me as being spiritually defunct. When you're as old as I am you'll have more trouble keeping track. How do they look?" She tipped her head away from Rayann so the light shone down on one comb, nestled in the salt-and-pepper masses.

Rayann clenched her fingers to keep from reaching for the sensuous textures that had swept her body last night. "They look great, if I do say so myself." Sapphire glinted at the delicate lobe of Louisa's ear. Rayann knew instinctively they were the Danielle earrings.

Louisa started to reply but was interrupted by a honk from the street. "Goodness, it's late." She looked out the front window. "Yes, that's Teddy. I can't believe he insisted on driving over here because of the fog. I've been driving since before he was born, and in worse than this. I've never even received a parking ticket."

"I think he considers himself the guardian of your welfare."

Louisa frowned. "I'm only fifty-six, Rayann. I have another half of life ahead of me. I'm healthy and I don't need people looking after me." She stared directly into Rayann's eyes. "I don't need a daughter or son looking after me . . . not yet. Hopefully never."

Rayann swallowed and tore her gaze away from Louisa's intensity. She could not recall such forcefulness in another person's eyes. "I'm not suggesting you do, not at all."

There was another honk. "Tucker will explode if he has to wait any longer to open his presents." Louisa shrugged into the black parka that hung on the same peg as the denim jacket she had worn to the bar. Rayann wondered why she didn't wear the denim which looked so smashing on her — it was foggy but not really cold enough to warrant the parka. "Well, it all works out. Now you can take the car to your mom's. See you tonight."

Rayann watched from the window as Louisa put her packages in the trunk and then got into the car. She looked up suddenly and caught Rayann's stare. Louisa smiled and closed the car door.

Rayann laughed when her mother groaned and pushed away her plate. "I can't eat another bite, but what a pie! It's so good I just want to dive face first into it."

"I thought a second piece was beyond your strength," Rayann said, "especially after seconds of everything for dinner."

"Let's open presents," her mother said. "I think I can waddle into the living room. We'll clean up later."

They collapsed in separate chairs and remained still for a few minutes. Then Ann pointed at the lavishly decorated tree with her foot. "Your present's under there."

"What makes you think I can get up?" Rayann patted her bulging stomach.

"You're young."

Groaning, Rayann got up and examined the two boxes under the tree. One was addressed to Jim and the other to Rayann. "Who's Jim?"

"What?" Her mother sat up with speed Rayann hadn't thought possible. "Oh." Incredibly, her mother began to blush. "A man I've been seeing for the last few months."

"Is he nice?" Rayann didn't know what else to say. As far as she knew, her mother had never dated after Ray Germaine's death. *How silly of me to think so.*

"Yes. I'd like you to meet him sometime. He's rather special." Her mother lounged back in her chair again. "Open your present."

Rayann put the gift on her chair and then went to get her mother's present. "Open yours, too."

"You first." Ann sat up a little more and watched indulgently as Rayann shredded the paper and expert ribboning on the box. "I know you work in a bookstore and all, but . . ." Her voice faded with a nervous quiver that Rayann had never heard before. "I hope you don't have them."

Rayann sat, stunned, then she slowly opened the books and fanned through them. The bookmark in one was a generous check like the others her mother had given Rayann every year, but Rayann hardly spared it a glance. Her mother had bought her two mysteries featuring lesbian detectives. She blinked back a rush of tears.

"I remembered you liked mysteries," her mother said softly, "and the man at A Different Light said these were both good."

"You went to A Different Light? Right into the Castro?" Her mother didn't answer and when Rayann looked up through the growing pool of tears she saw her mother wiping away tears of her own. It struck her then that their faces were becoming more and more alike as Rayann grew older. "Oh, Mom, I'll love them both."

"I'm glad. It was hard . . . hard to go inside, but once I was there and I looked around at all the gay people I found myself thinking of them as different. And then it came to me that while I was there I was the one who was different. I understood, a little, then, how you — all of you must feel. Made to feel different everywhere you go. And I felt so terrible." Her mother stopped, her voice choking off.

"Mom, don't —"

"Let me get this said, please, Rayann. I have to. I didn't want to think of you as different. That's why I shut out what I'd known since you were seventeen."

"You knew?" *And I was so careful. I wasted so much energy hiding it.*

"Of course I knew."

"Then why?" *Why did you practically throw Michelle and me out? Why did you try to send me to a shrink? Why did you send me those hate-books?*

"I don't know why. I love you and I knew what a difficult life you were choosing."

131

"I didn't choose. It's what I am."

"I understand that a little better now. I wanted to tell you this after you left Michelle. I didn't know how to bring it up and you didn't really give me a chance."

"I know I didn't."

"I've done a lot of thinking, mostly about what it feels like to know my daughter doesn't want me in her life. I pretended it was your fault for a while, but that doesn't last." Ann stared at her hands. "Not when I knew I was the one who was playing the judge." Rayann caught her lower lip in her teeth. Her mother wiped her eyes and continued, "The largest confession of all is that, when you finally brought it out in the open, my reaction didn't have to do with you so much as Michelle. I detested her, Ray, and I could never tell you that, not until now."

"Why did you dislike her so much?"

"At first I thought I was having some weird Freudian competitive urge, not wanting another woman to replace me in your affections. But in hindsight . . ."

"I see a lot of things about Michelle more clearly in hindsight," Rayann said with a half-laugh.

Her mother smiled, her tears fading as if they had never been. "I'm sure you do. In hindsight I think I disliked her because she wasn't a good match for you. She was completely absorbed in her own goals, and you're so giving that I knew you'd give every ounce of energy you had to helping her, not helping yourself. That's when I realized she reminded me of me — driven to achieve the goals we set for ourselves — and I knew you and I didn't get along for some of those same reasons, although I'd like to think I'm not as shallow as she appeared to be."

"I don't think I'm ready to deal with my relationship with Michelle on the level of Freudian analysis, Mom. She and I were simply not compatible in the end. I don't think it had anything to do with you." Rayann smiled. "And you're not shallow."

"Thanks for the vote of confidence. Well, I think I learned something when I stood on Castro and looked around, feeling very left out and lost. I never look at

132

French people, for example, and think of them as . . . alien. I just needed to give myself time to grow, to appreciate what I've never noticed before. Lesbian culture has a very rich history — I've been doing some reading of my own — and while I'll never understand it, just the same way I can't understand what it's like to be French either, I can appreciate it. And I can be proud you're a part of it."

"That's it," Rayann said, trying to smile. "I'm going to start really crying now." She fished a linty tissue out of her pocket. "I'll never have your emotional control."

Her mother turned shining eyes to her. "I'm not doing so well myself. But you've always been emotional — you're like your father that way. When you started dating I was going to keep such a close eye on you — but you never dated, not that I knew of."

"I dated, but not the boys from the country club." Rayann blew her nose.

Her mother laughed wryly. "I haven't belonged to the country club in years." She sighed. "I want so much for you, Ray. After your father died I knew it was all up to me. I want you to have a perfect life and find a perfect mate. Someone who would make you as happy and complete as your father made me. I don't care about who you spend your life with as long as the person's good to you. And I knew deep down Michelle wasn't good for you."

"I guess, now that I'm older, I'll have to start giving you credit for good judgment and good sense. I was never willing to do that before." Rayann swallowed, the lump in her throat easing. "And Michelle wasn't good for me. Living together was just convenient. I attached more importance to the concept of a relationship than she did."

"You can still come home if you want. I know living in Oakland suits you — you look so happy."

"I know. But I want to stay where I am. It suits me very well."

"The woman you work for sounds very nice."

"She is." Rayann didn't know what to say about

Louisa, so she groped for something her mother would understand. "She has some original Jimmy Dorsey recordings."

Her mother's eyes grew wide. "Really? Would she let me tape them?"

"I'm sure. I'll ask. But open your present now."

Her mother's eyes shone again when she examined the detailed pendant and earrings Rayann had carved out of glossy ebony. The pendant was a mass of flowers, vines and small birds embellishing the letter *A*, patterned after a fourteenth-century illuminated manuscript. The earrings matched the flower and vine pattern.

"I hope they're not too garish to wear to work," Rayann said tentatively.

"Garish?" Ann shook her head. "Not garish — gorgeous. Darling, not to bring up a tedious subject on Christmas, but I know women who would pay quite a bit for something so exquisite and unique. You should design yourself a catalog and take orders. Custom-made items and craftsmanship are in vogue again."

"I'll think about it," Rayann said. She would, too.

"I just remembered something." Her mother left the room and returned with a small pasteboard. "I swiped this out of the product file because I wanted you to see it."

Under the tissue covering the artwork was an ad for a new type of bank account. Rayann examined it for a few minutes and then said, "This is the same concept I developed just before I left Hibernia." Rayann had worked for the small, local bank years before.

"This ad was carried in national publications. It appeared in locally purchased ad space in seventeen markets throughout the United States," her mother said, her voice growing more urgent. "It was wildly successful. Ray, it won three national awards. You were ahead of your time, dear."

"I wish I'd stayed with it," Rayann said finally. "But I can't go back to it, not now."

"Maybe if you found a company you *liked* . . . But I didn't show it to you to pressure you — just to let you know that what you were doing *was* good, and someone besides me thought so."

"Thanks." Rayann felt a sting of regret, softened by a glow of self-esteem. She fingered her phoenix. Louisa had been right, the symbolism fit her. *That makes quite a few wonderful gifts in one day.* The thought of Louisa sent a hot flash through her body, followed by a cold flush. *But I could wish for one more.*

"It's nice to see you again," Louisa was saying. The voice that answered, faintly accented and attractively husky, brought a tinge of embarrassed heat to Rayann's cheeks. She took a deep breath and got up from behind the shelves that had kept Zoraida from seeing her when she first came into the store.

Zoraida smiled at her — an amused, knowing smile. "I am perhaps too optimistic, but could I hope you have no plans for the evening?"

Rayann didn't hesitate. "I'm free as the wind."

"I thought a movie, maybe some dancing to bring in the new year."

"Sounds wonderful."

"I've been after her to get out of the store," Louisa said. "She's been working like a mule."

You're going to get your wish. Rayann ran upstairs for her jacket. Zoraida was a gift from a kind goddess. For every day of the last week, Louisa had been unfailingly, unswervingly friendly — to the point where Rayann wondered if she'd dreamed the night they had spent together. But her body said it was no dream. Her heart knew it was in mortal danger every day spent with Louisa and every night spent alone. Her head knew a solution when it saw one. Zoraida would have no regrets tonight.

Zoraida, however, did not assume the same aggressive role she had played on their previous date. Rayann agreed to Zoraida's suggestion of *I Can Hear the Mermaids Singing*, which was showing in Berkeley. Except for a

135

heartfelt groan in Rayann's ear over the lethal, better-than Charbonneau looks of one of the movie's two lesbians, Zoraida stayed on her side of the shared armrest throughout the movie.

"Do you want to go dancing?" Zoraida asked, as they left the theater.

"Sure. But you know what I'd like to do first — walk on the campus a little. I haven't been back in ages." They crossed the street that separated the city from the campus and entered through the northside gate. They walked in silence for a while, Rayann leading the way over short bridges, through groves of eucalyptus, and past ivy-covered walls, then down the slope that took them to the base of the Campanile. "I've always thought this campus was romantic," Rayann said as they stood in the shadow of the belltower. It obligingly rang nine times.

"Is that why we're here?"

"Yes," Rayann said. "I'm sorry about last time."

"Is that all?"

"No." Rayann swallowed. She had to honest with Zoraida. "I . . . I'm hung up on Louisa. It's totally inappropriate. She's got Danny and I just don't share enough of her history. I . . . my body just needs a diversion. It's just an attraction, I think because we spend so much time together . . ." *If you want to be honest with Zoraida you have to be honest with yourself. Lust is not the only explanation.*

"*Novia,*" Zoraida said softly, "are you asking me to help you forget her?"

"I want to be honest," Rayann said. "I know it sounds hopelessly cold-blooded, but I . . . you said no strings, as long as you knew the score."

Zoraida was silent for a few minutes. When she spoke her voice was husky. "Have you made love to her?"

Not precisely, but she made love to me. "Yes. She regretted it the next day, and ever since she's been urging me to go out with my friends, reminding me how much I have in common with them, like . . . like she wants to be sure I don't expect anything of her. I don't want to lose her friendship and, well, I was thinking that my body just needs to fixate on someone else." *So I can stop staring at her hands and remembering my legs wrapped around her thigh.*

"That actually sounds like a pleasant prospect," Zoraida said, her voice clearing. "I accept the challenge, my damsel in distress. I will consider it my solemn duty to erase any imprint she may have made on your body."

Rayann remembered the way Zoraida had aroused her when they had been dancing. "You'll be successful. I think I've made too much of it already, *novia.*" She turned to Zoraida in the shadows and drew her away from the belltower to the grass-covered slope behind it.

They sank down to the earth, Rayann pulling Zoraida atop her, running her hands under the leather jacket to appreciate the muscled back and strong shoulder blades. Zoraida's hair fell around them in a curtain of black, shutting out the moonlight. Her lips found Rayann's, exploring slowly. Rayann's mouth invited Zoraida to probe deeper, faster. *Like liquid fire.*

Zoraida pulled up with a moan. "We have a drive ahead of us, and what I want to do can't be finished here." She hopped to her feet and gave Rayann a hand. "Come on, lover. Let's go dancing in private."

They walked briskly back to the 4x4, and Zoraida lost no time in negotiating the drive through campus, then onto Claremont. The entire bay glittered before them — dark patches of water broken by gold and silver bridges with a sweep of lights on hills across the bay in San Francisco. From the high Piedmont hills, they descended to the rolling slopes of the Glenview district.

"Aren't you warm?" Rayann slid across the bench seat to twine her fingers in Zoraida's hair. "Wouldn't you like to get out of that jacket?"

Zoraida shrugged out of the jacket and Rayann unceremoniously dumped it on the floor. She felt intoxicated. She kissed a slow line down the silk sleeve covering Zoraida's arm, ending with nibbles on the knuckles clutching the shift knob.

"Would you please stop that? I'm trying to drive."

Rayann stopped kissing and stroked the back of

Zoraida's neck lazily. Turning to face Zoraida, she tucked one leg under herself and slipped her hand down Zoraida's neck to caress the firm muscles under the collar.

"You are making concentration very difficult."

Rayann unbuttoned the top button of Zoraida's shirt and stroked the firm skin inside. Another button, and one finger slipped just under Zoraida's bra, tracing the top of one soft swell, the tantalizing valley in between, the top of the other softness.

"Stop that," Zoraida said, her voice brusque but edged with invitation.

Rayann drew her hand out with a sigh, and instead trailed her fingers over Zoraida's stomach, then the jean-covered thighs.

"*Novita,* you are making me crazy. If I drive any faster, we'll get arrested." Zoraida pushed Rayann away. "Sit over there where you belong and put your seat belt on."

Rayann complied, but not before she removed her own jacket and put on Zoraida's leather jacket. She put up the collar.

"You're really looking for trouble," Zoraida said. "Don't you know a woman's leather jacket is her domain?"

Rayann gave Zoraida what she hoped was a smoky look. She felt sultry and dangerous, but very much in control. *I feel like Lauren Bacall. You do know how to whistle, don't you Zoraida? Just put your lips together* . . . They stopped halfway down a quiet block and Zoraida pulled her truck into one of three parking spaces carved out in front of a long, low building.

"This is it," Zoraida said. "I'm on the second floor in the back." They ran up the stairs while Zoraida fumbled for her keys. "I'm freezing! You're going to pay for wearing my jacket, you know."

Rayann followed Zoraida inside. The chill air only accentuated how hot her hands were. Her palms were damp, which meant she was wet elsewhere.

"Hang on, let me get the light."

"There's no need," Rayann said. "Just lead the way."

In the darkness there was silence, and then Zoraida said, "If you trip on something soft and fluffy it'll be Whizzer. She's probably on the bed, though."

"Then take me in and introduce me." She found Zoraida's hand. In the dim light from the bedroom window she could make out a dark shape curled up precisely in the middle of a four-poster bed.

"Whizzer, this is Rayann and I think she really wants to lie down, so you're going to have to move." Zoraida picked the cat up gently and put it down on the floor. It glared at Rayann and then stalked out the door.

"It's not true, Whizzer. I don't want to lie down, not yet." She turned Zoraida to face her. "I want to undress you, but we have to pull the covers down. I'm allergic to cat hair."

"Well, that puts a damper on a perfect relationship," Zoraida said, throwing the covers back. "Actually, Whizzer only sleeps on the comforter, so the sheets and pillows should be relatively free of her presence."

Rayann's hands went to Zoraida's shirt. Button by button the silk shirt parted. Rayann kissed each new expanse of smooth skin then pulled the shirt out of Zoraida's jeans. She tasted Zoraida's shoulders, inhaling the faint saltiness and musk. Then she slipped the thin straps aside with her tongue and peeled away the fabric separating her mouth from Zoraida's breasts.

Zoraida gave a low moan and they moved to the bed. Rayann ran her cheek over Zoraida's stomach, then damply kissed the tender flesh. She fumbled with the button of the black jeans, but had no problem with the zipper. Her fingers slipped downward and teased, then withdrew. She nuzzled a hard nipple straining against her tongue. Zoraida stripped her upper body bare, murmuring, "Taste all of me."

Rayann buried her face against Zoraida's muscular thighs, stomach, shoulders, and then into the welcoming softness of her breasts, surprising softness she captured in her mouth and pleasured with her lips. Zoraida held Rayann against her, hips moving against Rayann's hand.

Rayann tugged at Zoraida's boots impatiently, then bared her completely. Hips lifting, Zoraida's legs drew her down and Rayann tasted her quickly, then teased deliberately. She raised her head and inhaled Zoraida's scent mixed with leather.

Zoraida groaned and pulled Rayann's head down. "*Devora me* —"

Rayann parted and drank, honey and wine, sweet and salt. She rode rippling waves of skin. Under rippling flesh and wetness she sank, drowning in delight, then groaning as Zoraida held her hands tighter. They crested, then surged together.

Rayann, still fully dressed, pinned Zoraida with the weight of her body. "I want to do that again," she whispered.

Zoraida's hands were working their way under the waistband of Rayann's underwear. "But it's your turn, *novita.*"

"I'll wait." Her mouth went to Zoraida's breasts again, aroused by the contrast of their caressing softness and the firm strength of Zoraida's shoulders.

"Don't go stone butch on me," Zoraida murmured. "I'll be truly disappointed."

Stone butch? Rayann raised her head. "I don't know what that means."

"Seriously?" Zoraida sat up on her elbows, her naked body reclining in the pale light.

"I'm starting to feel like I've led a sheltered life. I don't know anything about butch and femme."

"You don't have to *know* anything. It's how you feel."

Rayann rolled over on her back. "I don't know how I feel."

Zoraida rolled over to her, her brown skin gleaming as she wrapped herself around Rayann, moving sensuously against her. Soft lips found Rayann's throat. Fingers swept under the jacket, pulled up the sweater, then cupped Rayann's breasts. They swelled and the tips hardened.

"How do you feel?" Zoraida pushed Rayann's bra up, the rough texture of her palm further tightening the ache in Rayann's nipples.

"Like I'll die if you stop," Rayann gasped, swelling against Zoraida's palms.

"It's a dance, *novia*," Zoraida whispered in Rayann's ear. "Sometimes you want to lead, sometimes you want to follow." Her hand slid unerringly to the front of Rayann's jeans, unbuttoned and unzipped, then down. "I usually prefer leading, but tonight you made me feel like following. But I want to lead now, *novia*, I want to lead . . ." Zoraida's voice faded and a shudder swept her body when her hand found Rayann's wetness.

Rayann groaned and tipped her hips up, welcoming. "Yes."

Zoraida gasped something in Spanish too rapid for Rayann to even begin to understand, but Zoraida's fingers slid in and Rayann frantically shoved her jeans down. *Inside, yes.*

"How do you feel?" Zoraida's mouth covered Rayann's, as if tasting the answer.

"It must have been the jacket," Rayann said later, as they lay listening to the popping of firecrackers bringing in the new year. "Usually I'm shy." *But not with Louisa — I couldn't help myself with her.*

"*Novita*, I will never believe that. Would you like something? I'm going to get something to drink." Zoraida slipped out of bed and wrapped herself in a flannel robe.

"Some of whatever you're having," Rayann said. She huddled under the warm covers and listened to Zoraida telling Whizzer it was not dinnertime.

Comparisons were unavoidable. Michelle had been honey-sweet and very sensuous, but in a pattern — first

Michelle, then Rayann, then the two of them — that was nevertheless arousing and satisfying. Rayann hadn't thought there could be anything more mutually loving than how she felt with Michelle. Of course Michelle had been getting sex elsewhere, so perhaps it wasn't the best model to use as a comparison.

And then Louisa. At the memory of Louisa's power and passion, Rayann's body, so recently replete, flamed again. This is all your fault, she told her body, but the prickles and butterflies didn't go away. Rayann had been helpless in Louisa's grasp, utterly dependent on Louisa's touch. That night with Louisa had not had the shared give and take of tonight with Zoraida. *But the memory burns.*

Zoraida returned with two fizzing champagne glasses. "I opened a bottle of sparkling cider I've been saving." She handed one to Rayann, shed her robe and joined Rayann under the covers again. "To sex," Zoraida said, "and a happy new year."

They clinked glasses and tossed off their cider, then Zoraida took the glass away from Rayann. I've only got two. Can't have you throwing it in the fireplace." She turned back from setting the glasses on the floor and Rayann melted against her, pulling her mouth down for a languorous kiss.

"Hope you're not sleepy." Rayann bit gently at Zoraida's lower lip.

"*Novia,* I don't think you're ready for more."

"I'm on fire," Rayann moaned. She guided Zoraida's hand between her legs.

"Are you sure — *madre de dias.*" Zoraida's voice broke into a groan as her fingertips became slick with Rayann's passion. She said more, again in Spanish.

"What did you say? It sounds so passionate," Rayann moaned, moving against Zoraida's fingers.

Zoraida bent over her, lips nuzzling Rayann's chin. "I said something explicit about how wet you are and how I intend to make use of it."

"How will you . . . ?"

"Follow my lead," Zoraida murmured, her fingers taking and teasing as she slid lower against Rayann's body.

"As long . . . as I can lead . . . later."

"It will be my pleasure — *cuando quieras, donde quieras.*"

8

Chipped Away

"Rayann, if you don't hurry, you won't be ready when Zoraida gets here," Louisa reminded her for the fourth or fifth time.

Rayann was finishing the last of the day's restocking. "I swear I'll never do another flyer," she said, ignoring Louisa's urging.

"Knock on wood," Louisa said. "You may have single-handedly started a new trend for Valentine's Day. Calorie-free, wither-proof books."

"I thought you hated it."

"I was wrong — hearts and cupids do sell books. Who'd have thought it?" Louisa twitched an offending heart back into place so it hung from the back of the cash register. "And you'll be late if you don't stop now. I'm not so old that I can't finish those myself."

"That's not why I'm doing them," Rayann said, irritated. "And you're not old, much as you like to say so."

"Okay," Louisa said. She crossed the room and took the books out of Rayann's hands. Their fingertips brushed. "I'm not old, but you're late. Zoraida will think you don't want to go."

Rayann sighed. She wished her body would stop reacting each time Louisa inadvertently touched her. *It shouldn't be doing this anymore.* Zoraida had indeed left indelible impressions on her body, but Louisa's impact on her had never lessened. "I'll go shower."

As she dried her hair a few minutes later, Rayann mulled over, once again, her mystification at the way Louisa had practically rejoiced when Rayann had told her about Zoraida. Rayann understood why Danny had been pleased, particularly if Danny had suspected that Louisa and Rayann had made love one unforgettable night, but Louisa's reaction was a mystery. *She acts like a mother who's glad to see her daughter married off.*

Even as she recalled that night, Rayann shoved the memory away, replacing it with a memory of her last date with Zoraida. Then she replaced it with the anticipation of being with Zoraida tonight, dancing together at the Sweetheart's Ball. She chose black silk pants and a burgundy shirt topped by a casual black jacket. She and Zoraida would complement each other, no doubt. Glancing at her watch, she saw she had enough time to finish the shelving and hurried downstairs.

She stumbled to a stop when she saw her mother standing at the counter, having what appeared to be a very animated conversation with Louisa.

"I haven't seen anything like it since London," Ann

145

was saying. She smiled at Rayann, who walked uncertainly toward them. "Rayann won't remember the bookstore, she was just a baby, but I must have taken her there every week because they had a children's hour."

"One of the inspirations for opening this bookstore was the library back home," Louisa said. "Merced," she added in response to Ann's quirked eyebrows. "It must have been fifty years old even then and I thought it was the neatest place. Every Saturday I went there for the children's hour. The librarian would read for hours. They had to drag me away."

Rayann stifled a laugh. *Sounds like a first crush to me.* "I don't remember the bookstore or London," Rayann said. "I don't remember the cruise home or the plane to San Francisco. I remember moving into the house, though."

"I remember London as if it were yesterday," Ann said. "And now you're all grown up." She looked at Louisa. "They just grow up before your eyes, don't they?"

Louisa agreed and as they shared snippets about raising children Rayann felt a chill. They were glibly mentioning events and concerns that weren't part of Rayann's existence. How could she possibly imagine herself meeting Louisa's needs for friendship or anything else? She wasn't even sure she was necessary around the bookstore. Before the Valentine's Day rush Louisa could have managed everything herself. Rayann had to keep business booming to stay busy. If it got too quiet Louisa might regret renting her room. Rayann realized she could have been in the next county. Her mother and Louisa were having a jolly conversation. *Great, they're on Jimmy Dorsey now.*

"Could I borrow them? I'd be so grateful."

"You're more than welcome," Louisa said. "Could I interest you in a couple of Glen Millers?"

"Too precious, I couldn't." They drifted toward the doorway to the stairs.

"You could make me a tape as well," Louisa said, her voice eager. "I hardly listen to them because I'm afraid they'll get scratched."

Their voices faded away and Rayann looked around the empty bookstore in utter disbelief. Her mother had hardly acknowledged her presence. And Louisa had been more excited by the possibility of taped big band recordings than anything Rayann had ever seen — except for a certain night.

Back to that again. No matter what, Rayann thought of that night constantly. The precise images were blurred in her mind, but one sketchbook, the one stuffed to the farthest reaches of the closet, was filled with images of Louisa's face and hands. Details of her lips and eyes covered the corners of pages. Every time Rayann saw the ironwood block she saw Louisa in it. It was a project she would never start.

Louisa emerged from the stairway, followed by Ann with several records tucked under one arm.

"Did you want to see *me* about anything?" Rayann couldn't keep sarcasm out of her voice.

"Oh, no, not really, dear," her mother said. "I was over at Kaiser Center and had no appointments so I just stopped in." She smiled and patted the records lovingly. "I had ulterior motives. Jim knows a sound engineer who will make masters of these and put them on digital tape so they can be enjoyed for years to come."

"You're still seeing him? I'm glad, you said he was special."

"Very special. I'll even hazard a guess you might like him." Ann's smile was brilliant.

"I don't know, Mom," Rayann said, with a half-laugh. "We don't have a very good batting average when it comes to approving romantic relationships."

The doors chimed behind Rayann and from the pleased smile that creased Louisa's lips Rayann knew it was Zoraida. *I need this like I need leprosy.*

"Speak of the devil," Louisa said.

Rayann turned. She wanted to react as usual to Zoraida's presence but she was temporarily crippled by her mother's presence. Without nearly enough breath in her body she introduced Zoraida to her mother.

"A pleasure," Zoraida said, shaking hands. Rayann

saw that Zoraida's black hair carried a slight purple sheen that matched the vivid purple of her open-necked buccaneer's shirt.

"What have you done to your hair?" Rayann was sure her mother would think Zoraida a complete radical.

Zoraida's eyes widened. "You don't like it?"

"Of course I do —"

"It'll rinse out —"

"It's charming," Louisa said.

"Rayann's just jealous. She couldn't carry off such an elegant statement," Ann said. She ignored Rayann's gape. "Besides, she hates change. You should have seen the fit she threw when I put raisins in her oatmeal."

"*Mother!*" Rayann felt her face burn.

"It's true, dear," her mother said, then she laughed. "You should see your face right now. I'll bet you're glad I don't have that picture of you jumping up and down in the flour bin, stark naked."

"I'd love to see it," both Louisa and Zoraida said at almost the same moment.

"I want to die," Rayann moaned.

"Well, I never got the chance to embarrass you in front of a date before. Gosh, it's fun."

"I loved doing it to Teddy," Louisa said.

They're doing it again. Rayann wanted to crawl under a rock while her mother and Louisa detailed the most embarrassing things their children had ever done.

"Enough," Rayann cried when her mother started on the story about six-year-old Rayann's burning desire to be Mary Poppins when she grew up. "Zoraida, please, isn't it time to go?"

"Sure, *novia.* Ms. Germaine, it was a pleasure." Rayann watched in a numb state while Zoraida shook hands with her mother. As they left, Louisa and Ann were already deep in discussion of big band and swing.

"What's wrong, *novia?*" Zoraida patiently negotiated the side streets, then the freeway onramp.

"That was my mother."

"So?"

"I spent years hiding what I was from her and now she's so . . . so embracing. I'm not used to it."

"Do you know how many lesbians would give their eyeteeth to have their mothers embrace their lifestyle?"

"Okay, lots. I'm just not used to it." *Would they be happy if their mothers apparently had so much in common with someone they lov — had slept with?*

She liked being with Zoraida. She liked Zoraida's energy and strength. Rayann decided the only fair thing to do was concentrate on that. The setting sun limned Zoraida in a halo of purple. "I really do like your hair," Rayann said.

"Really? I'm glad. I wanted to do something for Valentine's, but the thought of pink made me gag."

"Purple's much more appropriate."

And suddenly everything with Zoraida was level again. They held hands when they blended into the crowd waiting to enter the Sweetheart's Ball, and danced the moment the music began. When they found Dedric and Judy in the throng, they split up, Dedric and Zoraida leaving the dance floor for the cool balcony outside the hall while Judy and Rayann fought through the crowds of dazzlingly dressed women to get to the buffet tables. They filled plates and headed for the balconies, passing Zoraida and Dedric on the dance floor, apparently having cooled off sufficiently.

"So how's business?"

"Very depressing. My phone's ringing off the hook," Judy said. She balanced her plate on one knee, perched on the concrete edge of a planter box. "I live with constant ambiguity. I like having enough cash to pay my share of the rent, but it means another woman needed therapy. What's new with you? You and Zoraida seem to have something steady going."

"Oh, yeah, she's nice. I enjoy being with her." Rayann nibbled on a canapé and then realized Judy had fixed her with a strange, penetrating stare.

"That does not sound like a declaration of love. Cut flowers are nice. You enjoy being with an elderly aunt."

"I didn't mean it that way. We get along very nicely, but I don't think it goes too deep with either of us."

"Nice arrangement, if it's true." Judy stripped a delicate skewer of shrimp and vegetables, then picked out the shrimp.

"You should eat your vegetables."

"Thanks. I get enough of that from Dedric."

"Judy," Rayann began tentatively. "I need some advice."

"Uh-oh. And no couch in sight."

"Oh, shush. It's just, well, what would you say if I said Louisa and I had had . . . you know . . ."

"You're kidding." Judy blinked and then stared at Rayann with both eyebrows hidden under her bangs.

Rayann shook her head. "Christmas Eve. She, I . . . we haven't repeated it."

"Why?"

"Because she's in a long-term relationship. She . . . doesn't want to."

"I see. She doesn't want to, but you do?"

"No," Rayann protested, but she knew she lacked conviction. "I'm just confused, because I can't put it out of my mind."

"I think it's shabby."

"What?"

"You are *also* in a relationship. I think using Zoraida like that is shabby."

"But Zoraida knows," Rayann protested.

"Then I think that's a little weird, but to each her own." Judy munched thoughtfully on a piece of zucchini. "Ray, why are you asking my advice?"

"Because I don't know why I'm so attracted to Louisa."

"And you think I can look deep into your psyche and explain it for you? Ray, if I could do that I'd be richer than God. No one knows why we're attracted to each other. But you obviously want to get over it."

"There's no future in it. But . . . I wish there were." Rayann said it so quietly she thought Judy might have missed it, but she hadn't.

"Then you should examine your options, and be serious about it."

"I had enough of that after I left Michelle."

"Rayann, what do you want me to say? I'm *not* your therapist." Judy stared at her.

"I want you to say it's okay. What I feel."

"Feelings are almost always valid —"

"No psychoanalytic bullshit, please."

"You think my life's work is bullshit. I'm glad we had this conversation." Judy stood up.

"I'm sorry, Jude, I'm sorry. I need a friend's advice."

"Good, because I don't deal in pat diagnoses. And wouldn't I love to get you on a couch," she finished, with a Groucho Marx leer that faded into a sigh. "I'm sorry, I didn't realize how involved you were. As a friend, Ray, I'm concerned for you. If, as you say, there's no future in this, then your staying under the same roof seems unhealthy. And the difference in your age . . . it concerns me, too. All the stereotypes of May–December romances portray the relationship as May making December feel young again which is what December wants. But Louisa — bearing in mind I've only met her once — does not strike me as someone who wants to change her life that way. She didn't strike me as a woman who would use someone else to make her feel younger. She seemed rooted in her sense of self, a very secure and confident person. Ray, as a friend — as a friend, dear — I'm not sure continuing to live with her, given the way you feel, is a good idea. Not when she has everything she needs already —"

"And has no reason to need me," Rayann finished. "I know, I know. And there's Danny. But I can't help myself and I keep hoping I'll wake up cured some day." Rayann stood up and stretched.

"You can always dream," Judy said.

"One last question?" When Judy smiled tolerantly, Rayann continued, "what would you do if some day I *did* show up with Louisa?"

"Do? Go right on loving you, of course."

"But what would you think?"

Judy laughed and put her arm around Rayann. Rayann hugged her back. "I'd think private thoughts."

"You wouldn't tell me?"

"I hated Michelle, but what would you have done if I'd told you that?"

Rayann sighed and she and Judy began to rock slowly to the music wafting onto the balcony. "I'd have chosen her over you, of course. I get the point."

"Don't let us interrupt," a voice said dryly.

Rayann looked over her shoulder and released Judy after the last hug. Dedric's tone was negated by the indulgent smile curving her lips. Zoraida had one eyebrow raised in mock disapproval.

"She's the best," Rayann said.

Dedric's smile widened. "I know."

"*Hola,* sweetheart. It's a million degrees in there." Zoraida handed Rayann and Judy glasses of punch. "I just grabbed as many as I could carry. Though I have discovered you in the arms of another, I'll share."

"So how's the dancing," Rayann asked. She moved slightly toward Zoraida while Dedric moved closer to Judy.

"They started a conga line, if you can believe it."

After the conga line of three hundred or so had bunny-hopped past them, Rayann swept Zoraida to the dance floor, inviting her to lead. The conversation with Judy still played in her mind, and she knew she was using Zoraida. It was only acceptable because Zoraida knew.

She made certain later, then, that Zoraida had no regrets.

"Wish you could stay the night," Zoraida murmured, her voice groggy with satisfaction and sleep.

"You know what happened last time." Rayann was not going to repeat the streaming eyes and asthmatic attack that arrived when she had stayed too long.

"I know." Zoraida kissed her. "Whizzer doesn't mean to make you sneeze."

"Probably not." But Rayann had the feeling Whizzer knew Rayann's time was limited, and her yellow eyes gleamed with satisfaction when Rayann left, so easily vanquished by a little well-placed fur. "You can't go to sleep. You have to drive me home."

"Okay," Zoraida murmured, dragging herself out of bed. "Good lord, I can hardly move. You are one hard-lovin' mama, *novia*. I'm worn out."

"I'm not so steady on my feet, either," Rayann said, picking her clothes off the floor.

Suddenly Zoraida grabbed her, pulling her onto the bed. "You are so beautiful when you bend over. Your spine makes me crazy." She tickled Rayann vigorously, but her fingers soon began to stroke Rayann's ribs instead of tickling them. "Stay a little longer," she said. "One more time."

"I'm so glad you couldn't think of a book-buying angle for St. Patrick's Day," Louisa said. She stretched, hands clasped over her head. Sunlight streamed through her fingertips in ribbons of gold and gray. Rayann itched for a pencil and sketchpad. "I'm still recovering from Valentine's."

Danny, leaning comfortably on the back of the chair she sat astride, hoisted her coffee cup in a toast. "Top o' the mornin' to ya." She sipped her coffee. "Damn, this is good stuff. What did you do, Lou, wash the pot or something?"

"Rayann made it. It's a special blend she grinds up."

Rayann squirmed under Danny's gaze. She thought Danny knew how Rayann felt about Louisa and she was glad Danny didn't know she had turned down a job offer because it would have meant having no reason to stay in Louisa's home. The job hadn't been all that great anyway. "I should probably go unlock the front door," she said nervously.

"Oh, there's fifteen minutes, at least," Louisa said. "You're a real slave driver." She started when there was a knock at the back door. "Who on earth?" Louisa went to the back porch. "Teddy, what a surprise!"

Rayann hardly had enough time to analyze what happened next. Danny leapt to her feet and dragged Rayann to the stairs with her, then down them, fiercely whispering. "Turn off the alarm and let me out the front door. For God's sake, hurry."

In a daze, Rayann followed Danny. "What are you doing? What's going on?"

"Will you get a move on? Louisa's life'll be hell if he sees me. He hasn't seen me since he went to college and it's better that he doesn't."

"But what about me?"

"I doubt he knows you're gay. I took one look and knew you were a dyke, but he'd never guess."

Rayann punched in the alarm code and shot back the bolts on the door, then unlocked the wrought iron gate. "But what about his mother? He loves her — how can he be like that?"

Danny didn't answer as she hurried through the door. Rayann followed her down the steps and grabbed her arm, pulling her to a stop. "Danny, wait! How can she live like this? Why do you cooperate with the lie?"

"Friends don't put conditions on their love. I visit at morning or late evening or she comes to my place. It's the price. Love's always got a price. She paid hers."

"But I don't understand."

"You wouldn't," Danny said vehemently. "You were in diapers when she made her choices. Keeping Ted's love has cost her plenty. She had to bury what she is to keep him."

"But why?" Rayann's bewilderment was complete.

"Because he was all she had. Bar dykes like me didn't accept her — kept trying to make her femme because she had a kid. And one word from an employer brought a social worker around to investigate. She walked to hell and back for that kid." Danny wrenched her arm away. "Not that he's got any more idea than you what it cost her."

"Hey, I'm a dyke, too. I understand."

"You ever been arrested? Ever been called bulldyke or

a fucking queer? Ever had a rock thrown at you because of the way you're dressed?" Danny's eyes blazed.

"No," Rayann whispered. "But I'm still a lesbian."

"You can't possibly understand."

"But I want to. Danny, I want to understand." She blinked back tears.

"I have to go before he sees me. For heaven's sake, go inside and support her. If you think this is easy for her you're crazy." Danny was in her aging half-ton pickup in a flash, and down the street within moments. Rayann went back inside, and hearing the murmur of voices, went upstairs after a few deep breaths.

Teddy sat in the chair Danny had vacated. There was no sign of Danny's coffee cup. He sipped from a different mug. "Hi there," he said. "How's business?"

"Booming," Rayann managed. She had started to like him, not knowing a bigot lurked within. *You bastard, you fake liberal homophobic bastard.* Rayann pictured a Ken doll with pins in it, particularly in the non-anatomically correct parts. *Bette Davis would have you for lunch.*

Louisa's color was unusually high, as was her voice. Rayann watched her talk to her son and saw, for the first time, uncertainty in her manner. She hated seeing Louisa so changed and pictured tweezers plucking out hairs one by one. *And not from his head.*

She could hardly stop herself from glowering at him, but the anger she felt began to spread from Teddy to Louisa. Whatever price she had paid during his youth was one thing, but Louisa was long since an adult. Rayann had never noticed that Danny's visits were at times when Ted was least likely to drop by. What did she have to lose now? What kept her from living with Danny now, if that's what she wanted?

"I almost forgot why I stopped," Teddy was saying. He reached into his breast pocket. "New school pictures."

Louisa's face softened into fond indulgence as she examined the photo of Tucker. Rayann knew she had her answer.

Teddy left a short time later, kissing Louisa goodbye.

Louisa watched after him for a few minutes, then turned away. Rayann saw that her hands were shaking. *Those hands, the most powerful hands I've ever felt.*

"Louisa, why?" Rayann's whispered question hung in the room while Louisa sank into the rocker and put her head in her hands.

"I don't have to justify myself to you," Louisa said, after a long silence. "I've done what I've had to do. God, it was such a close call."

"I wish I could help somehow," Rayann said quietly. "I wish there was something I could do."

"If you want to help then stop looking at me like that," Louisa said, raising her head. "Why do you think I don't embrace the community? Because every time I've met another lesbian and told her I wasn't out to my son she looked at me the way you are right now. Like I'm gutless."

"That's not what I think," Rayann protested. "I think you're one of the bravest women I know. That's why this doesn't make sense."

"You couldn't understand."

"But I want to," Rayann said sharply, then she calmed herself. "I want to understand, Louisa. Give me the credit for being able to."

"You're so young."

"I'm not a child," Rayann said intensely. "I can understand."

"But how can you?" Louisa shook her head. "I lived through a time you can't experience. Just the way I can't experience the time you're living in. You came of age when it was almost okay to be gay. You're free to choose so many things. That was not the way it was in Merced, California. Not by a long shot."

"Tell me about it," Rayann invited quietly. The chimes downstairs sounded and Louisa closed her eyes. "I'll go," Rayann said, hoping her voice did not sound as dejected as she felt. Louisa would not tell her because she thought Rayann couldn't understand. Rayann was a mere child.

Her dejection was a cloud around her all day. Louisa's shattered look slowly disappeared and when they sat

156

down to dinner she was almost her usual self — but still brittle. Rayann had trouble swallowing the stir-fry she had thrown together; her stomach was in turmoil. If Louisa would not accept her as even a friend close enough to confide in then she would have to leave. *Maybe the job is still open.* But she knew she wouldn't go. Not yet. Not before she had solved the riddle of Louisa.

Louisa spoke suddenly. "Chris helped me raise Teddy. He adored her. He never thought the living arrangement in the least bit odd until he went to college. I could tell he had figured it out."

A mixture of emotions flooded Rayann, but the primary one was relief. "Why did you wait for him to figure it out?"

Louisa spread her arms in a combined shrug and admission of regret. "I was a Doctor Spock mother. I was raised in a time when sex and sexuality were just not discussed with children. I have never been able to talk to him about it."

"And how did Chris feel about it?"

"She was . . . likeminded. Of the two of us, she was the more traditionally maternal."

"Do you have a picture of her?" *Teddy is why there aren't any of her in the curios cabinet. Had she felt compelled to erase Christina's existence?*

Louisa abandoned her nearly untouched dinner and went into her bedroom. She returned with a snapshot. "She really was a good photographer, and she hated having her picture taken." A small woman with fair hair and thin arms folded across her breasts stared at Rayann. She wore a work shirt, overalls and boots. Rayann had the distinct impression that Christina did not like the boots. "Chris hated that picture because it just didn't look like her. But that's how she looked most of the time at home." Louisa sighed. "The things we did to get by."

"Like what?" Rayann returned the picture to Louisa, who studied it as she talked.

"We had lesbian friends, but it was hard. We couldn't be ourselves around them. We had to play just as many games with them as with the people who held the lease on our lives — our bosses and landlords. I was a mother, so I had to be femme, right? And if I was femme, Chris had to be butch, right? We'll never really know what our true inclinations were, but we were forced into those roles so we accepted them, at least in public."

"Why did you play roles?"

"What else was there to do? Our friends were our sanity. There were so few of us that we had to socialize. The gay men would have nothing to do with us, and we couldn't even go to their bar. Not that that was a real drawback — it was burned down twice, and the local Bible-thumpers took down license plate numbers. I'd have lost Teddy. When we moved here we made friends again, but the fifties and sixties were very rigid in many ways."

"How did you stand it?"

"Stand it?" Louisa looked momentarily nonplussed. "How did we stand it? We were ecstatically happy whenever the doors were closed and we were alone. We were living together. We went right on leading our lives and never dreamed for more. After the fifties we both believed we had found the incredible, impossible dream. There was nothing to *stand*."

Rayann digested that for a few minutes. "I do understand that, a little. I know how relieved I was when my mother and I parted ways for a while. It felt like freedom."

"But I've always had something to lose."

"It's not freedom, anyway. It just feels like it."

"I know. I don't want to leave behind what I love." Louisa stared at the ceiling. "I'm too old to learn how to fly."

Rayann stopped herself from saying, once again, that Louisa was not old. "It's not any easier when you're younger." She picked up their uneaten dinners and busied herself in the kitchen.

"Thank you," Louisa said, still sitting in her chair.

"For what?" *I haven't done a damn thing.*

"For not saying I could change things if I had the courage to."

"Courage isn't the only thing you need," Rayann said quietly. " 'Courage is useless without a reason to fight.' "

Louisa turned to her, one eyebrow raised. "William Blake?"

Rayann shook her head and squirted soap into the dishpan. "Harvey Milk, I think. Or Mother Jones."

Louisa laughed and joined Rayann at the sink. "I'll wash. It's my turn."

I'll lead, Rayann heard in her head. *Chris tried to be butch, Louisa tried to be femme.* But she said they acted differently in private. *Did Louisa love Chris the way she did me? Probably.* For a few selfish moments Rayann hated Chris, but the emotion was gone before it matured. She couldn't understand the complexities. Louisa and Chris had survived a great deal of turmoil and however they had done it didn't matter. *She survived to stand next to me, and give me passion I'll never forget. And I'll never have again. What am I doing? I can't hold a candle to this woman. Why can't I be happy just knowing her? Why do I have to want more?*

A quiet knock at the back door startled them both, and Rayann went to the porch, turning on the light. Danny stared at her through the glass as Rayann opened the door.

"Is everything still in one piece?"

Rayann nodded. "We're doing the dishes," she said, as if it were an answer.

"Rayann, I'm sorry about this morning. I didn't mean to yell. It was just such a close call."

Rayann found the strength to smile. "You were honest with me. I appreciate that."

"Danny, is that you?"

"Sure is," Danny called, passing Rayann to go to the kitchen.

Rayann followed and froze in the doorway as Louisa threw herself into Danny's waiting arms. Their embrace cut Rayann, and the sight of Louisa's tears, tears she wouldn't shed in front of Rayann, was salt in the wound.

She left them and went down to the darkened

bookstore, huddling in the large easy chair Hazel and Greta had donated to the Poetry Corner, saying they couldn't wait to get rid of it. She knew the floor plan by heart now, and she could tell when two pairs of feet moved slowly from the kitchen, across the living room, then turned to the right to enter Louisa's bedroom.

Rayann rose from Zoraida's body. The sunshine of the first day of April poured through the windows, lighting Zoraida's skin to warm amber.

"No, *querida*, again," Zoraida groaned, pushing Rayann down. "I cannot get enough today."

Rayann went to her again, met the eager hips with her mouth. A fine film of perspiration covered them both; their bodies steamed in the sun.

"Don't stop, *querida*, *querida* Rayann." Zoraida clutched Rayann's hands, pulling and straining. Her hips arched up and Rayann clung to them, her tongue pulsing against Zoraida, plunging toward release.

"If that wasn't enough," Rayann panted, "I can probably do it again, if you'll let me catch my breath." She stretched out next to Zoraida who laughed lazily. She wiped Rayann's mouth with one hand, then kissed her.

"You have completely undone me," Zoraida said. "I can't imagine a more beautiful way to spend an afternoon. I'm happy you get days off now."

Rayann moved restlessly, not wanting to talk about the bookstore. The innovation of days off was a sore subject. Rayann didn't know why, but she thought Louisa was trying to get rid of her. But that was silly, because Louisa continued to make a point of how much Rayann's marketing efforts had improved business. Nevertheless Louisa had insisted Rayann spend some time away from the bookstore, and the free time had given Rayann more time to spend with Zoraida — which had seemed to please Louisa.

"Of course," Zoraida went on, "if you stayed here longer we could spend more evenings doing this as well."

"If I stay longer I'll sneeze my brains out."

"I've been thinking," Zoraida said slowly, her deliberateness negating the nonchalant tone of her voice, "that Whizzer could become an outdoor cat."

Rayann sat up. "Zoraida, please —"

"So you could stay all the time. Live with me."

Please don't. But it was too late. "Is this April Fool's?" Rayann kept her tone light, giving Zoraida a chance to laugh it off.

Zoraida sat up as well, sunlight illuminating every firm inch of her torso. She did not laugh, but sighed a little sadly. "No, *mi querida.* No joke."

"Zoraida," Rayann began, but Zoraida put two fingers over Rayann's lips, hushing her.

"You've answered. Forget I brought it up."

"I love being with you, Zoey, and heaven knows how much I love your body."

"I tried my best, but you're still in love with another." Zoraida rolled one shoulder expressively. "I wish it were not so."

If only I could love you that way. Rayann caressed the side of Zoraida's face. *You don't know how much I want to.*

"But we can go on as before." With strong arms tightening around Rayann, the warmth of Zoraida's body melted into Rayann's numbness.

"I can't use you anymore," Rayann said weakly.

"You can if I say you can. I know the score, so why can't we —"

"Because I know I'm using you. It's not fair to you. We'll end up enemies. It won't be hard to find someone who can love you better than I can."

"*Querida,*" Zoraida said wryly, "you sadly underestimate your prowess at lovemaking. I've grown used to wanting to follow from time to time and you lead so very well. And you follow well, too. How will I find someone so versatile?"

"I'm sorry," Rayann said.

"I'm not. I hope you're not either, really."

Rayann looked at Zoraida's passionate mouth, the

powerful shoulders, her incredibly soft breasts, then the smooth stomach ending in the dark silken hair. "I'm not sorry," Rayann said, her voice husky. "Only if I've hurt you."

"Oh, I'm bruised, but I'm tough." Zoraida traced Rayann's upper lip with a long finger. *"Novita, uno más, por favor.* For old time's sake."

"Con mucho gusto," Rayann answered. She kissed away Zoraida's groan, yielded to her mouth. "You lead."

9
Rough Wood

While Louisa picked out a video for the evening's entertainment, Rayann idly sketched some brochure ideas for a fundraiser to benefit a shelter for homeless women. She had visited the shelter earlier in the day and accepted the *pro bono* assignment. She missed Zoraida and was filling the empty hours with more work. She spent just as much time thinking about Louisa as before and she was beginning to get disgusted with herself.

"What would prevent you from giving money to a

homeless women's shelter?" Rayann's question broke several minutes of silence and Louisa blinked at her.

"What would prevent me? Well, I suppose lack of money. Or other charities I thought more important. Why do you ask?"

"We're tying to get money from people who don't identify with the problem, at least not yet. The director said that women who are at the poverty level, or just barely ahead, already give money to them because they identify. They know they're only a paycheck away."

"I identify," Louisa said. "I'm well aware that if Chris's insurance hadn't paid for this place I'd have to give it up. My life would have been pretty rocky. Ted would have been on his own for college."

It would have served him right — look how he's repaying you. "What would you have done?"

"Oh, probably gone back full-time to something in retail and found an apartment. We were both still working part-time because the income from the store didn't cover the mortgage." Louisa smiled fondly. "Chris and I worked at the same store when we met. I was in Children's Wear and she was in Notions. We talked woman-stuff about kids and clothes for almost three months and then I invited her over for coffee and to meet the kid I talked about all the time. She stayed the night and every night after that until . . . the accident."

Rayann had been doodling while Louisa talked, but she hung on every word. Since the near miss with Ted, Louisa had opened up a lot. To Rayann, it sounded as if Louisa was reminding herself of the reasons she had chosen to hide her sexuality from her son. "Did living together help with raising Teddy?"

"Oh, yeah. But a lot of other things got harder. We could pretend we lived together for monetary reasons. By and large that worked. Chris could never call Teddy's school, though, or pick him up if he was sick. And I couldn't put her name down for emergencies. We did what we had to do to hide our relationship. What really made it hard was keeping up appearances with our few lesbian friends. They had such definite ideas as to what a lesbian couple should look like. They expected me to do the housework and Chris was supposed to play with Teddy, show him how to be tough. Danny was the worst," she said, with a grin. "The absolute worst. She's softened up over time. I don't know what I would have done without her."

"Were friends so hard to come by that you had to pretend?" Rayann asked in curiosity, not critically.

"Correct me if I'm wrong, but I think *everyone* puts up appearances for their friends — even ones with demanding standards. Their approval helped us accept ourselves. We didn't have any role models except the Ozzie and Harriet variety and friends helped us. Oh, I don't know — they helped us put Ozzie and Harriet through a wringer and make use of what came out the other side. A little skewed and wrinkled, for sure, but the roles helped." Rayann watched Louisa's hand twine into her hair, idly coiling some of the curls around one finger. "And they helped me keep Teddy — they gave character references to social workers and lied through their teeth for me."

"They said you had character? They *were* lying," Rayann joked. She looked away from Louisa's fingers and back to her sketchpad.

Louisa laughed. "Oh, they said I dated men, they'd seen me themselves, but not too many men, in fact I'd had a steady boyfriend for a while but he'd moved away, what a pity. The phantom male's life history was kept up to date, just in case of a surprise phone call from a social worker. They were so cooperative with information that I'm surprised the social workers didn't get suspicious."

"Why did they harass you?"

"Because I kept getting into trouble in places where I worked." Louisa pushed the tape into the VCR and then settled into her easy chair with the remote control. "One place I made a fuss because the women's bathroom door didn't close properly. Another place I mentioned the word 'union' in the hearing of my supervisor. Then I got arrested at a war protest march. My bosses would tell me that they thought I'd be better off if I stayed home with my son, and when I didn't take kindly to advice they'd call up social services and report a negligent mother, and somehow I always ended up looking for another job. And because I had something to hide, the situation frightened me, but I never got angry. I accepted it as a price to be paid."

"Once you've given into blackmail you keep paying — but you can stop," Rayann said quietly.

"I know. I get angry now, but it's all over and done. Almost," Louisa said, just as quietly. Then she cleared her throat and spoke more lightly. "But there's always that last payment to be made and it's got a lot of interest accumulated. And with Chris gone, there's no reason to force the issue." Louisa stared blankly at Rayann, then blinked and turned her head. She pressed the play button, effectively changing the subject.

Rayann went back to her sketching, playing with words and icons while half-watching the movie. She didn't want to assimilate what she'd just learned about Louisa because it only widened the gulf between them in time and experience. She wondered if there were something she could take that would make her twenty years older. *It's not my fault I came of age during disco. Face facts, you can't change to please others. They have to take you as you are.* Rayann sighed. Louisa could take her anywhere she liked.

She couldn't concentrate on the movie, so she went on doodling and thinking. Her mental meanderings were interrupted by a prolonged banging on the back door — the hallmark of Danny's arrival. Rayann put down her sketchpad and stood up, preparing to make herself scarce. It was hard to watch Danny and Louisa together. They talked to each other almost without words sometimes. Jealousy was not a nice emotion and Rayann was trying to conquer it.

"Well, I got a job," Danny was saying as she and Louisa came into the living room. "Hi, Ray. How's tricks?" She immediately went to the kitchen for coffee and then sat down in the chair Rayann had vacated. "Would you look at that." She stared at Rayann's sketchpad.

Alongside her sketches for the women's shelter was an explicit sketch of Louisa's shoulders and breasts.

"Who does this luscious body belong to?" Danny looked up, a teasing edge to her voice.

Don't you recognize her? Rayann dug her fingernails into her palms. "It's . . . from my imagination. I — I've been sketching ideas for the ironwood block downstairs."

Louisa said, "Ray, I had no idea your imagination was so detailed." Rayann reached for the sketchpad, but Louisa stopped her. "I like it. The body isn't perfect. One boob is just a little bigger than the other."

"I tried to make it realistic," Rayann choked. She snatched the sketchpad and closed it.

"And they sag," Danny added. "Now *that's* realism."

"Not at Rayann's age," Louisa said with a laugh. "She's got a few years till she sags."

Rayann's cheeks flamed as both women evaluated her chest, their heads tipped to one side in a similar pose.

"We've embarrassed her," Danny said.

"She'll be a better person for it," Louisa said philosophically, then she turned her attention to Danny. "Hey, so what's this about a new assignment?"

Danny stared into her coffee cup. "You're going to be really pissed off, Lou."

Rayann returned from the bedroom, after cramming the sketchpad as far under the bed as it would go, and listened to Danny describe the job. She knew Danny was a specialty mechanic, working free-lance on rare cars when there was work and less rare cars in between.

"Remember when I went to Kansas City last month to get a Rolls for the guy in Blackhawk?" Louisa nodded. "Well, he decided to buy it."

"So why is that going to piss me off?" Louisa looked both amused and suspicious.

"Because he wants me to drive it back from Kansas City for him and I have to be back here by Saturday morning. His daughter's getting married on Saturday and he wants to drive her to the church in style. He had been going to buy a different one but that fell through and now it's too late to get a commercial carrier to bring the car out in time."

"But — opening day is day after tomorrow," Louisa said. Her voice had a wail. "We were going to have hot dogs and beer!"

"Knew you'd be pissed," Danny said. "Normally I'd have told him to get another driver because I do not like short notice for something like this, but the engine needs to be drained and tuned up before it hits the road, and, well, I can't walk away from the two grand bonus he's willing to give me."

"Two thousand dollars?" Louisa and Rayann gasped at the same time.

"Two grand, plus my usual rates and all expenses of course. Reagonomics at last — I'm being trickled on, finally. Ain't het'rosexuality grand?"

"I'd be really mad if you turned it down," Louisa said. "I can get through the game alone."

"Don't have to be alone," Danny said. She dug in her pocket and handed her ticket to Rayann. "You seem to like baseball."

Rayann grinned and didn't know what to say. "You don't have to give it to me," she said, even as her fingers tightened around it. "But thanks. I'll have a beer in your honor."

"Don't forget the nachos," Danny said. She drained her coffee. "Well, I got to throw some things in a suitcase and head for the airport. I'm not looking forward to the Great Salt Flats, but this Rolls is a 'forty-nine in just about mint condition — pure decadence."

"Oh, drive safely," Louisa said. She hugged Danny enthusiastically.

Danny hugged Louisa back and told Rayann to have fun at the game. Rayann assured her she would, while thinking to herself what she'd really enjoy was the company of the woman who would be sitting next to her.

* * * * *

A light breeze took the edge off the brilliant sunlight
as Rayann trudged up the connecting walkway from the
BART station to the Oakland Coliseum. She was lagging
behind Louisa who cut through the crowd with agility.

When Rayann came abreast of her, Louisa said, "I
love the first sight of the ballpark. The grass seems so
pure and untouched. There's just something so clean
about baseball."

"That's Astroturf for you," Rayann said.

Louisa's eyebrows shot up. "This park is a real park
with real grass and real dirt. I'd be seriously upset if
they ever changed that."

"I thought they had."

"You're nuts," Louisa said. "One look and you'll see."

Their seats were just beyond the A's dugout only four
rows back from the barrier. The vivid green, yellow, red
and white of the various uniforms on the field were
scattered against the lush grass and blazing blue sky, all
combining to assault Rayann's eyes, making her feel as if
she'd never seen color before. The bright white of the
balls rolling across the field left traces of afterburn in her
vision, despite sunglasses. The heat of the sun warmed
her skin. *It's like a big yellow tongue, licking me all
over . . . Stop that right now. You do not need to think
about things like that.*

They toasted the absent Danny by touching their cups
of beer. After they consumed their first jumbo dogs,
Louisa pointed at the field where various dignitaries were
now milling around, preparing for the first pitch of the
season. "That is real grass."

"Looks too green to be real."

To Rayann's surprise, Louisa got up and went down to
the barrier above the dugout. She leaned over, leaving
Rayann to admire her flexed body.

"Hey," she heard Louisa call. "Will somebody down
there get me a blade of grass? This young person up here
thinks it's Astroturf."

Rayann gaped when a uniformed player sauntered out of the A's dugout, uprooted a little of the sod and brought it over to Louisa. Clump in hand, Louisa loomed over Rayann. She held the clod over Rayann's head and slowly squeezed. A fine sprinkling of dirt sifted through Louisa's fingers onto Rayann's head and shoulders.

"Okay, okay, it's real," Rayann said. She squeaked in alarm as a blade of grass fell in her beer. "I was wrong, I admit it." She ducked and tried to cover herself. Louisa laughed and settled into her seat again.

During the course of the game Rayann was delighted that she could actually concentrate on it, and not on Louisa, though every time Louisa jumped up to follow a long ball into the outfield Rayann would appreciate how shapely her sweatshirt was. *Only natural appreciation for beauty.*

In the top of the eighth inning, the young player who'd given Louisa the clump of dirt put his first major league home run, and the first home run of the season, over the fence at dead centerfield. From the crack of the bat Louisa and Rayann were on their feet, following the ball way, way back. "Tell it goodbye," Louisa whooped. She threw her arm around Rayann.

Their hips met and they rocked as "Can't Touch This" pulsed from the stadium's loudspeakers. Rayann felt the surge of heat flowing through her — the same surge she'd been trying to forget ever since Christmas Eve. It was no use. When Louisa moved away again her body went cold. She could not stop staring at Louisa's clapping hands.

If only she wouldn't touch me, or look at me, or stand next to me, and if only she'd cover up her hands somehow. She'd lost track of the game. Her legs were rubbery and between her legs she was on fire, melting into her seat. A lengthy at bat was underway, with the A's renowned lead-off man fouling off pitch after pitch, looking for a good one. Rayann couldn't have cared less. Her vision blurred as her body seized energy and used it to fuel the waves of heat that were washing over her. The part of her mind that controlled her senses wasn't capable of thought — deep, burning longing had hijacked her brain and was taking no prisoners.

Bat connected with baseball yet again, and the resounding crack brought a gasp from the crowd. Rayann looked up and her eyes began to clear. When they focused it was on the baseball, headed straight for her face. No time to react. She scrunched her eyes shut and flinched for the impact.

She heart it hit something, then someone said, "Nice catch, lady." She opened her eyes. Directly in front of her nose was Louisa's hand, fingers spread and curled around the baseball. Rayann stared at that hand, noting every tendon and freckle. The movie reel in her head started playing back the way she had felt, the way she had moved, the way Louisa had taken her and made love to her — every moment, from the first brush of Louisa's lips to the last surge of her fingers, played on Rayann's body. Even as Louisa dropped the ball into Rayann's lap and shook her hand, flexing and extending her fingers, Rayann slumped in her seat. *I can't go on like this.*

"I thought you were on your way to the hospital for sure," Louisa said. She was still shaking her hand. "What on earth were you looking at — it sure wasn't the game."

I was looking at you. "Thanks," Rayann managed. She picked up the ball in her lap. "I believe you earned this. Is your hand okay?"

"Oh, yeah," Louisa said nonchalantly. "It's just surprised. Will the ball fit in your coat?"

Rayann squeezed it into her pocket. The A's eventually won on a two-out, two-strike bases-loaded bunt in the bottom of the twelfth inning. Rayann watched the ball spin like a top, toying with the foul line, threaten to go foul as it spun toward first base. It made her dizzy to watch it, so she closed her eyes, missing the third base runner's triumphant slide and the crowd's roar when the ball stopped a quarter-inch fair. She just didn't care.

* * * * *

At home, Rayann emptied her pockets, and tried to ignore the shudders that went through her when she looked at the baseball. "Think fast," she said. As soon as Louisa turned, Rayann flipped the ball to her.

Louisa tried to catch it, but the ball thudded to the floor as Louisa winced.

"You *did* hurt yourself," Rayann said. She was at Louisa's side in a flash. "Oh, my God," she moaned when she saw the red, bruised palm.

"It's just sore," Louisa said, her nonchalance at odds with the proof of the bruise. She gave an involuntary "ouch" when Rayann prodded gently. Her color was unusually high.

"Why didn't you tell me? I could have gotten some ice from the concession stand." She pressed the protesting Louisa into her easy chair and then hurriedly dropped some ice into a baggie and wrapped it in a paper towel.

"It's nothing. You don't have to fuss. I don't need a nurse."

"Hold this in your hand," Rayann commanded.

"It's not neces— oh, all right. I had no idea you could pout like that."

"How does it feel?"

"Good," Louisa said reluctantly, after the ice pack had rested in her hand for few moments. "It's terrible getting old."

Rayann wanted to drop to her knees and kiss the injured hand tenderly. She wanted to cup it against her face and give it T.L.C. until it felt better. And once it was healed and strong again, she wanted to bring it to her body, invite it to learn her again. "Age has nothing to do with it," she said. "Why do you think the players wear gloves?"

"To extend their reach," Louisa answered dryly. "I know age is a state of mind, but it's also a state of the body. Mine's about twenty-seven years older than yours."

Why do you do that? Why do you keep reminding me? There was nothing to say to that, nothing that could be said. "Well, now you have a souvenir for Danny." *That's*

172

right, bring up Danny and remind yourself that Louisa is happy the way she is.

"Danny? Oh, she'll love it." Louisa closed her eyes and Rayann could see she was in quite a bit of discomfort despite her bravado — flush still covered Louisa's cheeks. She fetched a glass of water and some ibuprofen and forced them on Louisa who submitted with good grace. "Doctor, do I have your permission to go downstairs and take down the 'Closed for Baseball' sign?"

"No. I'll do it," Rayann said. "And don't take off that ice pack."

Louisa stared at Rayann. "Dominating type, aren't you?"

Rayann stared back, blinked, and said, "Not all of the time." Then she escaped to the bookstore, her heart racing. She wiped her palms on her pants, but all the wiping in the world wouldn't keep them dry.

"Ray, could you get this gentleman a copy of *Absalom, Absalom* while you're up there?"

Rayann put two new E.M. Forsters in place and reached over for the Faulkner. When she glanced over her shoulder to tell Louisa she had it, she was startled by the expression on Louisa's face — almost fierce as she watched Rayann clamber down the ladder. She handed over the book and then wondered if she had imagined the look. Louisa's face was as composed as usual.

"I thought you were going to knock off early," Louisa said as she rang up the purchase.

"Work is therapy. I'm really blocked on this brochure and the deadline is rapidly approaching. Restocking is so mindless it actually helps me think." *Ask me if I'm going to see Zoraida.* Rayann was still trying to slip the information that she and Zoraida were no longer seeing each other into the conversation. She didn't want to call too much attention to it, but she wanted Louisa to know.

"Thanks for stopping in," Louisa said to the customer.

She started the cash register printing out the day's receipts. "Get the gate, would you, Rayann?"

Rayann closed and locked the iron gate and shut off the porch lights. Louisa was already heading up the stairs. "Any plans for the evening?" Rayann called after her.

"Ironing — I'm sick of looking at the pile."

The store had been busy earlier so Rayann cleared away the remains of their hastily eaten supper while Louisa got out the ironing board and started on the pile of workshirts and pants. The dishes finished, Rayann retrieved her sketchpad and pencils again and sat down in Louisa's easy chair to work.

She had the overall design finished — what she lacked was a theme. It didn't help her concentration that if she looked just to the left of her sketchpad she could watch Louisa's hands settling a shirt on the ironing board. Her fingers smoothed the collar and straightened the pockets as the iron pressed its way around the button. Then her palms smoothed the cloth as the iron passed over it, long strokes over the back, faster strokes on the sleeves. Her fingers carefully eased each button closed. In Rayann's mind she saw the buttons easing open, not closed.

The tablecloth was next under Louisa's touch. *If those linens were alive they'd be fighting to get in line.* Rayann envied the tablecloth from the bottom of her heart. Her palms were so damp the sketch paper was sticking to them. *I've got to stop.* Rayann knew she was going insane, but there didn't seem anything else to do. *Except tell her.* But Rayann knew she couldn't. Because it would only embarrass Louisa. Because she'd have to leave afterward. Because there was Danny.

Almost as if Rayann's thoughts had conjured her up, Danny was pounding on the back door. Louisa turned the iron off with a grateful sigh and went to let Danny in. Rayann heard her voice drop from her usual ebullient greeting to a more refined and formal tone, telling someone she was glad to meet them.

Danny entered first, her usual heel-to-toe swagger

more pronounced than ever. She was followed by another woman whom Rayann guessed was in her late forties, maybe early fifties, with neatly styled brown hair and pale blue eyes. She looked nervous. Danny sat down on the sofa and patted the place next to her. The woman sat where Danny had indicated, perched right on the edge.

Louisa said, "Can I get you both some coffee?"

"Sure," Danny said.

"Here, let me," Rayann said. *What on earth is going on?*

"Marilyn, this is Rayann. Rayann, this here is Marilyn." Rayann shook hands and answered Marilyn's shy greeting. She went to the kitchen and poured the cool coffee they'd made around dinnertime into mugs and then heated them in the microwave. She nearly dropped both steaming cups when she realized what Danny was saying.

". . . finally said she'd live with me. Took her long enough to make up her mind."

"I never had any doubts about you, sweetie," Marilyn said in a quiet voice. "I just wasn't sure I could make you any happier than you were."

"Well, I'm happy for you both," Louisa said. "Danny's just been a bear lately."

Rayann carefully set the stoneware mugs on the counter, then gripped the edge to keep from falling over backward. "Cream or sugar, Marilyn?" Her voice cracked.

She saw Louisa give her a puzzled look, but she added a spoonful of sugar to Marilyn's coffee without spilling more than half on the counter. She managed to bring the mugs out to Danny and Marilyn without spilling anything, but once she'd sat down she had to stuff her hands under her thighs to hide their shaking.

"What do you do, Marilyn," Louisa asked. Marilyn gained confidence when she talked about her career as a physical therapist, a little color creeping into pale cheeks.

It took Rayann about fifteen minutes to completely process the incredibly stupid mistake she'd made, and another fifteen minutes to reevaluate her perception of Louisa and Danny as lovers. There was no doubt that Louisa and Danny loved each other very much, but

Rayann really hadn't any concrete evidence that they were lovers. *If they're not lovers, then why didn't she want me again? Why doesn't she want me now?* Rayann's mind kept turning over. She watched Danny relax as Louisa and Marilyn talked. She realized that Danny had brought Marilyn to Louisa for approval. She needed to know that her best friend and lover would get along. *I am so stupid, so stupid.*

When Danny and Marilyn left, with Louisa's assurance that it had been a pleasure and they'd all be getting together soon, Louisa turned to Rayann with a concerned look. "You're white as a ghost," she said. "What's wrong?"

"Nothing," Rayann said. *I can't tell her. Yes, I can. I have to.* "I thought — I thought you and Danny — you and Danny were — were lovers."

"What?" Louisa stared at Rayann, astounded.

"You stayed the night with her after the party at the Lace Place."

"I thought you might be bringing Zoraida home."

That threw Rayann. She thought about it and said, "Danny's slept over here a couple of times."

"Slept, yes. I needed to talk to her, needed comfort. I've done the same for her."

"Comfort?"

"It's possible to have a long friendship with someone and never want to have sex," Louisa said defensively. "I save sex for love."

Rayann was suddenly drenched with a cold sweat. "I'm not seeing Zoraida anymore," she blurted out. Louisa paled. Rayann knew without doubt that her life was hanging on what she said next. "I found out I have to save sex for love." Rayann took a step closer to Louisa. "And I didn't love Zoraida, not that way. I'm in love with someone else." She took another step. Louisa didn't answer, only watched Rayann's slow approach with wide eyes. A frantic pulse beat in Rayann's throat. "Louisa, I love you."

Louisa closed her eyes. "You can't."

"I do."

"It's just — you feel grateful." Louisa opened her eyes again, and Rayann withstood the piercing gaze.

"No."

"We spend so much time together, it's just —"

"No," Rayann said again, shaking her head. Now that she had said the words, a wonderful rush of confidence surged through, buoying her. "I'm in love with you. I want to make love with you very, very much."

"You can't," Louisa said again.

"I do." Rayann took the final step and stood so close to Louisa that all she had to do was lean forward if she wanted to kiss her. And she wanted to kiss Louisa.

Louisa put her hands to her face. "Rayann, I can't do this to you."

"Do what?" Rayann realized Louisa was trembling.

"Hold you back. Keep you from the rest of your life. Your future."

"Let's build a life together. My life, your life. Our life."

"I'm so much older," Louisa whispered. "Have you considered that?"

"I'm so much younger," Rayann said. "I have so much to learn it scares me."

"No," Louisa murmured. "Dear God."

Rayann took Louisa's hands from her face, and placed them on her own flushed cheeks. The strong hands trembled there as Louisa drew in her breath sharply. "I don't need charity."

"I can't afford charity. All I have to give is love." Rayann focused on Louisa's trembling lips. Louisa made a sound — a tiny gasp. The inches separating their lips melted away and Rayann kissed her.

Louisa's hands slid down Rayann's face, to her throat, then her shoulders. The uncertain grip on Rayann's shoulders became firm as Rayann brushed her lips against Louisa's chin, then the corners of her mouth.

"I want you so much," Rayann murmured.

Control slipped away as Louisa's hands moved slowly and deliberately on her back, then down. Her fingers eased under Rayann's sweatshirt, brushing the bare skin. One hand remained on her back, holding Rayann tightly against Louisa while the other hand slid slowly around to the button and zipper of Rayann's jeans, easing them open.

Louisa captured her mouth as Rayann moaned. Rayann had no strength to move away even if she had desired to do so; she was held fast and secure against Louisa. She could feel Louisa's body molding to hers. Her heart thudded as fingers sought their way under her clothing, lower, down, then between.

"How can you be so wet, so fast," Louisa said. Her voice came from back in her throat, each word a groan.

"I've been like this for weeks . . . for months," Rayann thought she answered. She couldn't tell if her vocal chords were working. The fingers found her swollen flesh and an oh of pleasure filled her and flowed to Louisa's demanding mouth, searching hers.

Louisa's fingers teased and promised, but didn't quite enter. "Do you like that?"

"Yes. But I can't . . . not like this . . . I need to lie down." Her body had strength in only one place, the part that followed Louisa's fingers.

"I've got you." Louisa moaned into Rayann's throat. The arm that gripped Rayann's back tightened. "I have hold of you."

"I'm falling," Rayann said, her voice breaking. "Don't let me fall."

"Never," Louisa answered.

Rayann's hips thrust forward, begging, but the terror that she would fall filled her. "No," she whimpered, even as Louisa's fingers glided inward. Her knees gave way.

The room whirled. There was a wall at her back now. Louisa's body pinned Rayann to it and her fingers met Rayann's frantic arching. In Rayann's mind she was still falling, spiraling toward the hand that held her. Her body flamed like a shooting star, then burst into sparks, burning in release.

"Don't stop," Rayann moaned. She could have stayed

where she was forever, but Louisa's fingers were sliding away.

"Darling, I want to do that again, but now *I'm* the one who needs to lie down."

Rayann nodded. Her limbs felt unbearably heavy. Louisa's arm, still around her, held her up. In the bedroom, Rayann shakily removed her clothes. Louisa swept back the comforter, then pulled Rayann down beside her, under the tapestry of sun and moon.

I've never felt so naked. Louisa's shirt and jeans grazed Rayann's skin as Louisa placed her on the bed, then moved next to her, then on top of her, her mouth finding Rayann's breasts. Rayann hissed as her body filled again with shameless and selfish desire, too heavy to lift her hands — she needed Louisa to touch her again. She didn't know how she could want so much. "Please . . . your fingers . . ."

She arched her breasts to Louisa's mouth again and again as Louisa teased with the tips of her fingers — they promised more — and Louisa's tongue caressed and stroked. Rayann clasped Louisa's hand in her own, drawing the elusive fingers into her body, hips meeting them. Louisa's breath, quick and rasping, filled Rayann's ears.

In the darkness, she could see Louisa's face — a mask, austere in concentration. *I need her so badly.* Rayann shuddered as Louisa's voice came to her, urging her to finish, begging her to come. *She needs this . . . this.* Rayann arched one last time, hands clutching Louisa's shoulders.

Louisa held her fast, frozen against her, moaning, "How can you? Dear God, so wet."

She was no longer falling. The bed seemed secure under her as Rayann fought off the last vestige of dizziness. She was still leaden with desire, but her head was clear. She knew what she wanted.

Louisa was on her back, breathing hard, eyes closed. They snapped open when Rayann's hand touched her.

"So beautiful," Rayann murmured, tracing the outline of Louisa's nipples though her shirt. She shook off her lethargy and lowered her mouth to the nearest peak.

Louisa lay quiescent for a moment, a soft sigh escaping her, then she rolled away, evading Rayann's hands which followed her. "You don't have to do that," she said.

Rayann, her responses slowed by the passion that drained her, said, "Don't you want me?"

"I thought I'd just proven the answer to that." Louisa's glance at Rayann's wet thighs made them open slightly.

Rayann wanted to protest as Louisa bent to her body again, kissing her thighs, tongue gliding over the wetness, then toward the source. Louisa's shirt scraped against her thighs, reminding her again how naked she was. *Falling again, I can't stop falling.* Her hair . . . *her hair* . . . Rayann filled her hands with it, held it against her stomach as Louisa's mouth captured all of her. She opened herself to take all Louisa offered, to show Louisa how much she needed — and how much she could give.

The last shudder had passed before Rayann was aware that Louisa had rolled away. Rayann slid after her, spooning to Louisa's back. She was surprised to find the back of Louisa's shirt damp. "God, you're incredible," Rayann murmured, her arm snaking around Louisa's waist. Only then did she feel Louisa's body shaking. "What's wrong, darling, what's wrong?"

"Nothing." Louisa's voice was muffled by her arms.

"Tell me," Rayann said. "I need to know what you're feeling."

Louisa was silent and the shaking had eased before she raised her head. "I don't know why you're being so . . . good. To me."

"Good," Rayann echoed. "I haven't done anything yet." She lifted Louisa's hair and kissed her neck. "Let me make you feel the way you've made me feel."

"Why?" Louisa turned over onto her back. "Why do you want to?"

"Because I love you. Because I want you."

"Ray, you don't have to."

"You don't . . . want me to?"

"You don't have to. I'm so much old—"

Rayann's mouth stopped Louisa, stifling the words that would separate them again. She kissed Louisa gently, then more fiercely as Louisa finally responded to her. She raised her head, gasping. "What does that matter when I love you, when I want to fill my hand with your beautiful softness." Her fingers stroked Louisa's breasts. "What does that matter when I want to learn every inch of your body over and over again. I want to feel your skin against mine. What do I have to do to make you believe that?"

"It's hard, so hard to believe. But I want to believe you, I do."

"I'll do whatever it takes to make you sure," Rayann murmured. She unbuttoned Louisa's shirt slowly. When her hand slipped inside, cupping the wonderful abundance of Louisa's breasts through her bra, she was rewarded by Louisa's deep sigh. She felt some of the tension drain out of Louisa's body. She realized then that she did not know what Louisa wanted or needed, or if she could possibly fill that need. "Tell me what to do," she said. "You frighten me a little."

Louisa held Rayann's hands against her breasts. "I frighten *you?* You can't imagine . . . I've been telling myself I couldn't possibly know what a woman your age wants."

"Sshhh. It's not important."

"Oh, but it is." Louisa swallowed and let go of Rayann's hands, moving her shoulders back slightly in a gesture of offering.

Rayann slid her hands around, unhooked and then freed the wondrous softness. With a groan she lowered her mouth to them.

Louisa groaned in answer. "How can you want me so? After Zoraida . . ."

181

Rayann didn't want to stop, but knew she had to answer. She replaced the attention of her mouth with her hands, delighting in the texture and grain of Louisa's skin. "I can't compare her to you. I was shockingly and wantonly casual with her. I won't lie and say it wasn't good, but it was *not* . . . oh, not like this." Rayann sighed and helplessly brought her mouth to Louisa's breast again, capturing one hardened nipple between her teeth, then gently caressing it with her tongue. "She knew I was in love with you, that I longed to be with you again. I've never felt with anyone the way you make me feel." Rayann's voice grew intense as one hand went to Louisa's thighs, slipping between. "I've never wanted anyone like this."

Louisa's thighs closed on her hand. "Ray, I . . . there's only one way I've ever . . ."

"Show me," Rayann said. "Teach me."

Louisa shed her clothes. Rayann bit her lower lip as she gazed on what she had wanted for so long to see again. Louisa shook her hair down, then returned to Rayann, pressing her onto her back.

"Like this, like before," she said in a low, intense voice. She lowered herself astride Rayann's thigh, moving languorously while a low moan rippled through her throat.

"God, you're beautiful," Rayann said. She slowly brought her fingers to her thigh, slipping them gently between her skin and the throb of Louisa's passion.

Louisa's hands were at her shoulders, pulling her up. "Hold me," she said. She rested against the arm Rayann slipped around her waist. Her hips moved faster. "Too good."

Rayann held her, praying she could be enough. She brought her mouth to Louisa's breast. Louisa's hand came to the back of her head, holding her there.

"Dear God, Rayann."

Rayann responded to each nuance of Louisa's groans, her tongue and lips giving up Louisa's breasts when Louisa clasped her tightly, held her frozen except for rapid jerks of her hips which ended with one final gasp, one final thrust, one final grip of Rayann's fingers inside the trembling flesh.

"Hold me," Louisa murmured, sinking slowly to the sheets, pulling Rayann with her.

10

Touch Wood

When Rayann opened her eyes the next morning, she knew she wasn't alone. She wrapped herself in the scent and sound of Louisa next to her. She surfaced out of the covers to find Louisa watching her.

"You're pretty adorable with your hair all messed up like that," Louisa said.

"Well, I'm glad you like it. This is what I look like in the morning."

"I can live with it."

Rayann rolled over on her back. The moon seemed to

be winking at her. "Tell me about the tapestry. I've been dying to ask."

"Chris and I found this bed at an estate sale. We were supposed to be buying books. The tapestry came with the bed and we had the feeling the family was only too eager to see the last of it. They were Mormons, and judging from the pattern, the dearly departed was not."

"It's beautiful."

"I'm glad you like the view." Louisa stretched and sat up.

"I'm quite attached," Rayann said. She was not looking at the tapestry.

"Flatterer. It's time to get up, you know."

"I know. Can I change your mind or will you insist on the mundane tasks of the day?" Rayann let her gaze caress Louisa. They had a lot to talk about, a lot to discover, but right now it felt good to just . . . feel good.

" 'There's nothing so fatiguing as the eternal hanging on of an uncompleted task' — William James," Louisa quoted.

"Make love, not work," Rayann said.

Louisa gave her a sidelong look. "Who said that?"

"I did. Just now." Louisa laughed and got out of bed. Rayann sighed and followed her. "Can I at least take my shower with you instead of waiting?"

Louisa looked over her shoulder. "I guess so. But no funny business." Rayann gave Louisa her most innocent look, but she knew Louisa was not fooled.

Rayann stood under the hot water, letting it wake her up. It seemed almost uncivilized to leap from a warm, cozy bed into water. It must have been the feline instinct in her that hated it. She gave up the hot water when Louisa complained of cold and shampooed her hair while Louisa rinsed. She relaxed more and more in the steam, until Louisa started washing her back. Despite the heat, her body goose-pimpled in response and she shivered.

"I thought you said no funny business."

"I'm just washing your back," Louisa said. Her voice sounded sultry to Rayann, but maybe it was just the steam.

"I'm going to get soap in my eyes."

"Spoilsport," Louisa said. Rayann rinsed her hair and then turned.

"Oh yeah?" Her fingers slid between Louisa's thighs and curled in the thick hair. She wanted desperately to touch Louisa again, to satisfy her. She wanted to taste and adore but Louisa had not indicated that she wanted Rayann's mouth on her. She heard Louisa take a deep breath, then exhale slowly.

"Okay, okay," she said weakly. "I'm going to fall down if you don't let go of me. As erotic as it may sound, the shower is no place to make love."

"I know," Rayann said, releasing her. "I've tried it. Got water up my nose."

Louisa gave a shout of laughter as she stepped out of the shower to dry off. "I know exactly what you mean."

"It really interfered with the mood."

Rayann gathered her clothes of the night before and returned to her bedroom. They met again as they both emerged from their respective rooms, dressed and ready for breakfast. Rayann took in the near-white blue chambray shirt and the swell of the body that had been next to her the night before.

"What are we doing?" Louisa stared at Rayann.

"Pretending last night didn't happen," Rayann said.

"Every inch of me knows it did happen," Louisa said. She put her hand on her stomach as if she were in pain. She moved toward Rayann.

"Same here," Rayann said. Louisa began unbuttoning Rayann's shirt. "I just put that on." Louisa unzipped Rayann's jeans. "It was a waste of time getting dressed."

They spent the day like adolescents in love. Every time Rayann turned around Louisa was close by, watching, smiling a secret smile. Rayann found she couldn't make the simplest decision without consulting Louisa, standing close, breathing in the same air. The customers and ringing phone seemed nuisances. When it was quiet enough to grab a bite to eat they gobbled their food and then necked in the stairwell until a customer came in. Rayann longed for night.

Louisa answered yet another call, but after the usual pleasantries she said, "The Count Basie Orchestra? I'd love to." Her gaze searched out Rayann who stood across the room. "Well, I don't know — it's not her type of music, but I think she's free. Would you like to talk to her?"

Rayann took the phone and said hello to her mother.

"You don't have to come if you don't want to, dear, no pressure, but there's a wonderful concert tomorrow night that I just found out about. I thought of Louisa immediately because I haven't met anyone in a long time who loves swing the way I do. You're welcome to come — it'll be fun."

Rayann was unsettled by the entire proceedings, but heard herself agreeing to go to the concert. She hung up the phone slowly. Her mother still had a great deal more in common with Louisa than she did herself.

"Sounds fun, doesn't it?" Louisa spoke over her shoulder as she rang up a purchase.

"Sure. You can teach me all about swing."

"Be glad to," Louisa said. She waved goodbye to the customer. "Danny hates swing. She's a blues baby from way back."

"I like the blues, too," Rayann said. "Stevie Ray Vaughn, Robert Cray."

Louisa stared at her blankly. "I was thinking more in the lines of John Lee Hooker and Muddy Waters."

It was Rayann's turn to stare blankly, a frightening sensation seizing her stomach. She swallowed, then smiled as provocatively as she could manage. "Looks like I have a lot to learn, but you're a good teacher."

"I might learn a thing or two myself," Louisa said, her lips pressing together in a delectable smirk.

"Stop that," Rayann whispered. "Do you want to be compromised right in front of the cash register?"

Louisa laughed, but suddenly her face froze — the laugh died. Rayann didn't have to turn to know Teddy had just come into the store.

"Oh, my God," Louisa said. "Ray, give me just this once, just this once. I never thought you'd . . . I hadn't thought this far ahead."

Rayann swallowed her protest. No conditions on love, as Danny would say. So she smiled and joked and made small talk, every word choking her. As soon as she could, she took Tucker upstairs for cookies and milk. She didn't have to pretend with Tucker. When Louisa and Teddy joined them Rayann went downstairs, taking as long as she could to close up and run out the day's receipts.

She went upstairs again when she could no longer avoid it and agreed to play cards with Tucker. *That's right I'll just sit over here with the children.* She was aware that Louisa and Teddy were both watching them as they talked. Her concentration was so bad she wasn't surprised when she lost three hands of gin in a row. She got up from the floor and manufactured yawns and stretches, then made the necessary excuses and escaped to her bedroom.

Teddy and Tucker left a short time later, while Rayann was still fully dressed, sitting on the edge of her bed. Though her mind had never stopped turning, she had come to no conclusions. She didn't know if she could live like this. She heard the door close and the creak of the floor as Louisa came back from the back porch.

Come to me. Please Louisa, come to me now.

There was a soft knock on the door, and Louisa looked in. "You're a pretty good actress, all in all, but I didn't think you were sleepy."

"I'm not." Rayann stood up and moved to Louisa's side. "And I didn't particularly want to sleep in here, either."

"I don't want you to," Louisa said slowly. She closed her eyes, her face tightening. "Ray, can we not talk about it. Not yet. Can we just go to bed?"

"Yes." For now it was enough.

After last night Rayann wasn't sure she would or

could reach the same levels of desire as she had before, but her body responded — swelling and opening as Louisa undressed her. Her fingers fumbled with the buttons of Louisa's shirt, but finally her hands were smoothing the bare skin of Louisa's stomach. She stroked the soft plane of Louisa's back. Bare skin to bare skin, they rolled over and over on the bed. Rayann found herself beneath Louisa. Louisa held her down, and kissed her thoroughly.

"Wait," Rayann said, when she was able. "I wanted to —"

"You're intoxicating," Louisa said. She parted the satin folds between Rayann's legs.

"So are you . . ." Rayann knew she said more, but she didn't know what. Her mind was absorbed with the smoothness of Louisa's body against her as Louisa swirled within her. Her hands traced the curves of Louisa's sides and back. Louisa rolled atop Rayann and feasted on her lips, her mouth and then her breasts.

"Touch me," Rayann urged her. "I want —"

Teddy faded into the background as Rayann lived another day on the edge of her emotions, showing Louisa every thought, every desire, welcoming every smile, every innocent glance that hid smoldering looks. Louisa touched her a thousand times that day, as if making up for lost time.

As they dressed for the concert Rayann chose a thin turtleneck sweater, slipping the phoenix necklace over it. She slung her black silk pants over one arm, then went into Louisa's bedroom where Louisa was shrugging into Rayann's favorite high-collared blouse. Rayann held her black pants up to her waist. "How will this look?"

Louisa turned, her blouse still unbuttoned. "D'lovely, d'lightful, d'licious." She smiled and her hand went to the buttons of her blouse.

Rayann swayed. *Not again.* She was turning into warm honey just watching Louisa button her blouse. The flash of passion must have shown in her face because

189

suddenly Louisa was in front of her, hands cupping her breasts, mouth seeking them through the thin fabric of the turtleneck.

Rayann pulled her clothes off in a frenzy, offering her body to Louisa yet again. Louisa pulled her down to the bed, mouth never leaving Rayann's breasts. The silk of Louisa's shirt, sensuous against Rayann's stomach, moved in a warm wave down Rayann's body, between Rayann's open knees.

"We'll be late," Louisa said later. "We have to get dressed."

Rayann got up. She felt groggy and heavy lidded. Whenever she went near Louisa she wanted to move against her. She managed to dress and was very glad Louisa was driving.

They met her mother at the entrance to the Orpheum Theater just as the last bell rang. "Sorry, Mom," Rayann said, after she had hugged her in greeting. "We couldn't find a parking place." A lie, Rayann thought as they hurried to their seats. They'd found a space right away but Rayann had kept Louisa in the car for a few extra minutes, her mouth hungry and demanding. Once they were seated, Louisa between Rayann and her mother, Rayann put her fingers to her mouth. It felt bruised and tender. *I'm still falling.*

The curtain rose on a white tuxedo-clad orchestra, with the principal performers — men and women alike — in baby blue. The music started smooth and sexy, then built to melodic frenzy. Rayann wanted to hold Louisa's hand, but propriety kept her hands on her own knees, keeping time and trying to enjoy the music when all she could think about was Louisa in a baby-blue tuxedo.

At intermission her mother and Louisa shared music stories — the first time they'd heard "Take the A Train," "In the Mood" and favorite songs. Rayann listened, glad she could add that the Platter's version of "Smoke Gets in Your Eyes" was also her favorite. She wondered what her mother would say if she knew that Louisa was now her daughter's lover. *I can just guess.*

After the concert, Ann Germaine invited them home for dessert. "I've got this wonderful chocolate marble torte from Il Fronaio — it's early yet. Besides, I forgot to bring back Lou's records and the tapes of them. They sound wonderful."

Rayann rode with Louisa, "to show her the way." As Louisa's car slid into the driveway behind the slowly closing garage door that hid Ann's BMW from sight, Rayann said, "This is very hard for me, Louisa. I want to tell her, but it's up to you."

"No, it's your decision."

"Louisa, you have to decide. She already knows I'm a lesbian. You have to come out yourself to your friends. And she is your friend now. You tell her about yourself. I'll tell her about us if you like."

"I'm not very good at this. Everything is happening too quickly. Somehow I thought I'd get through life the easy way."

"It strikes me that your life has never been particularly easy. But whatever you decide," Rayann said. She slid over the bench seat, her lips finding Louisa's throat. "Right now I can't think of anything but being with you again. I want you so much I feel drugged with it. I'm still falling in love with you, over and over."

Louisa drew her breath in sharply, then gently pushed Rayann away. "Let's go, sweetie."

Jimmy Dorsey and his orchestra sounded almost as if they were in the next room. Ann dished up torte and poured coffee while she and Louisa discussed the music rolling out of the tape player. Rayann could see how Louisa was searching for the right way to mention ever so casually that she was a lesbian. *Except there never is a right, easy way.*

When Ann went to the kitchen for more coffee, Rayann reached over to Louisa, cupping her face. Rayann's voice held compassion but was mostly desire. "Would you like me to tell her? It's up to you."

There was a startled gasp from the doorway. Ann

191

stood frozen, the coffee pot in one hand. Her gaze went from her daughter to Louisa and back to her daughter. Rayann's hand fell away from Louisa's face. She tried to penetrate her mother's expression — shock and a smoulder of anger.

"Why didn't you tell me?" The question was directed at Louisa, not Rayann.

"It just happened, Ann. I — we've been trying to find a way."

Ann let out a short, explosive breath, then came to the table and set the coffee pot down. Rayann took measure of her mother's distraction — she had set the hot pot on the wood. Rayann moved it to the brass trivet.

"Ann, I'm a lesbian. I've always been a lesbian."

Ann said nothing. She turned her fixed gaze to her daughter.

"And we're in love, Mom. At least this time you like her." Rayann saw her mother swallow, but she still said nothing.

"Ann, I know you're worried about your daughter giving the best years of her life to someone my age —"

"Louisa, that's not true," Rayann began, but her mother interrupted.

"Well, they didn't prepare me for anything like this at the support group." Ann's tone was wooden.

"You went to a support group?" Rayann could not imagine her mother talking about herself in front of other people.

Ann nodded, her face unreadable. She did not look at Louisa or Rayann. "I concentrated on opening myself up for my daughter's choices, but . . ." another short breath, "I'm not ready for this."

"Ann," Louisa said, "I understand how you feel."

"Do you?" Ann's voice was edged with bitterness.

"I think so. If my son brought home someone my age I'd be upset. I'd want him to be happy, but I'd be worried. I *am* worried about the way I feel for Rayann. She's convinced everything will be fine, but I'm scared."

Rayann put her hand on Louisa's sleeve. "I do know

192

we have to work at this." She turned to her mother. "Mom, don't make this hard for us. Please, don't do it —"

"Don't do it again," Ann finished. "I — forgive me. I'm just completely taken by surprise. I didn't know there were lesbians my age. I mean, I *knew*, but . . ." She looked at Rayann's hand resting on Louisa's sleeve.

"I love your daughter very much," Louisa said.

Why haven't you said that to me? Rayann tightened her fingers on Louisa's arm.

Ann's mouth trembled. "I like you, Louisa." Gone was the informal "Lou" of earlier in the evening. "But I can't accept this with open arms."

Rayann put her napkin on the table. "Let's go, Louisa. I can't do this entire scene again. Once was enough."

Louisa looked at Ann again, then rose. "Can't we talk about it?"

"I'm — speechless." Ann sat down suddenly, as if her legs wouldn't support her.

"Louisa, let's go."

Louisa turned back to Ann, pulling Rayann close. She swallowed. "I think we can spare a few minutes."

Rayann put her arm around Louisa's waist, her body automatically molding itself to Louisa's hip.

"I'm sorry," Ann said, her words cutting. I'm sorry I can't just leap up and say how happy I am."

"Mom," Rayann said quietly. "You're not losing a daughter, you're gaining a permanent partner for swing concerts."

"There are some definite benefits here," Louisa said. "You're just about all I could hope for in a . . . a mother-in-law."

"You can't ever break up with her, Rayann," her mother said without looking up. "I think it would break my heart." Suddenly she started to cry. "I love you both. I'm happy for you, really."

"You're convincing us," Rayann said dryly.

"Let me get a tissue," Ann said. She returned quickly, regaining some of her composure. "Well, I don't suppose we could start this conversation over."

"Fine by me," Louisa said. She looked at Rayann, eyes pleading.

Let the past go. Rayann managed a smile. "Mom, Louisa and I are lovers."

"How wonderful for you both." The doorbell rang, startling all of them. Ann said, "Who could — oh, I'll bet that's Jim. I told him to drop by if he was free and maybe he'd get a chance to meet you." She hurried away, obviously relieved.

Rayann was starting to feel shell-shocked. And what was she supposed to do? Like him and accept him without question, while her mother had had to get used to Rayann's relationship with Louisa. It was not fair.

A silver-haired man strode directly toward Rayann. He was a few inches taller, with a close-cropped silver beard. "You must be Rayann. I'm glad we've met at last." After a firm handshake, he turned with a questioning look to Louisa.

Before Rayann could say anything, her mother said, "Jim Dove, this is Louisa Thatcher, Rayann's lover."

Rayann waited for Jim to freeze up, but he didn't. "Oh wonderful, I'm glad I'm meeting you, too. Ann, I could have sworn you told me your daughter was currently single." He shook Louisa's hand, and they murmured "Pleased to meet you" at each other.

"I thought so until tonight." Ann put her hand on Jim's arm. "I'm not sure you'd be proud of the way I reacted." She turned to Louisa and Rayann. "Jim leads a support group for parents of˙gay and lesbian children. That's where we met." She smiled fondly at him, with a dash of pride. "In his spare time he's a municipal court judge."

Louisa gave a surprised gasp. Jim Dove heard it and smiled at her. "I know it's a shock. There aren't too many of us who openly support lesbian and gay rights — about two in twenty." Despite not wanting to, Rayann found him charming. He went on, "But San Francisco is really opening up now, with our lesbian supervisors, a fellow member of the robes, and domestic partners legislation."

"I'd be pleased if Oakland could move in that direction," Louisa said.

"I don't want to sound like an incredible liberal," he continued, "because it's actually simple expediency. Like Harry Truman, I know I'm going to be a father all my life and my son is gay."

The four of them sat down. Jim went to the kitchen to get himself dessert and Rayann recognized that he knew his way around. Unable to help herself, Rayann leaned over to her mother. "Okay, he's wonderful."

"I knew you'd like him," Ann said. "Now I really feel ashamed of myself. I can't believe I thought I had the right to approve or disapprove of you. I'm sorry."

"Forget it, Ann." Louisa poured herself more coffee and then filled the cup Jim brought to the table. "As a mother, I understand how you feel. Mother to mother, I'll never hurt your daughter."

Ann and Louisa looked at one another, then Ann nodded slightly. She smiled at Jim as he slid into the chair next to her.

"Well," Louisa said. "I hope what I have to do next turns out even half as well." She sipped her coffee with an air of resolve, but Rayann saw a tiny tremor in her fingers.

"What?" Rayann didn't know what Louisa meant.

"Teddy," she said. Louisa turned to Ann and Jim. "My son. We've never talked about my . . . sexuality and until a few days ago I didn't think I'd ever have a reason to force the issue." Her brown eyes swept over Rayann. "Now I have every reason in the world."

Rayann's skin prickled under Louisa's gaze. The earlier passion of the evening, which had died down, flared again, snapping and popping through her nerves. She hoped it didn't show in her face. There were some things her mother didn't need to know. She bit her lower lip. "You don't have to — not for me."

"For myself." Louisa looked at Ann and Jim. "Until tonight I thought compromising and accepting conditions was the only way to get by. I expected your initial reaction, Ann. I was ready to discuss the terms by which you would allow me to go on loving your daughter." She stopped, took a deep breath, then continued, "God, it's how I got along in the world because I was the queer one."

"I can't stop you from loving my daughter," Ann said. "I'm slowly accepting the fact that if I tried, I'd lose her. In a second. And you — I'd lose my new friend."

"Why do you think your son won't accept this new love in your life?" Jim looked at Louisa intently. "Doesn't he want your happiness?"

"I think he wants me to stay his mother forever. Always there in the same way."

"Well, he'll just have to get used to it like the rest of us," Ann said with asperity. "If I can, anyone can. Didn't you say he has a child?"

Louisa nodded. "A ten-year-old boy."

Ann grinned. "Well, if he'll just do the sensible thing I'll have a grandchild and my life will be complete. If my family keeps expanding like this I might just fill this mausoleum of a dining room on some Thanksgiving in the future."

Louisa smiled uncertainly. "I wish I had your optimism."

Rayann was in a daze as they all said goodbye. Her mother and Louisa had another concert planned. *I'm double-dating with my mother.* She wanted to tell Louisa how weird she felt. She wanted to be sure Louisa understood that Rayann did not enter their relationship lightly. But when they arrived home, Louisa unraveled her again with a small glance, a mere touch of her hand.

Much later, Rayann reached for Louisa, her limbs liquid with satisfaction. Her body was replete but she was filled with an urgent lover's desire to satisfy Louisa as well. "Won't you let me do something for you?" She nuzzled Louisa's chin.

"You're awfully sleepy."

"Isn't there anything you'd like?" Her hands drifted over Louisa's body.

Louisa pulled Rayann against her. "Go to sleep, baby."

"I'm not a baby," Rayann mumbled. The pillow of Louisa's breast was inviting. "If you'd just leave me a little strength." Louisa's laugh was quiet and filled with satisfaction. The music of it filled Rayann's ears as she dozed off.

"Well, I was just wondering if you'd be stopping by sometime this week." Louisa looked up at Rayann while she talked to her son. "I do need to talk to you about something the next time I see you. No, it can wait until then."

Rayann had watched Louisa's hope and resolve wax and wane over the last few days, building to this phone call, but she kept her thoughts to herself. She could help Louisa in only one way — by making no demands, and accepting everything at the pace Louisa could give it. She kept a handle on her patience but was frustrated in her attempts to establish anything like equality in bed. They balanced each other so well while they worked — why couldn't it be that easy in bed?

"You'll have to ask her that yourself." Louisa's voice was suddenly strained and high. "Give me a call when you're going to drop by."

"What was that all about?" Rayann asked after Louisa hung up the phone.

"He wants to know if you might be over your bad love affair — I had told him that much after I first met you — to consider going out. With him."

Rayann's heart gave a painful thud. "No. You're joking."

"Would I joke about something like that?" Louisa's eyes were wide. "I knew he liked you, that's what's been giving me hope."

"Louisa, this is getting too . . . too Greek for me. I have no intention of having a date or anything else with your son unless I'm sitting by your side."

"I know." Louisa reached for her address book and then dialed a number. The chimes sounded downstairs and as Rayann went down to help the customer she heard Louisa say, "Ann? Do you have a few minutes?"

Rayann handed the bag to the customer. "Thank you for stopping by," she said sweetly. The customer left and Rayann slammed the register shut and stomped over to the box of books that had been delivered that morning. She viciously sliced it open with the packing knife. *She won't tell me about it. She won't ask me for advice. But she'll call my mother up. Ask anybody but me. Don't push, I told myself. And what did it get me?* Anger helped her shelve the books in record time. She stabbed the box corners until they were flat, then took the box out the back door, threw up the garage door and heaved the box in. She let the garage door slam shut again. For good measure she slammed the back door after her. *I've had it being supportive. It's got me nothing.*

"What on earth is going on?" Louisa appeared from the stairwell.

"Nothing," Rayann said sweetly.

Greta and Hazel Schoernsson came in to top off their evening walk, distracting Louisa. Rayann continued her work with a little too much vigor, causing the three other women to look at her several times. Each time Rayann responded with an angelic smile. When Greta and Hazel left, Rayann avoided Louisa by running upstairs, but Louisa followed her.

"Are you going to tell me what's wrong?"

"Nothing is wrong," Rayann answered, her tone honeyed.

"I can tell you're upset." Louisa's tone was scolding, but still indulgent.

"It's just a child's tantrum," Rayann said in the same sweet voice. "Why don't you just leave me to kick my heels on the ground. Or send me to bed without my supper."

"If taking you to bed will help," Louisa began.

Rayann clapped her hands over her ears. "Don't. It won't work. We can't settle anything there."

"Ray," Louisa said, her voice filled with bemused

198

tolerance, "I don't understand. I thought everything was fine. Tell me what's wrong."

"Why should I? You don't tell me anything. You'd rather tell anyone but me."

"Oh, baby, it's that —"

"I'm *not* a baby," Rayann yelled. "I'm almost thirty. I've been around. I smoked pot in college, you know." She was so furious she hiccupped.

Louisa laughed. It didn't matter that it was a gentle laugh of bewilderment — it was the last straw. Rayann burst into tears.

"You don't need me," she said through her tears, fending off Louisa's comforting arms. "I'm just a built-in toaster to you."

In the last light of the setting sun Rayann saw Louisa bite her lower lip. Then Louisa said in a shaky voice that sounded too much like laughter and not enough like apology, "Darling, you are not a household appliance. I'm very sorry if I've treated you like one."

"I may as well be one for all the use I am to you." Rayann's tears slowed. She sniffed. "Oh, God. I *am* behaving like a child. No wonder you treat me like one."

"Have I been doing that?" Louisa's laughter was gone. "I really am sorry, darling. I'm not used to you. I'm not used to having you there for me. I don't mean to shut you out, but I don't want to burden you with my problems. Some of them are older than you are."

"If we can't share our problems, what can we share?" Rayann hiccupped again. *Great, now I sound like I need to be burped.* She found a tissue and blew her nose.

"It's my . . . instinct to want to protect you, Ray. You're young and free. I don't want to hold you down."

"I'm not a child and I'm not free," Rayann answered. "Can't you be a little bit selfish for once — burden me, make demands on me. I'm supposed to be your lover."

"It's not easy for me." Louisa bit her lower lip again, but this time there was no laughter.

"You have my heart and just about every inch of my body." Rayann smiled slightly. "I think the little toe on my left foot is the only part of me you haven't left an indelible impression on."

"I'll have to take care of that," Louisa said. "If it's any comfort I was never able to share my problems with Chris, either. With Danny, but never Chris."

Rayann snapped, "I won't be an emotional femme for you."

Louisa's eyes widened and her expression hardened slightly. "Chris was not a femme. You aren't either."

"But you treat me like one."

"You don't know what you're talking about. If you were my femme I wouldn't have let you build shelves, or —"

"I'm talking about in bed. You won't let me touch you."

"Ray, it's not that I don't want you to."

"Then what?" Rayann felt a wave of relief. *At least she wants me.*

"I . . . you can't teach an old dog —"

"Will you *stop* calling yourself old! You're doing it deliberately."

"Because you seem to forget."

"I don't. I just know that you're the woman I love. With the body I'd love to pleasure and taste if only you'd let me."

"I'm afraid I'll disappoint you. I'm not up on the latest dance steps. There, satisfied?" Louisa turned her back.

Rayann went to her, putting her arms around Louisa from behind. She whispered in her ear, "My darling, have you noticed me complaining in any way? The female body is just the same as it was four thousand years ago. Maybe we know a little more about why it feels good, but it doesn't change the fact that lips and tongues and fingers combined with mouths and breasts and . . . you know." Rayann was suddenly shy and glad Louisa was not looking at her. She swallowed. "It feels good. Some things more than others. Teach me what feels good to you."

Louisa turned in Rayann's arms. "You are amazing, quite beyond your years. I think in the deep recesses of my mind I thought if I got on my back for you you'd suddenly appear with electrical devices, latex and —"

"Whips and chains, and so on?" Rayann laughed, hugging her. "Not all us young folk are into that scene, *Macho Sluts* to the contrary — but who knows what people do in private — no two lesbians are alike. Except of course that we're the newest development on the evolutionary ladder."

"Wise child," Louisa said. She kissed Rayann on the nose.

Rayann lowered her head. "And you don't have to . . . get on your back, so to speak. Just let me have a little control. Let me touch you. Let me taste you." She was encouraged by Louisa's shudder.

"Chris didn't, she —"

Rayann kissed Louisa swiftly. "You get to start over with me."

They rocked in each other's arms, slowly swaying to music from the radio downstairs.

"Who's going to go close up?" Louisa's voice was distant and dreamy.

"It's not quite time," Rayann said. "I'll go." Rayann floated downstairs and impatiently waited for closing time. *Thank goodness it was a quiet night.* At five minutes to the hour the chimes rang. *Figures.* Rayann's heart leapt into her throat as Ted smiled congenially at her. *You were supposed to call!*

"How's business?"

"Business is fine. I . . . need to make a phone call, excuse me." She hurried to the stairs. "Louisa," she called. "Ted's here." The sudden creak of the floor and where it came from told her Louisa had been waiting for her in bed.

"I'm sure she'll be right down," Rayann said. She was in a bind. If she talked to him he might ask her out; if she didn't talk to him he might go upstairs and discover Louisa dressing. "I'll just make that phone call." She dialed their bank's teleservicing line and started writing down anything the computer told her, the balance, the checks that had cleared recently, the most recent deposits.

201

By the time she had exhausted her options Louisa appeared at the door to the stairs.

"Hi, son," she said. She kissed him as she usually did. "Want some coffee?"

He glanced over at Rayann who was in the middle of asking the operator if she could get a copy of a canceled check.

"Ray will be up in just a second. Won't you?" Louisa looked at her for agreement. Rayann nodded.

She emerged at the top of the stairs as Teddy was saying, "Mom, you sound so serious. Is something wrong?"

"No, I just need to tell you a story. You too, Ray. You haven't heard this one."

Rayann selected Louisa's easy chair while Louisa paced in front of them. Teddy leaned back on the sofa, watching his mother intently.

"You have to promise to hear me out, Ted. Promise me."

"Of course."

"When I was growing up there were three kinds of acceptable women. Young girls not yet married, married women or widows. Remember that because it makes some of what I've done with my life make sense. I didn't have any other choices in a tiny place like Merced. I didn't know there were any other choices. All I knew was that I looked awful in pencil skirts and my shoulders were too broad for the sleeveless tops that were supposed to make me ultra-feminine." She smiled wryly. "I once had the bright idea of using my height and black hair to imitate Leslie Caron, but when I cut my hair short it frizzed. All the Dippity-Dew in the world wouldn't make it into the 'shining black cap' they described in the fashion magazine. I never fit in. I thought it was the way I looked, but it was something inside me, something different."

She was silent for a moment or two. With a puzzled sigh she shook her head and went on. "Out with it. I thought I was the only girl ever born who didn't like boys. I didn't even know the word *lesbian* existed." She stopped when Teddy suddenly sat forward.

"Mom, why are you doing this?"

"You promised you would hear me out."

He sat back, but not before he looked at Rayann. She stared back at him and his eyes suddenly narrowed. She gave the merest nod of the head, a slight lift of one eyebrow. *Yes, I'm one too.* His jaw tightened.

"I once kissed a classmate. I told her I loved her. I look back on it and I realize how frightened she must have been. Though she'd kissed me back, she told me I was a queer and she'd just been finding out how far I'd go. I didn't kiss another girl for years. That's what fear does to you. Her rumors, coupled with the fact that I didn't date, made every girl who tried to befriend me decide I was definitely one of *those* women nobody talked about but everybody knew existed. The other kind of woman. At least I knew I wasn't the only one anymore."

"I remember when that horrible lonely feeling went away," Rayann said quietly. Teddy glared at her.

"They were incredibly powerful sights to me. I would see butches and femmes walking together, and they frightened me because I was afraid someone would look at them, then at me, and know I was one, too. And during the seventies I kind of went along with the sentiment that there was something regressive about butch and femme relationships and I tried to unlearn what I'd learned in the bars and with Chris. I feel so different now, looking back — they were *there.* They were the ones who were getting beat up and arrested and the rest of us got a little freedom for what it cost them," Louisa said passionately. She took two quick breaths and rushed on, "I never had the guts for it. That's why I got married, an act of non-defiance, complete compliance. That's how you came to be, Teddy."

"Don't do this." Rayann could see that he was embarrassed and angry. *But he loves her too, or he wouldn't still be sitting here.*

"I have to. This is my life I'm giving you, the life you guess at, but never wanted to recognize. I still remember why I did everything, as if it were a movie I'd seen hundreds of times. This was the moment my life changed irrevocably — every detail is clear. Christmas vacation.

The street lights had been wrapped like candy canes by the Jaycees. I was shopping for something to wear for Christmas at my mother's. I went into a dressing room to try on a blue sweater with a large rose applique. "Silver Bells" was playing in the background. I heard voices in the room next to mine. I recognized the voice — it was the girl I had kissed, the one who had spread rumors about me. I blamed her for the fact that I was so unhappy, so I justified spying on her, just to get even. She and another girl were kissing, that was all. They were completely dressed, not even really touching." Tears gleamed in Louisa's eyes. "Just like when she had kissed me."

"You were hurt, and it was a long time ago," Rayann said soothingly.

"I felt so betrayed. I got dressed and waited for her outside the shop. When she left the store with the other girl, I asked her if I could talk to her. Being seen with me put her on the spot, but I really begged. I told her I'd seen her in the dressing room and all I wanted to know was if she still thought it was wrong. I must have frightened her to death. She said everyone knew I was queer, and if I didn't get married right away and leave her alone forever she was going to tell my mother everything."

Rayann said, "I was so frightened my mother would find out, I didn't tell her for years. I wasted time — she knew all along, and you've seen how she's starting to get over her homophobia." She used the word deliberately, with a glance at Teddy. He was staring at her as if she were a sub-creature. *He blames me for this.*

"Rayann has nothing to do with my past," Louisa said quietly. "But she has everything to do with my future."

Teddy swallowed and looked back at his mother. "So how *did* you get married?"

"Much the same way I told you. I just left out the beginning. I was crazy with fear. My mother wasn't very healthy, and I thought finding out would kill her. I thought maybe I could be arrested. I decided I needed to prove I was a normal woman so that if my friend did talk, no one would believe her. I went in and bought the sweater. Then I got in my car, put on some lipstick, Ravishing Red, and drove to a dance joint where G.I.'s hung out. I loosed my distributor cap and waited until one came along and offered to help. He wasn't married, didn't have any family. He had a two-week furlough and then he was being shipped to Korea. He said he could get killed, and he'd always wanted to get married so he could have someone to write to. So he put the distributor cap back on, then we drove over to Nevada and got married. I now had proof I was a normal woman. I called my mother the next day and she was happy, relieved I think. Like I said, she wasn't well. I was something she didn't have to worry about anymore."

"That doesn't explain how I came into being, not if you don't like men."

Louisa's tone hardened. "If you had ever bothered to notice, you'd see that women have always done things they do not like in order to survive. It's the ongoing story of one half of the species." Her voice softened again. "Your father wasn't any more experienced than I was. He was kind. After two weeks he went back to the army and never came home from Korea. He did write once or twice, then he was killed. You have his purple heart, Teddy. That's really the only trace he left. But I had you. You were all mine and adorable. As a war widow I was perfectly respectable, and I could work because I had a mouth to feed and my sainted husband had been tragically killed in action. I wasn't soft and feminine, but I'd been married, so there was just no way anyone would think I was a lesbian. So I worked and raised you, and I was as happy as I thought I deserved to be. And then Christina came into our lives."

Rayann saw Teddy's hand clenching on his knee. "I don't want to talk about her."

"She was your other mother for most of your life. I still feel a hole in me because she's not there." Louisa glanced at Rayann with a smile. "A hole you're beginning to fill, darling."

Teddy stood up. "Are you through?"

"No," Louisa said. "Sit down. You promised."

He hesitated, then finally sat again, staring at the floor. Rayann sensed his barely controlled anger.

"Teddy, for so many years I wanted to talk to you about it, but I never did. I want you to be happy that I've found someone who loves me."

"Happy? You're my *mother*. You're not supposed to be —"

"A lesbian? Sexually active?" Louisa's voice dropped to a whisper. "I'm both."

"Then why didn't you tell me before?"

"Because no one ever knew what Ward Cleaver did for a living," Louisa said vehemently. "He was a *man* and his identity was still completely secondary to the identity of the children. One mistake with your psyche and you could have become Jack the Ripper. I was convinced of it because every woman's magazine told me it was true. I was used to accepting things the way they had to be — you see, I was a queer and queers had to accept their lot in life. We told each other that all the time. I went on believing it, until Rayann taught me it wasn't true." Louisa's voice caught. Rayann sensed the shudder that swept through her body.

Teddy folded his arms across his chest as if to shield himself. He suddenly got up and began pacing.

"Teddy, are you upset because I'm sleeping with somebody, because I'm sleeping with another woman, or because I'm sleeping with Rayann?"

"I don't know," he said in a low voice, intense with emotion.

"Louisa, I don't think I should be here now," Rayann said.

"I agree," Teddy muttered. "Well, what do you have to say for yourself?" he asked Rayann angrily. "Weren't there lots of women to choose from in San Francisco? Why do you have to screw *my* mother?"

"Teddy!" Louisa gasped.

Rayann stood up with all the control she could muster. "I don't *screw* anybody," she said intensely.

"Maybe that's how you make love, but not me. How can you think that of your mother — that all she wants is a good lay?"

"I don't know what she wants or what you've convinced her she wants."

"Teddy! Rayann! Please stop," Louisa said.

Rayann took several deep breaths and turned away from Teddy. "I love Louisa," she said slowly, carefully. "She is the best thing that ever happened to me."

"A couple of months and you can tell?"

"Yes, I can tell. My life is never going to be the same." Rayann couldn't keep her voice from creeping upward. She dropped her voice back to an intense whisper and faced him again. "You can't change the way I feel, and you can't change the way Louisa feels. If you don't like to think of us loving each other, then don't think about it. But it's real. Ignoring it won't make it go away."

"This has nothing to do with Rayann," Louisa said. "I'm a lesbian. That's what you have to accept."

He stared at Louisa for a few moments, then turned away. "I'm not thinking this through," he said, scooping up his coat. He crossed the living room and back porch before Rayann started moving.

She ran down the stairs, catching him when he was opening his car door. "How can you do this to her? Don't you see how much she loves you? She's done just about everything for you."

"I can't see anything," he said, turning back so quickly to face her that Rayann recoiled. "Except everything was fine until you showed up."

"From your point of view. She could never introduce you to her friends, or carry certain kinds of books in her store — all to protect your precious picture of her. And this isn't about me, it's about you and your mother." Wind whipped her hair into her face and she brushed it aside angrily. "You don't have to like me. But go back to her now. Please."

"I can't."

Rayann let her anger take over. "You . . . phony bastard. All your liberal posturing is just a lie — you're a bigot."

"That's not true . . ." He looked at her for a long moment, then his face twisted and he turned away. He stared for a moment or two through the darkness to where Louisa stood at the bottom of the stairs. Then he got into the car and drove away.

11

Heart Wood

Rayann overslept. They had both had a terrible time falling asleep — Rayann wasn't sure Louisa had slept at all. Her pillow hadn't been pulled and poked into the shape of a horseshoe as it usually was by the time morning arrived. One glance at the clock sent Rayann scurrying to the bathroom.

In a record fifteen minutes she was downstairs, and her panic eased when she saw Louisa was on the phone and several customers were milling around as usual. *Life does, after all, go on.* Rayann remembered how she had felt when she had walked in on Michelle — firm ground dissolving under her feet. She knew Louisa must be feeling that way though Louisa hadn't said anything beyond, "Good for you," after Rayann confessed she'd called her son a phony bastard. Louisa's face had closed up, eyes shuttered and distant. Rayann had decided it was best to leave her alone for the moment. *I'll just be here when she needs me.*

"Good morning," Louisa said. She looked up from a page of notes, adorned by arrows, dollar amounts and dates. Rayann saw the brown eyes were as intense as ever but it would have taken a bucketful of Murine to get the red out of them. Nevertheless, Louisa's gaze brushed Rayann with warmth as she said, "I have a project for you."

"Goody, I was getting lazy. What is it?" Rayann was relieved. Life was apparently moving forward with direction. She tried to send a similarly warm message back. *I'm here for you.*

"I want you to build as many shelves as humanly possible in the storeroom, floor to ceiling and some up the middle — leave room for bodies to move around. How long would it take you?"

Rayann was a little startled. Louisa was usually not so succinct with her instructions. *She's usually only this way in bed.* "Maybe two weeks if I worked on it exclusively. The lacquer takes the longest." *How she — we are in bed has nothing to do with how we are down here.*

"Perfect. What about relocating the cash register and moving those tables —" she waved a hand, "over here so the door to the storeroom won't be obstructed."

"A day or two."

"Good. The first boxes will start arriving in maybe four weeks, but it'll be six to eight weeks for most of them. Everything has to be finished by the third week in June. We've only got about ten weeks."

"Okay." Rayann looked around, then back at Louisa. "I'm a little confused."

"I've been busy this morning. Walk this way," Louisa

said. Her smile was almost natural, but the lines of her face were cut deep with stress — and pain.

"If I could walk that way, I wouldn't need the talcum powder," Rayann whispered at her, aware of the customers.

Louisa laughed and held back the curtain to the empty storeroom. Newspaper had been spread out to approximate where shelves would be. Rayann saw immediately that Louisa had already planned out the best use of space — it would be full but not too cramped.

Louisa walked to one wall and spread her arms in front of it. "Women's studies, sociology and herstory." She walked to the opposite wall, spreading her arms again. "Health, psychology, child rearing, parapsychology, spirituality." Then she went to the third wall, the one directly opposite the doorway. She rested her hands on it. "My favorite wall. Fiction for lesbians."

Rayann reached up and pushed her jaw shut when it wouldn't close by itself.

"And these," Louisa said, turning and indicating the shelves that would be in the middle of the room, "are for magazines and journals, with display cases on top for consignments from local women artists — one in particular whom I happen to know rather well." Louisa raised her eyebrows suggestively at Rayann. "I don't want them any more than four feet tall — I want everyone to be able to see everything that's here for them. I don't want that wall —" she pointed at the wall for fiction for lesbians, "to be hidden in any way. No more hiding. I've paid my price."

Rayann was swallowing rapidly, forcing back the welling tears so she could engrave the image she wanted to keep for the rest of her life — the image of a free woman. "I'll get started right away," she said, trying to keep her voice level. "What about the regular customers?"

"If they can't accept something bigger in their life then screw 'em. I don't want to alienate them, I don't want them to feel as if they've lost anything, but they'll know there is another world in here if they want to enter

211

it. Besides, I have a marketing director extraordinaire on my staff who will probably find the right pitch to make everyone feel served."

"You said we'd have to be done the last week in June." Rayann looked into her lover's face, drawing on the strength.

"Specifically, the second to last weekend in June." Louisa laughed when Rayann shook her head, not understanding. "Some lesbian you are if you don't know. It's a natural for marketing the expansion."

Rayann grinned as she realized the significance of the date. "The Lesbian and Gay Pride Parade. We'd have to open the day before."

"Of course."

"And get the word out that we're here."

"Of course."

"I want to call it The Woman's Reader," Rayann said. She stopped. "But it's your bookstore, your choice."

"Not anymore," Louisa said. "It's finally getting bigger than me. And the Rubicon is finally behind me."

"This doorway is not big enough," Rayann muttered. She had yet again smacked an armload of cut planks into the frame, bruising herself — yet again. The "Pardon Our Dust — The Woman's Reader will be open soon" sign fell down, again.

"You're trying to move too fast," Louisa said.

Rayann dropped the load with a clatter. "Well, that's the last of shelf wood."

"Good," Louisa said. She suddenly smiled brilliantly. "I'm going out to dinner with my son, sweetie. You don't mind eating alone tonight, do you?"

"He called?"

"He had to. I wasn't going to call him. I thought he'd hold out longer than this, though."

"He misses you, I'm sure," Rayann said. "Of course I don't mind eating alone. I hope everything goes . . . the way you want it to." Last night she had caught Louisa

212

staring wistfully at the last school picture of Tucker. She could sense the empty space in Louisa but she had no way of filling it.

The bookstore seemed particularly empty after Louisa left, but Greta and Hazel stopped in. Rayann was glad they were alone. She told them about her new relationship with Louisa and after accepting their congratulations, she showed them the plans for the expansion.

"I may not be reading espionage novels for quite a while," Hazel said. She was perusing one of the order lists with promising titles such as *The Love of Good Women* and *On Strike Against God: A Lesbian Love Story.* "I'm going to be very busy."

"I didn't realize," Greta said with a pleased smile. "There are so many books."

"I used to feel that way," Rayann said with a laugh. "But now I feel there just aren't enough. Of course after I shelve all these books I'll probably think there are too many."

"This is very exciting," Hazel said in a matter-of-fact voice. "I would be delighted to help in any way I can."

"It would give us both something to do — if there's any little thing," Greta said.

"Thank you both." Rayann was touched. She impulsively hugged Greta, but knew better than to hug Hazel. "Louisa and I will keep it in mind, you can be sure. Of course I'll have to tell her about the two of you."

"Of course, of course," Hazel said. Her hungry gaze rested on the book list again.

The store was even quieter after the two older women left. When Louisa came in Rayann said, "Hello, you gorgeous thing you," from her comfortable perch on Louisa's high stool. In lieu of dinner, she was redrawing her brochure layout for the battered women's shelter so she could show it to the director in the morning.

"Hello yourself. I take it there's no one here."

"No one but us chickens."

"Good." Louisa took a deep breath, put her hands on either side of her head — as if to hold it on — and then let loose a screaming groan of chagrin, anger and despair. "How could I have raised such a devious, stubborn *worthless* child!" She gave another groan, dropped her arms on the counter and banged her forehead once on her arms.

"I take it things didn't go well," Rayann said tentatively. She could see Louisa was angry, but her sense of humor appeared to be intact.

"I thought everything was peachy. We went to a nice restaurant and talked generally through dinner, like we always did. Then he says he thinks we should do it more often. I got the idea he thought we should do it instead of the way we used to see each other — here. And there was no mention of my grandson."

"And?"

"I asked him if he ever planned to set foot in my house again or did he think we could have a meaningful mother-and-son relationship in restaurants. Do you know what he had the *nerve* to say — I know how Lear felt! He said he hasn't made up his mind. *He* would decide if I could see him again, apparently forgetting that I was in complete control of whether he ever saw *me* again. I walked out and took a cab home. I'm still speechless."

"Not exactly speechless," Rayann said with a gentle smile.

"I'm so angry at him, but — I don't feel as if I've had an amputation anymore. I just feel sad it has to be this way. I spent thirty years telling myself I didn't have a right to my feelings and that his were more important, more valid. Now that I've seen what a crock that is," Louisa looked fiercely into Rayann's eyes, "I won't get trapped again. He has to understand that I can live without him. I can get by without seeing my grandson, though it will hurt. Whether *he* can live without *me* is what he has to decide — that is what he's choosing."

"Mom."

Rayann almost jumped out of her skin. Louisa whirled around to face Teddy. They had been so intent they hadn't heard the quietly opening door.

214

"Unless you have an acceptable counteroffer, counselor, there's no point in discussing anything." Rayann cringed at the cutting tone of Louisa's voice. She was glad Louisa's sarcasm was not directed at her.

"Can we go upstairs?"

"What's wrong with here?" Louisa stood her ground.

Ted bit his lower lip in a gesture that reminded Rayann of Louisa. "If I learned one thing from the very fine law school you worked so hard to put me through, it's that negotiations are better handled in private." He glanced at Rayann. "I don't mean to be rude to you, Rayann."

"I agree with you. This is private between you and Louisa," Rayann said. Louisa glanced at her, then nodded at Teddy, leading the way to the stairs.

"I will warn you that only a one hundred percent reversal of your current attitude is acceptable," Louisa said as they disappeared.

Rayann heard Teddy say, "That's my offer. I still have some reservations, but I can't live without you in my life, Mom, but . . ." His voice faded away, but Rayann had heard enough. Her anxiety faded into hope.

She finished the sketch of the brochure while trying to ignore the creak of the floorboards overhead — someone was doing a lot of pacing. For the brochure she had decided on the theme, "Because You Can," and shamelessly aimed the copy at people who liked to pat themselves on the back for helping the less fortunate. She thought it was effective and she hoped the shelter director agreed.

It was almost an hour and a half before Louisa came downstairs. She looked exhausted but her face was glowing. "Everything I said before, about the worthless child I raised, I take back most of it."

"It's going to be okay?"

"I think so. I asked him how he'd feel if I remarried and he admitted he'd probably feel some of the same sense of loss. It's been just him, Tucker and me for so long that this sudden development really threw him for a loss. He said he'd been thinking about dating you not because he had any particular romantic urges toward you, but because I liked you so much and Tucker seems to like you, too. He sensed that you would be a perfect addition to the family. I had to agree, of course."

"Does he forgive me for calling him a phony bastard?" Rayann put down her finished drawing and slid off the stool. She'd locked up and closed the blinds some time ago.

Louisa laughed — a clear, uninhibited laugh of joy. "He said it really shook him up and he started to question his liberal credentials. I told him perhaps he should get them renewed. But my walking out on him made him realize I had all the cards and he knows when he's beaten."

"So he basically gave in?" Rayann didn't like the sound of that.

"When he first got here that was how he put it — giving in. But I think he's ready to see this isn't a battle with me winning and him losing, not like a court case. He's ready, I think, to grow a little at a time and discover the new joy of a larger family. I expect him to keep making up conditions, but we'll work it out. I can't wait for him to meet Jim Dove. They probably already know each other, now that I think about it, but Teddy could use a role model."

"Louisa," Rayann said slowly, "not to change the subject, but before this all started, we had reached a new understanding about a certain something and the . . . the, well consummation, so to speak, of the new understanding, was rudely interrupted. I know you just needed me . . . to be there, and . . . but now that you can forget about Ted. Well . . . everything in bed has been great, you have been just incredible for me and . . . I'd still like to . . . you know . . . equalize things a little."

Louisa buried her hands in her hair, removing her

combs. "Darling, you've been wonderful. You can't understand how knowing I'm making you happy has given me strength."

"I do understand, a little."

With a deep, heartfelt sigh, Louisa shook the silver-black masses of her hair down her back and around her shoulders. "Right now I'm ready to try anything."

"Ooooh," Rayann said, keeping the moment light. Despite Louisa's apparent ease, she sensed that Louisa was a little nervous. "That is an offer I have no intention of refusing."

They ran upstairs and breathlessly collapsed on the bed. Louisa laughed then assumed a stiff, prone position. "Okay," she said. "I'm ready. You take over."

Rayann smiled and kissed Louisa, knowing that Louisa's laughter was a symptom of her vulnerability. "Darling, it isn't . . . I don't want to take over. I just want to reciprocate and share in lovemaking that pleases both of us." Rayann stood up and slowly removed her clothing, then returned to the bed, sliding herself along the length of Louisa's clothed body. "I like this," she whispered. "I like being naked first. I never thought blue jeans could be so erotic."

"Shall I take them off?"

"When you want to. When you can't stand having them on anymore," Rayann said. She moved on top of Louisa, seeking her mouth. Louisa's lips captured hers. "I have an idea," Rayann said, when she raised her head. "Let's try kissing with my lips on the outside."

"What?"

"Well," Rayann said, aware that Louisa was tensing again, "your lips are usually more on the outside, you know, like this." She demonstrated.

"It feels — right," Louisa said.

"I agree, but let's try it this way."

They pressed their lips together, Rayann consciously shaping her mouth in a new way. Two, three, four seconds passed and then she raised her head. They stared at each other for a few more seconds then burst out laughing.

"That was *so* strange," Rayann said. "I like your way much better."

The laughter relaxed Louisa again. "I like it, too. Kiss me again," she said.

Lips against lips, their mouths melted together. Rayann opened her mouth to Louisa's exploration, rolling her back so she was cradled in Louisa's arms. The knit of Louisa's polo shirt was soft against her breasts. The denim covering Louisa's legs brushed the inside of Rayann's knees.

Louisa raised her head at last, and Rayann looked dizzily up at her. "It isn't fair," Rayann whispered.

"What isn't?" Louisa's mouth found Rayann's breast, heat on cool skin.

Whatever Rayann was going to answer came out as a soft "ah" as Louisa traced a path with one lazy finger between Rayann's breasts, across the soft down of her stomach, then lower. Rayann closed her eyes, feeling the searing touch of Louisa's finger . . . lower. *Oh, don't tease.*

She didn't know when Louisa had taken her clothes off, only recognized the velvet press of Louisa's body against her. Her hands found the alluring angles of Louisa's back, smoothing across and around. *This texture . . . like the ironwood, so warm and yielding but strong.*

She could picture the block finished now. *Louisa kneeling, resting back on her haunches. She is lifting her hair from her shoulders, pulling it above her head, arms at rest as she arches her neck . . .* "Louisa, oh . . ." Her hands explored everywhere, recording and learning again, engraving the memories deeper and deeper so they would come to her when she applied chisel and hammer to the block. *What do her breasts feel like . . . I have to touch them again.* Rayann rolled over and over, caressing the voluptuous flesh with her mouth and fingers. *She'll have to pose for me . . . too good.*

"Rayann, darling — whatever you want."

218

Louisa's hands were on her again, sweeping over her stomach and arms, then clutching her hands as Rayann knelt, her tongue brushing the length of Louisa's trembling thigh . . . from knee to hair line, gathering Louisa's hips in her arms.

Her mouth drank the desire she found, tongue sweeping through the tender flesh. *Too fast, too soon.* Louisa's legs were stiff, her body tense. Rayann lifted her head. *Slowly.* She kissed gently, then Louisa's hands were behind her head.

"Don't tease me," she pleaded.

Tears welled up in Rayann, mingling with the other wetness on her face. *Never, darling.* She knew her hands would ache tomorrow from Louisa's fierce hold of them, but she set that aside, channeling all her love to her lips and tongue, tasting each change in Louisa, interpreting every gasping shudder or moaning quiver into a response that gave more pleasure. She heard her name cried out in her lover's passion-charged voice — the sound mingled with the smell and the taste, mixing into the vivid moment of frozen tension before Louisa called to her again, in a softer, crooning tone. Rayann recognized the quality of Louisa's voice — it sounded like Rayann's so often sounded as she tried to catch her breath after Louisa had touched every nerve.

"Come hold me," Louisa said, her body slumping as she released Rayann's hands.

"You're so beautiful," Rayann whispered, rocking Louisa gently in her arms. "I hope you'll let me do that again sometime."

Louisa stirred, her voice groggy. "After that I'm willing to let you try anything."

Jubilation surged into Rayann's head, making her giddy and dizzy. "Anything. Hmm. I'm not afraid to make demands." She spread herself under Louisa's body, pulling Louisa's hips to her own.

"Which are?"

"Let's start over and do everything again."

* * * * *

"We're going to run out of paper bags," Louisa muttered anxiously as she peered under the counter at the dwindling supply.

"We'll just ask people if they have to have one, that's all. Just be sure they get a bookmark," Rayann said. "Will you be okay here?"

"Of course," Louisa answered. She turned to the next woman in the line waiting to pay for her books.

Rayann eased her way through the crush, stopping to say hello to women she knew, accepting Judy's exuberant congratulations and pointing out several books to Dedric when she asked for something "really hot."

She expected to be inundated with "do you have" and "where would I find" as she had the last time she had ventured into The Woman's Reader, but to her delight Hazel Schoernsson was fielding all questions, faultlessly pointing out the location of books, along with a general description of size and color that helped the customer find it. Hazel's cheeks were glowing as she gazed at all the young women milling around her.

Grinning, Rayann headed for the counter to help Louisa. She had never expected the bookstore to be wall-to-wall women — she had even thought that pre-Parade activities would keep women involved elsewhere throughout the area. For a Friday evening, it was a good crowd. She returned the smiles and nods of several women she recognized before delivering flyers announcing the "Just For You" addition to The Common Reader Bookstore.

As she gained the counter she realized Louisa didn't need her help. Greta Schoernsson was comfortably seated on Louisa's stool, stacking books and inserting bookmarks and making pleasant conversation with the women who were waiting patiently to check out.

Maybe it was the word sale *that did it*. Rayann noted that many of the women had taken advantage of the discounts on "all other books" they purchased with the purchase of two books from the new Woman's Reader.

"Rayann, dear, what on earth is going on?"

Rayann whirled around to her mother with a huge

smile. "Effective niche marketing, that's what." She hugged her mother and without hesitation hugged Jim Dove as well. "This is why we've been too busy to see you lately."

"It looks like Filene's Basement the day after Thanksgiving," Ann said.

"Isn't it great?" Rayann suddenly took in her mother's corsage and Jim's spiffy gray suit. "Why aren't you two still at work?"

"We took the afternoon off to go get our marriage license, and then thought we'd find out if you two could join us for dinner and champagne."

"Marriage license?" Rayann repeated.

Ann clapped her hand over her mouth. "I thought Louisa had told you!"

Louisa's voice sailed over the customers. "Ann, I thought *you* were going to tell her!"

"Oh, my God," Ann said. "Darling, how thoughtless of me."

"Mom," Rayann said, managing a stunned smile, "I'm pleased as punch, just surprised as all get out. Congratulations," she said to Jim. She hugged him again. "When's the happy day?"

"That's one of the things we wanted to discuss with you and Lou," Jim said, patting her back.

Rayann had barely regained her composure when she felt a tug on her arm. She looked down. Tucker was pulling on her sweater. "Rayann, you moved the Black Stallion books. Where are they?"

She looked up. Where Tucker went, Ted was sure to follow. She saw him before he saw her, his head a good six inches above that of the sea of women he was attempting to safely navigate. He looked very relieved when he saw a familiar face.

"I didn't realize there was some sort of party today," he said when he finally reached her.

"Grand opening of The Woman's Reader," Rayann told him. She knew Louisa had told him the plans and warned him that the word *lesbian* would be featured prominently in several places. Evidently, he gathered up enough nerve to visit. "We're taking advantage of Lesbian and Gay Pride week."

"Of course," he said, his voice neutral. "I should have known."

"Rayann," her mother said. She inclined her head at Ted with raised eyebrows.

"Oh, how rude of me. Ted Thatcher, this is my mother, Ann Germaine, and her fiancé, Jim Dove."

"I thought you looked familiar, sir," Ted said. "In fact, I think we've met —"

"At a Bar fundraiser," Jim said. "Please, don't call me 'sir.' Especially not when we're soon going to be related — although I'm still trying to figure out how my step-daughter-to-be's lover's son is related to me." He shuddered in mock horror. "I just came up with step-grandson and that's completely unacceptable. I'm too young."

"Hear, hear," Ann said. "Let's not bother with all that intermediate stuff. A member of the family is a member of the family."

Rayann led Tucker to the new location of children's books, mechanically pointing them out while her stunned brain absorbed what her mother had just said. *Family.* It was such an exclusive word in a legal sense but her mother and Jim had expanded and liberalized it to an extent Rayann hadn't even hoped possible. *Like Louisa did for so long, I just accepted that the word never applied to us.* She helped customers and watched the trio of her mother, Jim and Ted as they talked together. Louisa urged her son to play host and take them upstairs for coffee. If Louisa was as stunned as Rayann felt she didn't show it.

The store was finally quieting down an hour later. Many women were hurrying to get ready for the dances and celebrations that would be held all over the Bay Area to celebrate gay pride. Rayann walked Greta and Hazel to their door. They were both very happy, but exhausted.

Upstairs it was calmer and her mother stood at the

counter chatting with Louisa while Jim Dove and Ted were engrossed in conversation in the living room.

"Now, who forgot to tell me my mother was getting married?"

Ann immediately relented in her long-suffering pose. "Darling, I am sorry. I asked Louisa for some advice and just assumed she would tell you."

"I thought you would want to tell her yourself."

"Of course you did," Ann said. "It was stupid for me to have thought otherwise."

"Well, I didn't say it," Rayann commented to no one in particular. Her mother pursed her lips in response.

The conversation lulled, then Jim said, "Well, we wanted to compare calendars and find out when everyone has a week free."

"A week?" Louisa said.

"For a wedding?" Rayann looked at her mother.

"Not for a wedding, but for a family . . . celebration," Ann said. "Jim and I thought Greece would be nice and were hoping anyone who could would join us."

"My son and his lover are both free most of August," Jim said. "I went to law school with a fellow who's now a member of the Greek National Assembly and will loan us a villa in Athens —"

"On the water facing Corinth," Ann said. "It's huge and you wouldn't even have to know we're there." She glanced at Ted. "Think what a wonderful opportunity your son would have to see such a historic place." She turned to Louisa. "And a vacation — it's been just ages since you've had one. Air fare," she finished, looking at Rayann, "is our treat."

"But who would watch the store?" Louisa said.

"I can certainly afford air fare for Tucker and me," Ted began.

"Mom, you two are nuts," Rayann managed to say.

"We're in love," Jim said. "And all the sages and poets agree that love is carte blanche for odd behavior. Besides, we're both delighted to be able to share our happiness with a suddenly large and diverse family. Patrick — my

223

son — can't wait to meet you all. He said he's sick of being an only child."

"But who would watch the store?" Louisa had at first sounded as if no one minding the store would be her excuse to bow out gracefully, but now she sounded as if she really wanted to solve the problem.

"Darling," Rayann said, "this very day we'll put up a sign that says we're having reduced hours while we're gone. I'm sure that Greta and Hazel would love to watch the store during the peak hours. I think they'd be offended if we didn't ask."

Louisa looked at Ann with a relieved smile. "A week in August?"

"Or two if you can stand being away that long," Ann said.

Louisa reached for her calendar. Rayann handed her an indelible red marking pen.

"I believe I don't want this journey to end," Louisa said.

Rayann rested back in her lover's arms, aware that the other women in the tour group still stole glances at them occasionally.

She didn't blame them — after all, she and Louisa were newcomers to their tour, and only joining them for the next three days. And she and Louisa were the only ones whose entire family had seen them off at the dock in Athens.

"I still can't believe they all got up at the crack of dawn," Rayann said. "It's been a lovely day."

"I've got bird seed in my bra," Louisa said.

"At least I managed to pick all the confetti out of your hair."

"I don't know why I got the worst of it."

"Tucker was aiming for you." Louisa squeezed her for a moment, then they both relaxed into the rock of the

224

ferry. Her hair tickled Rayann's ear every time the warm Mediterranean breeze lifted it.

Never in a million years would I have thought I'd be so happy. Rayann closed her eyes to better sense the rhythm of the waves. Behind her lids she still saw the impromptu bon voyage party on the dock. Their decision to make this pilgrimage had been spur-of-the-moment. She could picture her mother and her new husband, and his son and son's lover laughing and throwing confetti while Ted took pictures as they boarded the gangplank. She wondered if Louisa had noticed that Ted, burdened with his cameras, had instead set Tucker on Patrick's shoulder so he could more easily see his grandmother. Patrick's new lover threw the last of the streamers. *What a picture — and it wasn't a dream!* Rayann had spent the first few hours of the ferry ride making sketches from memory. Louisa said she liked Rayann's sketches better than photographs.

The Greek sun was still hot when they disembarked at their destination almost twelve hours after first boarding the ferry. Rayann complained of her behind having gone to sleep. Louisa stretched to get a kink out of her back.

"This is one photograph we have to have," Rayann said, pulling Louisa into the line-up of women. One by one or couple by couple they posed in front of the sign welcoming visitors to the island. There was always a happy volunteer willing to take the picture.

Louisa handed over her camera. "Take an extra one just in case."

Rayann stood within the curve of Louisa's arm. She knew that many of the women were still figuratively rubbing their eyes every time they looked at Louisa and her together. The send-off at the dock had made it clear to all the other women that she and Louisa were lovers. Some had looked enviously at the well-wishing family, and some were unabashedly curious about the way she and Louisa related to each other. Others just looked mystified.

"Hey, cuddle closer," the photographer said. "You're covering up the L."

Rayann hugged Louisa to her. "Can't have that. Who wants a picture that says we went to ESBOS."

She heard the shutter click as Louisa's mouth claimed hers for a laughing kiss.

A few of the publications of
THE NAIAD PRESS, INC.
P.O. Box 10543 • Tallahassee, Florida 32302
Phone (904) 539-5965
Toll-Free Order Number: 1-800-533-1973
Mail orders welcome. Please include 15% postage.

NOT TELLING MOTHER: STORIES FROM A LIFE by Diane
Salvatore. 176 pp. Her 3rd novel.   ISBN 1-56280-044-2 $9.95

GOBLIN MARKET by Lauren Wright Douglas. 240pp. Fifth
Caitlin Reece Mystery.   ISBN 1-56280-047-7   9.95

LONG GOODBYES by Nikki Baker. 256 pp. A Virginia Kelly
mystery. 3rd in a series.   ISBN 1-56280-042-6   9.95

FRIENDS AND LOVERS by Jackie Calhoun. 224 pp. Mid-western
Lesbian lives and loves.   ISBN 1-56280-041-8   9.95

THE CAT CAME BACK by Hilary Mullins. 208 pp. Highly praised
Lesbian novel.   ISBN 1-56280-040-X   9.95

BEHIND CLOSED DOORS by Robbi Sommers. 192 pp. Hot, erotic
short stories.   ISBN 1-56280-039-6   9.95

CLAIRE OF THE MOON by Nicole Conn. 192 pp. See the movie —
read the book!   ISBN 1-56280-038-8   10.95

SILENT HEART by Claire McNab. 192 pp. Exotic Lesbian
romance.   ISBN 1-56280-036-1   9.95

HAPPY ENDINGS by Kate Brandt. 272 pp. Intimate conversations
with Lesbian authors.   ISBN 1-56280-050-7   10.95

THE SPY IN QUESTION by Amanda Kyle Williams. 256 pp. 4th
spy novel featuring Lesbian agent Madison McGuire.
  ISBN 1-56280-037-X   9.95

SAVING GRACE by Jennifer Fulton. 240 pp. Adventure and
romantic entanglement.   ISBN 1-56280-051-5   9.95

THE YEAR SEVEN by Molleen Zanger. 208 pp. Women surviving
in a new world.   ISBN 1-56280-034-5   9.95

CURIOUS WINE by Katherine V. Forrest. 176 pp. Tenth
Anniversary Edition. The most popular contemporary Lesbian
love story.   ISBN 1-56280-053-1   9.95

CHAUTAUQUA by Catherine Ennis. 192 pp. Exciting, romantic
adventure.   ISBN 1-56280-032-9   9.95

A PROPER BURIAL by Pat Welch. 192 pp. Third in the Helen
Black mystery series.   ISBN 1-56280-033-7   9.95

SILVERLAKE HEAT: A Novel of Suspense by Carol Schmidt.
240 pp. Rhonda is as hot as Laney's dreams. ISBN 1-56280-031-0   9.95

LOVE, ZENA BETH by Diane Salvatore. 224 pp. The most talked
about lesbian novel of the nineties! ISBN 1-56280-030-2   9.95

A DOORYARD FULL OF FLOWERS by Isabel Miller. 160 pp.
Stories incl. 2 sequels to *Patience and Sarah.* ISBN 1-56280-029-9   9.95

MURDER BY TRADITION by Katherine V. Forrest. 288 pp. A
Kate Delafield Mystery. 4th in a series. ISBN 1-56280-002-7   9.95

THE EROTIC NAIAD edited by Katherine V. Forrest & Barbara Grier.
224 pp. Love stories by Naiad Press authors. ISBN 1-56280-026-4   12.95

DEAD CERTAIN by Claire McNab. 224 pp. 5th Det. Insp. Carol
Ashton mystery. ISBN 1-56280-027-2   9.95

CRAZY FOR LOVING by Jaye Maiman. 320 pp. 2nd Robin
Miller mystery. ISBN 1-56280-025-6   9.95

STONEHURST by Barbara Johnson. 176 pp. Passionate regency
romance. ISBN 1-56280-024-8   9.95

INTRODUCING AMANDA VALENTINE by Rose Beecham.
256 pp. An Amanda Valentine Mystery — 1st in a series.
ISBN 1-56280-021-3   9.95

UNCERTAIN COMPANIONS by Robbi Sommers. 204 pp.
Steamy, erotic novel. ISBN 1-56280-017-5   9.95

A TIGER'S HEART by Lauren W. Douglas. 240 pp. Fourth Caitlin
Reece Mystery. ISBN 1-56280-018-3   9.95

PAPERBACK ROMANCE by Karin Kallmaker. 256 pp. A
delicious romance. ISBN 1-56280-019-1   9.95

MORTON RIVER VALLEY by Lee Lynch. 304 pp. Lee Lynch at
her best! ISBN 1-56280-016-7   9.95

THE LAVENDER HOUSE MURDER by Nikki Baker. 224 pp. A
Virginia Kelly Mystery. Second in a series. ISBN 1-56280-012-4   9.95

PASSION BAY by Jennifer Fulton. 224 pp. Passionate romance,
virgin beaches, tropical skies. ISBN 1-56280-028-0   9.95

STICKS AND STONES by Jackie Calhoun. 208 pp. Contemporary
lesbian lives and loves. ISBN 1-56280-020-5   9.95

DELIA IRONFOOT by Jeane Harris. 192 pp. Adventure for Delia
and Beth in the Utah mountains. ISBN 1-56280-014-0   9.95

UNDER THE SOUTHERN CROSS by Claire McNab. 192 pp.
Romantic nights Down Under. ISBN 1-56280-011-6   9.95

RIVERFINGER WOMEN by Elana Nachman/Dykewomon.
208 pp. Classic Lesbian/feminist novel. ISBN 1-56280-013-2   8.95

A CERTAIN DISCONTENT by Cleve Boutell. 240 pp. A unique
coterie of women. ISBN 1-56280-009-4   9.95

GRASSY FLATS by Penny Hayes. 256 pp. Lesbian romance in
the '30s.   ISBN 1-56280-010-8   9.95

A SINGULAR SPY by Amanda K. Williams. 192 pp. 3rd spy novel
featuring Lesbian agent Madison McGuire.   ISBN 1-56280-008-6   8.95

THE END OF APRIL by Penny Sumner. 240 pp. A Victoria Cross
Mystery. First in a series.   ISBN 1-56280-007-8   8.95

A FLIGHT OF ANGELS by Sarah Aldridge. 240 pp. Romance set at
the National Gallery of Art   ISBN 1-56280-001-9   9.95

HOUSTON TOWN by Deborah Powell. 208 pp. A Hollis Carpenter
mystery. Second in a series.   ISBN 1-56280-006-X   8.95

KISS AND TELL by Robbi Sommers. 192 pp. Scorching stories by
the author of *Pleasures*.   ISBN 1-56280-005-1   9.95

STILL WATERS by Pat Welch. 208 pp. Second in the Helen
Black mystery series.   ISBN 0-941483-97-5   9.95

MURDER IS GERMANE by Karen Saum. 224 pp. The 2nd
Brigid Donovan mystery.   ISBN 0-941483-98-3   8.95

TO LOVE AGAIN by Evelyn Kennedy. 208 pp. Wildly
romantic love story.   ISBN 0-941483-85-1   9.95

IN THE GAME by Nikki Baker. 192 pp. A Virginia Kelly
mystery. First in a series.   ISBN 01-56280-004-3   9.95

AVALON by Mary Jane Jones. 256 pp. A Lesbian Arthurian
romance.   ISBN 0-941483-96-7   9.95

STRANDED by Camarin Grae. 320 pp. Entertaining, riveting
adventure.   ISBN 0-941483-99-1   9.95

THE DAUGHTERS OF ARTEMIS by Lauren Wright Douglas.
240 pp. Third Caitlin Reece mystery.   ISBN 0-941483-95-9   9.95

CLEARWATER by Catherine Ennis. 176 pp. Romantic secrets
of a small Louisiana town.   ISBN 0-941483-65-7   8.95

THE HALLELUJAH MURDERS by Dorothy Tell. 176 pp.
Second Poppy Dillworth mystery.   ISBN 0-941483-88-6   8.95

ZETA BASE by Judith Alguire. 208 pp. Lesbian triangle
on a future Earth.   ISBN 0-941483-94-0   9.95

SECOND CHANCE by Jackie Calhoun. 256 pp. Contemporary
Lesbian lives and loves.   ISBN 0-941483-93-2   9.95

BENEDICTION by Diane Salvatore. 272 pp. Striking,
contemporary romantic novel.   ISBN 0-941483-90-8   9.95

CALLING RAIN by Karen Marie Christa Minns. 240 pp.
Spellbinding, erotic love story   ISBN 0-941483-87-8   9.95

BLACK IRIS by Jeane Harris. 192 pp. Caroline's hidden past . . .
                                            ISBN 0-941483-68-1   8.95

TOUCHWOOD by Karin Kallmaker. 240 pp. Loving, May/
December romance.   ISBN 0-941483-76-2   9.95

BAYOU CITY SECRETS by Deborah Powell. 224 pp. A Hollis
Carpenter mystery. First in a series.   ISBN 0-941483-91-6   9.95

COP OUT by Claire McNab. 208 pp. 4th Det. Insp. Carol Ashton
mystery.   ISBN 0-941483-84-3   9.95

LODESTAR by Phyllis Horn. 224 pp. Romantic, fast-moving
adventure.   ISBN 0-941483-83-5   8.95

THE BEVERLY MALIBU by Katherine V. Forrest. 288 pp. A
Kate Delafield Mystery. 3rd in a series.   ISBN 0-941483-48-7   9.95

THAT OLD STUDEBAKER by Lee Lynch. 272 pp. Andy's affair
with Regina and her attachment to her beloved car.
    ISBN 0-941483-82-7   9.95

PASSION'S LEGACY by Lori Paige. 224 pp. Sarah is swept into
the arms of Augusta Pym in this delightful historical romance.
    ISBN 0-941483-81-9   8.95

THE PROVIDENCE FILE by Amanda Kyle Williams. 256 pp.
Second espionage thriller featuring lesbian agent Madison McGuire
    ISBN 0-941483-92-4   8.95

I LEFT MY HEART by Jaye Maiman. 320 pp. A Robin Miller
Mystery. First in a series.   ISBN 0-941483-72-X   9.95

THE PRICE OF SALT by Patricia Highsmith (writing as Claire
Morgan). 288 pp. Classic lesbian novel, first issued in 1952 . . .
acknowledged by its author under her own, very famous, name.
    ISBN 1-56280-003-5   9.95

SIDE BY SIDE by Isabel Miller. 256 pp. From beloved author of
Patience and Sarah.   ISBN 0-941483-77-0   9.95

SOUTHBOUND by Sheila Ortiz Taylor. 240 pp. Hilarious sequel
to *Faultline.*   ISBN 0-941483-78-9   8.95

STAYING POWER: LONG TERM LESBIAN COUPLES
by Susan E. Johnson. 352 pp. Joys of coupledom.
    ISBN 0-941-483-75-4   12.95

SLICK by Camarin Grae. 304 pp. Exotic, erotic adventure.
    ISBN 0-941483-74-6   9.95

NINTH LIFE by Lauren Wright Douglas. 256 pp. A Caitlin
Reece mystery. 2nd in a series.   ISBN 0-941483-50-9   8.95

PLAYERS by Robbi Sommers. 192 pp. Sizzling, erotic novel.
    ISBN 0-941483-73-8   9.95

MURDER AT RED ROOK RANCH by Dorothy Tell. 224 pp.
First Poppy Dillworth adventure.   ISBN 0-941483-80-0   8.95

LESBIAN SURVIVAL MANUAL by Rhonda Dicksion.
112 pp. Cartoons!   ISBN 0-941483-71-1   8.95

A ROOM FULL OF WOMEN by Elisabeth Nonas. 256 pp.
Contemporary Lesbian lives.   ISBN 0-941483-69-X   9.95

MURDER IS RELATIVE by Karen Saum. 256 pp. The first
Brigid Donovan mystery.   ISBN 0-941483-70-3   8.95

PRIORITIES by Lynda Lyons 288 pp. Science fiction with
a twist.   ISBN 0-941483-66-5   8.95

THEME FOR DIVERSE INSTRUMENTS by Jane Rule. 208
pp. Powerful romantic lesbian stories. ISBN 0-941483-63-0   8.95

LESBIAN QUERIES by Hertz & Ertman. 112 pp. The questions
you were too embarrassed to ask.   ISBN 0-941483-67-3   8.95

CLUB 12 by Amanda Kyle Williams. 288 pp. Espionage thriller
featuring a lesbian agent!   ISBN 0-941483-64-9   8.95

DEATH DOWN UNDER by Claire McNab. 240 pp. 3rd Det.
Insp. Carol Ashton mystery.   ISBN 0-941483-39-8   9.95

MONTANA FEATHERS by Penny Hayes. 256 pp. Vivian and
Elizabeth find love in frontier Montana. ISBN 0-941483-61-4   8.95

CHESAPEAKE PROJECT by Phyllis Horn. 304 pp. Jessie &
Meredith in perilous adventure.   ISBN 0-941483-58-4   8.95

LIFESTYLES by Jackie Calhoun. 224 pp. Contemporary Lesbian
lives and loves.   ISBN 0-941483-57-6   9.95

VIRAGO by Karen Marie Christa Minns. 208 pp. Darsen has
chosen Ginny.   ISBN 0-941483-56-8   8.95

WILDERNESS TREK by Dorothy Tell. 192 pp. Six women on
vacation learning "new" skills.   ISBN 0-941483-60-6   8.95

MURDER BY THE BOOK by Pat Welch. 256 pp. A Helen
Black Mystery. First in a series.   ISBN 0-941483-59-2   9.95

BERRIGAN by Vicki P. McConnell. 176 pp. Youthful Lesbian —
romantic, idealistic Berrigan.   ISBN 0-941483-55-X   8.95

LESBIANS IN GERMANY by Lillian Faderman & B. Eriksson.
128 pp. Fiction, poetry, essays.   ISBN 0-941483-62-2   8.95

THERE'S SOMETHING I'VE BEEN MEANING TO TELL
YOU Ed. by Loralee MacPike. 288 pp. Gay men and lesbians
coming out to their children.   ISBN 0-941483-44-4   9.95

LIFTING BELLY by Gertrude Stein. Ed. by Rebecca Mark. 104
pp. Erotic poetry.   ISBN 0-941483-51-7   8.95

ROSE PENSKI by Roz Perry. 192 pp. Adult lovers in a long-term
relationship.   ISBN 0-941483-37-1   8.95

AFTER THE FIRE by Jane Rule. 256 pp. Warm, human novel
by this incomparable author.   ISBN 0-941483-45-2   8.95

SUE SLATE, PRIVATE EYE by Lee Lynch. 176 pp. The gay
folk of Peacock Alley are *all cats*.   ISBN 0-941483-52-5   8.95

CHRIS by Randy Salem. 224 pp. Golden oldie. Handsome Chris
and her adventures.   ISBN 0-941483-42-8   8.95

THREE WOMEN by March Hastings. 232 pp. Golden oldie. A
triangle among wealthy sophisticates.   ISBN 0-941483-43-6   8.95

RICE AND BEANS by Valeria Taylor. 232 pp. Love and
romance on poverty row.   ISBN 0-941483-41-X   8.95

PLEASURES by Robbi Sommers. 204 pp. Unprecedented
eroticism.   ISBN 0-941483-49-5   8.95

EDGEWISE by Camarin Grae. 372 pp. Spellbinding
adventure.   ISBN 0-941483-19-3   9.95

FATAL REUNION by Claire McNab. 224 pp. 2nd Det. Inspec.
Carol Ashton mystery.   ISBN 0-941483-40-1   8.95

KEEP TO ME STRANGER by Sarah Aldridge. 372 pp. Romance
set in a department store dynasty.   ISBN 0-941483-38-X   9.95

HEARTSCAPE by Sue Gambill. 204 pp. American lesbian in
Portugal.   ISBN 0-941483-33-9   8.95

IN THE BLOOD by Lauren Wright Douglas. 252 pp. Lesbian
science fiction adventure fantasy   ISBN 0-941483-22-3   8.95

THE BEE'S KISS by Shirley Verel. 216 pp. Delicate, delicious
romance.   ISBN 0-941483-36-3   8.95

RAGING MOTHER MOUNTAIN by Pat Emmerson. 264 pp.
Furosa Firechild's adventures in Wonderland.   ISBN 0-941483-35-5   8.95

IN EVERY PORT by Karin Kallmaker. 228 pp. Jessica's sexy,
adventuresome travels.   ISBN 0-941483-37-7   9.95

OF LOVE AND GLORY by Evelyn Kennedy. 192 pp. Exciting
WWII romance.   ISBN 0-941483-32-0   8.95

CLICKING STONES by Nancy Tyler Glenn. 288 pp. Love
transcending time.   ISBN 0-941483-31-2   9.95

SURVIVING SISTERS by Gail Pass. 252 pp. Powerful love
story.   ISBN 0-941483-16-9   8.95

SOUTH OF THE LINE by Catherine Ennis. 216 pp. Civil War
adventure.   ISBN 0-941483-29-0   8.95

WOMAN PLUS WOMAN by Dolores Klaich. 300 pp. Supurb
Lesbian overview.   ISBN 0-941483-28-2   9.95

SLOW DANCING AT MISS POLLY'S by Sheila Ortiz Taylor.
96 pp. Lesbian Poetry   ISBN 0-941483-30-4   7.95

DOUBLE DAUGHTER by Vicki P. McConnell. 216 pp. A Nyla
Wade Mystery, third in the series.   ISBN 0-941483-26-6   8.95

HEAVY GILT by Delores Klaich. 192 pp. Lesbian detective/
disappearing homophobes/upper class gay society.

                                               ISBN 0-941483-25-8   8.95

THE FINER GRAIN by Denise Ohio. 216 pp. Brilliant young
college lesbian novel.   ISBN 0-941483-11-8   8.95

THE AMAZON TRAIL by Lee Lynch. 216 pp. Life, travel & lore
of famous lesbian author.   ISBN 0-941483-27-4   8.95

HIGH CONTRAST by Jessie Lattimore. 264 pp. Women of the
Crystal Palace.   ISBN 0-941483-17-7   8.95

OCTOBER OBSESSION by Meredith More. Josie's rich, secret
Lesbian life.   ISBN 0-941483-18-5   8.95

LESBIAN CROSSROADS by Ruth Baetz. 276 pp. Contemporary
Lesbian lives.   ISBN 0-941483-21-5   9.95

WE WALK THE BACK OF THE TIGER by Patricia A. Murphy.
192 pp. Romantic Lesbian novel/beginning women's movement.
                                         ISBN 0-941483-13-4   8.95

SUNDAY'S CHILD by Joyce Bright. 216 pp. Lesbian athletics, at
last the novel about sports.   ISBN 0-941483-12-6   8.95

OSTEN'S BAY by Zenobia N. Vole. 204 pp. Sizzling adventure
romance set on Bonaire.   ISBN 0-941483-15-0   8.95

LESSONS IN MURDER by Claire McNab. 216 pp. 1st Det. Inspec.
Carol Ashton mystery — erotic tension!. ISBN 0-941483-14-2   9.95

YELLOWTHROAT by Penny Hayes. 240 pp. Margarita, bandit,
kidnaps Julia.   ISBN 0-941483-10-X   8.95

SAPPHISTRY: THE BOOK OF LESBIAN SEXUALITY by
Pat Califia. 3d edition, revised. 208 pp. ISBN 0-941483-24-X   10.95

CHERISHED LOVE by Evelyn Kennedy. 192 pp. Erotic
Lesbian love story.   ISBN 0-941483-08-8   9.95

LAST SEPTEMBER by Helen R. Hull. 208 pp. Six stories & a
glorious novella.   ISBN 0-941483-09-6   8.95

THE SECRET IN THE BIRD by Camarin Grae. 312 pp. Striking,
psychological suspense novel.   ISBN 0-941483-05-3   8.95

TO THE LIGHTNING by Catherine Ennis. 208 pp. Romantic
Lesbian 'Robinson Crusoe' adventure.   ISBN 0-941483-06-1   8.95

THE OTHER SIDE OF VENUS by Shirley Verel. 224 pp.
Luminous, romantic love story.   ISBN 0-941483-07-X   8.95

DREAMS AND SWORDS by Katherine V. Forrest. 192 pp.
Romantic, erotic, imaginative stories.   ISBN 0-941483-03-7   8.95

MEMORY BOARD by Jane Rule. 336 pp. Memorable novel
about an aging Lesbian couple.   ISBN 0-941483-02-9   9.95

THE ALWAYS ANONYMOUS BEAST by Lauren Wright
Douglas. 224 pp. A Caitlin Reece mystery. First in a series.
                                         ISBN 0-941483-04-5   8.95

SEARCHING FOR SPRING by Patricia A. Murphy. 224 pp.
Novel about the recovery of love.   ISBN 0-941483-00-2   8.95

DUSTY'S QUEEN OF HEARTS DINER by Lee Lynch. 240 pp.
Romantic blue-collar novel.   ISBN 0-941483-01-0   8.95

PARENTS MATTER by Ann Muller. 240 pp. Parents'
relationships with Lesbian daughters and gay sons.
ISBN 0-930044-91-6   9.95

THE PEARLS by Shelley Smith. 176 pp. Passion and fun in
the Caribbean sun.   ISBN 0-930044-93-2   7.95

MAGDALENA by Sarah Aldridge. 352 pp. Epic Lesbian novel
set on three continents.   ISBN 0-930044-99-1   8.95

THE BLACK AND WHITE OF IT by Ann Allen Shockley.
144 pp. Short stories.   ISBN 0-930044-96-7   7.95

SAY JESUS AND COME TO ME by Ann Allen Shockley. 288
pp. Contemporary romance.   ISBN 0-930044-98-3   8.95

LOVING HER by Ann Allen Shockley. 192 pp. Romantic love
story.   ISBN 0-930044-97-5   7.95

MURDER AT THE NIGHTWOOD BAR by Katherine V.
Forrest. 240 pp. A Kate Delafield mystery. Second in a series.
ISBN 0-930044-92-4   9.95

ZOE'S BOOK by Gail Pass. 224 pp. Passionate, obsessive love
story.   ISBN 0-930044-95-9   7.95

WINGED DANCER by Camarin Grae. 228 pp. Erotic Lesbian
adventure story.   ISBN 0-930044-88-6   8.95

PAZ by Camarin Grae. 336 pp. Romantic Lesbian adventurer
with the power to change the world.   ISBN 0-930044-89-4   8.95

SOUL SNATCHER by Camarin Grae. 224 pp. A puzzle, an
adventure, a mystery — Lesbian romance.   ISBN 0-930044-90-8   8.95

THE LOVE OF GOOD WOMEN by Isabel Miller. 224 pp.
Long-awaited new novel by the author of the beloved *Patience
and Sarah*.   ISBN 0-930044-81-9   8.95

THE HOUSE AT PELHAM FALLS by Brenda Weathers. 240
pp. Suspenseful Lesbian ghost story.   ISBN 0-930044-79-7   7.95

HOME IN YOUR HANDS by Lee Lynch. 240 pp. More stories
from the author of *Old Dyke Tales*.   ISBN 0-930044-80-0   7.95

SURPLUS by Sylvia Stevenson. 342 pp. A classic early Lesbian
novel.   ISBN 0-930044-78-9   7.95

PEMBROKE PARK by Michelle Martin. 256 pp. Derring-do
and daring romance in Regency England.   ISBN 0-930044-77-0   7.95

These are just a few of the many Naiad Press titles — we are the oldest and
largest lesbian/feminist publishing company in the world. Please request a
complete catalog. We offer personal service; we encourage and welcome direct
mail orders from individuals who have limited access to bookstores carrying
our publications.